Not f ☑ S0-BCR-926

No friends
Cyber bullying -
predictable

How did Noor's mother get
money to send her to school?
ESP. with a new baby?
father?

under the bed.
Hiding, hidden, Monster
dark Dank
Birth coffin

S. J. LAIDLAW

significance
FIFTEEN
of
nine
LANES

TUNDRA BOOKS

Library and Archives Canada Cataloguing in Publication

Laidlaw, S. J., author
    Fifteen lanes / S.J. Laidlaw.

Issued in print and electronic formats.
ISBN 978-1-101-91780-0 (bound).–ISBN 978-1-101-91782-4 (epub)

    I. Title.

PS8623.A394F54 2016   jC813'.6   C2015-901054-3
                                             C2015-901055-1

Published simultaneously in the United States of America by Tundra Books of Northern New York, a division of Random House of Canada Limited, a Penguin Random House Company

Library of Congress Control Number: 2015931503

Edited by Sue Tate
Designed by Rachel Cooper
The text was set in Bell MT

Printed and bound in the United States of America

Tundra Books,
a division of Random House of Canada Limited,
a Penguin Random House Company

www.penguinrandomhouse.ca

1 2 3 4 5   20 19 18 17 16

Penguin
Random
House

How can I dedicate a book to girls who may never have the freedom, education or leisure to read it? How can I not?

Noor

What I remember . . .

I was asleep on the floor under Ma's bed when I was awakened by the creaking of rusty springs straining under the weight of a heaving mattress. I feared it would break and crush me so I slithered out. This was not allowed. I was never to come out from under the bed until Ma said. I didn't know why I had to stay quiet, or why I couldn't sleep in the bed with her at night, like I sometimes did on hot afternoons. My heart pounded as I emerged.

The terror of being caught in the darkened room eclipsed my earlier fear. Too late, I realized the rashness of my disobedience. Without looking, I knew Ma was not alone. The deep grunting of her visitor punctuated her own soft mewling. I scuttled on all fours toward the curtain that separated our small section of the room from the other three occupants. I was not accustomed to seeing it closed, though it didn't surprise me. Its soft rustle always accompanied the heavy footsteps of her guests. I moved quickly, brushing against clothes that hung from a low peg on the wall next to the bed. They hadn't been there when I fell asleep. I recognized Ma's crimson skirt with the gold-sequined border. I resisted the urge to touch it, though the diaphanous fabric held endless fascination. I had no desire to touch the man's clothes. Their smell of sweat and earth was trapped in the fetid air around the bed.

Only when I reached the curtain did it occur to me to worry about who might be with Deepa-Auntie on the other side. I went cold when I heard an unfamiliar male voice. If it had only been Deepa-Auntie I wouldn't have hesitated. She was kind, not like the other two aunties who shared our room. Deepa-Auntie gave me sweets and never scolded me. She called me her beautiful baby, though my too-dark skin proved her a liar. Deepa-Auntie couldn't have babies. That part of her was broken. I liked to pretend she was my real mother. I even called her Ma, but only when my own was not around.

I reached for the edge of the curtain, listening hard to the voices. Deepa-Auntie was using her sex-me voice. That's what Ma called it when Deepa-Auntie shouted to the men who passed by under our window. I don't know why Deepa-Auntie's shouting made Ma angry. She got angrier still when the men came inside and went behind Deepa-Auntie's curtain. Ma stood in the street, where Deepa-Auntie was not allowed to go, and cajoled the men to come inside. They often did, but when they saw Deepa-Auntie it was her they wanted.

The man with Deepa-Auntie sounded angry. He called her bad names and said he would bring police to arrest her if she didn't let him do what he wanted. Her voice quavered. No one at Binti-Ma'am's house talked to the cops. Not ever. Police were wicked, even more wicked than Binti-Ma'am. They arrested mummies and put little girls in cages. Real cages, not like the barred window boxes the aunties sat in at Binti-Ma'am's, which overlooked the street but were open to the bedroom. Police cages had bars on all sides.

Deepa-Auntie said she'd never let anyone put me in a cage. I asked if she meant a police cage or Binti-Ma'am's cage. Ma said it made no difference because Deepa-Auntie couldn't even keep herself out of a cage. Besides, she said, Deepa-Auntie, with her pale-pale skin and slanted eyes, was not "our kind." I wasn't sure what our kind was, but when Deepa-Auntie got a beating I was the only one who could make her smile again. Nothing I did made Ma smile, so I thought Deepa-Auntie may not have been Ma's kind but maybe she was mine.

I held my breath and slid silently under the curtain. I did it so carefully I imagined the curtain barely stirred, but when I glanced up, Deepa-Auntie was looking right at me. Her eyes went wide and her lips pressed together. I think she wanted to say something but only her eyes told me to go back.

Deepa-Auntie wasn't wearing any clothes; neither was the man who loomed over her. I felt embarrassed. I'd seen Deepa-Auntie without her clothes many times but not like this, never like this.

The man clutched a fistful of her hair and tried to kiss her. Deepa-Auntie's face twisted away. The man yanked her hair so hard it stretched her neck back and I thought it might snap. Deepa-Auntie's eyes rolled back in her head. She let out a sound like the whoosh of a sugarcane press. I wanted to shout at the man to let her go. Kissing wasn't even allowed. Everyone knew that. But I kept silent. I would be in far bigger trouble than him if I was caught roaming at night.

I crawled toward Deepa-Auntie's bed. To get past them and reach the door, I had to slip under the bed and out the other side. I pretended I was invisible, a cockroach, just part of the landscape. If the man raised his head he would see me. I worried he could hear my thudding heart.

As I got closer I saw Deepa-Auntie's cheeks were wet. I wasn't sure if it was sweat or tears. I couldn't think of anything I could do to make her smile. I mouthed the word *chootia*— stupid—it was the worst word I knew. I added a few threats. If words could pierce flesh, that man would have run from the room screaming.

I reached her bed and dropped flat on my stomach. The cold cement chilled my body through the thin fabric of my dress but its worn smoothness made it easy to slide. I was almost completely under when the mattress juddered and there was a loud exclamation of surprise. A huge hand wrapped round my ankle. Without thinking, I shrieked.

I was jerked backwards and my head cracked on the metal bed frame. The man let go of my ankle only to grab my arm and swing me up to his eye level. I dangled helplessly in his clutch and whimpered in fear as much as in pain. (The next day, when Ma took me to the hospital, we were told that I should have had stitches right away for the gash on my head. By then it was too late. To this day I have a bald patch under my hair.)

Ma appeared on Deepa-Auntie's side of the curtain and slapped me hard across the face. This shocked me into silence. I still wanted to cry so I bit down on my lip to hold it in. A man stepped out behind Ma and shouted at her. He towered over her with his fist raised. His arm was as sinewy as a buzzard's neck. Ma would have got the better of him if he'd tried to hit her. He wanted her to give him his money back, which showed how little he knew. Only Binti-Ma'am had money. Ma couldn't give him what she didn't have. He shoved Ma back toward her bed. She got tangled in the curtain that was still half closed.

Ma looked angry rather than frightened as she scrabbled behind her to push the curtain aside. I didn't want her to leave me but I knew enough not to call her back. Deepa-Auntie was sobbing now, much louder than I was before. I wanted her to stop because this would only make things worse.

Suddenly the lights came on. Seconds later, Binti-Ma'am and her son Pran pushed through the curtain nearest the door. The man holding me let go and I dropped to the floor. I tried to scoot back under the bed but I was grabbed again, this time by Pran. He smacked me, once on each cheek, even though I was no longer making noise and my head was already bleeding profusely. The last thing I saw, as he dragged me out the door, was Binti-Ma'am pummeling Deepa-Auntie with a mop handle. Ma was nowhere in sight.

Pran carried me down the hall. I realized immediately where he was taking me. I struggled and pleaded hysterically. As he threw open the door to the kitchen cupboard, I heard the rats scuttling behind the wall. They'd wait for him to lock me in before they crawled through the holes to attack me. I begged for mercy one last time. He laughed.

It was years of this before I finally understood it was what he wanted. He fed on fear like a mosquito feasts on blood. The more I fought, the more he enjoyed it. Eventually, I learned to submit quickly, but on that night, when I was five years old, I still had hope.

Grace

I feel I ought to give this day a dramatic name, like in a murder mystery. I could call it *Before the Apocalypse* or *The Beginning*. More than anything I'd like to give it a soundtrack. The shark's music from *Jaws* would capture it nicely, except that would imply that I had a sense of foreboding, and honestly I hadn't a clue.

I knew I wasn't in for a great school year. We'd been back in class only three weeks but that had been long enough to get a pretty good idea of what I was in for. I'd been trying desperately to ingratiate myself with a group of girls who'd made it very clear I wasn't welcome. Madison, the queen bee, questioned my motives. According to her, I was a snob who, in the three years we'd all been together at Mumbai International School, had never shown the slightest interest in being friends until I had no other options. She wasn't completely wrong.

I was never under the illusion that I was too good for

Madison, or anyone else for that matter, but it was true that for the first time in my fifteen years I was out of options. The summer break had seen not only the departure of my über-popular brother Kyle to university but the move of my best and only friend, Tina, back to her home in Singapore.

Tina and I had been inseparable since our very first day of school, when we'd met at orientation three years earlier. Ours was by far the longest friendship I'd ever had. To be perfectly honest, it was the only friendship I'd ever had. Losing Tina had been a painful and unexpected blow. I'd had time to get used to the idea that Kyle would be leaving, but Tina and I had always talked of graduating together. In fact, we'd made a lot more plans than that. This year, for example, we were going to start dating. I wasn't entirely sure how we were going to find boys to date, since none had ever shown the slightest interest, but that didn't faze Tina. She said the only thing we had to worry about was finding boys who got along well with each other since we weren't going to sacrifice our own time together just because we had boyfriends. We also had to find boys who were serious about school. Both of us were in the International Baccalaureate program, which was mega-challenging, and Tina said we only wanted boys who would not hinder our studies. She was mainly talking about me when she said that because Tina could pull straight As standing on her head. Tina was determined I was going to get good enough grades that I could apply to the same universities as her. We were going to apply only to the top schools. Like I said, we made a lot of plans.

The one thing we never planned on was the possibility of her moving away. It never occurred to us, though I don't know why. Before Mumbai, my family had moved every couple of years. I'd gone to four different schools on three continents by the time I was twelve. I was so used to the idea that relationships, like schools and homes, were at best temporary that when we first arrived in Mumbai and Dad announced we wouldn't move again until I graduated I thought he was joking. And I was not amused.

To my mind, spending five years in one place was unbelievably risky. What if I didn't like the school? What if no one liked me? The latter was a distinct possibility. At my previous schools I'd always hung on the fringes of groups, never really fitting in. No one ever picked on me; it was more like I was invisible, which at the time I thought was almost as bad as being bullied. I knew it was my own fault I had no friends, especially since Kyle slid into every new school like he'd been there his whole life, proving it could be done. I was just too shy.

The one thing that kept me from giving up completely was the chance that things would be better at the next school, that I'd hit the right combination of kids, or I'd figure out the secret to fitting in. Moving gave me hope. Dad's decision to stay in Mumbai meant the end of hope. Perhaps that's what gave me the unprecedented courage to make the first move with Tina.

I liked the look of her immediately long black hair tied in a messy knot on top of her head and cherry-red, horn-rimmed glasses. She looked dorky and bold at the same time. I didn't approach her immediately, though. I waited through the tour of the ground floor (gym, pool and playing field), the second floor (offices, cafeteria and library), the third floor (humanities classrooms), the fourth floor (foreign languages and arts classrooms) and the fifth floor (science labs). Only when we got to the top floor, Fine Arts and Theatre, did I finally work up the nerve.

By this time I'd had more than ninety minutes to prepare my opening line. I was convinced it was the perfect combination of witty, yet sincere. I sidled over to her and waited until I caught her eye.

"Rockin' goggles."

That's what I said. You can see why I wasn't more popular, right?

She burst out laughing.

I couldn't believe it. It was like a solar eclipse or a meteor shower. Not only had she understood my humor but she'd laughed out loud. No one had ever done that before, unless you counted my parents' dutiful fake laughs or my brother's bemused groans. But this was different. Tina laughed for real.

So Madison was right when she said I wasn't interested in being her friend until I had no other options. There was even a grain of truth to her accusation that I thought I was superior. I did feel elevated. But I never thought I was better, just luckier. I didn't care that Tina and I weren't part of any particular group, or that some kids probably considered us losers. I never even thought about it. I had a friend, a best friend. I never wanted another.

Uppermost in my mind, as I dragged myself to the cafeteria on a Friday, the day after saying good-bye to my brother at the airport, was how much I wished Dad would get transferred again. I wanted to leave this school, these girls and this country. I wanted another do-over. I could see Madison and her posse at the usual table. There wasn't a chair for me, though there was room for one. This wasn't the first time this had happened. I suspected they got rid of empty chairs before my arrival, to discourage me. It worked. I was discouraged. I almost walked right past them to the library, but then I remembered Kyle.

My brother loves to give advice. It's partly an inherited trait, being my mom's favorite pastime as well, and partly his conviction that, with guidance, I, too, could become popular. It's irritating and flattering at the same time. The night before, as we drove to the airport, he'd given me a final pep talk. Though I was mired in my own misery, one thing he said stuck.

"You don't try hard enough, Gracie. You assume people aren't going to like you. You've got to take more risks, put yourself out there."

I didn't state the obvious—that it's a lot easier to put yourself out there when you're smart, good-looking and athletic, like Kyle—because I knew he was partly right. My heart pounded with anxiety even when I was called upon in class to answer a question I knew the answer to. I hated being the center of attention, at any time, for any reason. Even at home I was happy to let Kyle monopolize our parents. He cast a long shadow, and I was content to hide in it.

With Kyle in mind, I dragged a chair from a neighboring table, dropped my schoolbag on the floor next to it and sat down. For the past week, Todd Baker, a boy in the year ahead of us, had been the subject of lunchtime conversation. Today was no exception. I did my best to look interested.

"He pretty much asked me out," said Madison. "I'm just not sure I want to go."

"What did he say—exactly?" asked Kelsey. You could tell she was trying not to sound skeptical. While Madison was undeniably the queen of our little group, her popularity quotient was nowhere near Todd's. Not to mention the fact that he was a senior. I also thought he had a girlfriend.

"Isn't he going out with Anoosha Kapur?" I asked, immediately wishing I'd kept quiet. Despite Kyle's advice, it was rarely a good idea to join in their conversations.

"Are you saying I'm trying to steal someone else's boyfriend?" Madison glared at me.

"No, I—"

"Or maybe you think I'm not in the same league as a girl like Anoosha?"

I hesitated. I'd never thought about it till she brought it up. Anoosha was really gorgeous, and nice as well. She and my brother had dated, only for a short time, but even after they broke up she always said hi to me in the hallways.

I shouldn't have hesitated.

"Really?" Madison broke into my thoughts. "Well, thank you very much! Perhaps you'd like to sit with girls who are more worthy of you. I don't know why you even waste your time with us."

"As if she could get any guy, much less a guy like Todd," added Kelsey.

"I'm sorry," I said. Madison was blowing this way out of proportion.

"I suppose you think because you hung out with the popular kids when your brother was here that you were one of them," said Madison venomously.

I stared at her in shock. I didn't know where she was getting her information. The only person I hung out with was Tina. Sure, I might have said hello to my brother's friends, but it never went further than that.

"You've got it all wrong—"

"No, you've got it wrong," Madison cut in. "Just because Todd was your brother's friend doesn't mean he'd ever be interested in you."

This conversation had spiraled so far out of control that I was speechless, though Madison's comment about Todd and Kyle got me thinking. They definitely weren't friends, which was a little strange since they played on all the same teams and hung out in the same crowd. In fact, I'd always had the feeling that Kyle didn't like Todd, but ours was a tiny school, less than two hundred kids, so Kyle was savvy enough not to be openly hostile.

Madison startled me by jumping to her feet. The rest of the girls stood up with her.

"In future, we'd appreciate it if you ate lunch somewhere else," she said.

Tears sprang to my eyes. I knew they hadn't welcomed me, but I'd thought, at least I'd hoped, that over time they'd warm up. Before Tina, I might have expected to be shunned, but hadn't our friendship proven that I wasn't a complete freak?

I was grateful when the lot of them flounced out. Reaching for my bag, I dug out my Math book and buried my face in it. Equations swam across the page in front of me. I'd really thought I had a shot with Madison's group. They weren't populars, or brainiacs, or socialites. They were just ordinary, in a nice way, like me. Why wouldn't they give me a chance?

I missed Tina and Kyle so badly I wanted to scream or hurl something. The effort of holding back tears was suffocating. Grabbing up my books, I ran for the nearest bathroom. I just made it inside a cubicle before the tears spilled out. I shoved my fist into my mouth so I wouldn't make a sound. How was I going to get through two more years of this?

Perhaps you're thinking this was the terrible event that warranted the sinister theme music.

Not even close.

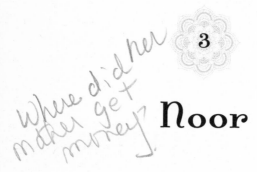

3

Noor

Starting school . . .

I could barely contain my excitement the first time I put on my
school uniform. It was a light-brown shirt with a darker skirt,
white kneesocks and black leather shoes. I'd never worn shoes
before. They pinched. I kept catching my reflection in their gleam.
If I twisted my feet the light danced across them. Deepa-Auntie
and I laughed to see it.

Ma fixed my hair into two braids. They were very short and
stuck straight out on either side of my head. I was happy my
hair was long enough to braid at all. The year before, Ma had
shaved off every inch of it because of lice.

"Easier to keep you bald than bug free, dirty girl," she said.

"It's not her fault, Ashmita-Auntie," argued Deepa-Auntie.

Deepa-Auntie always called Ma "auntie" rather than "sister,"
so Ma knew she respected her greater age and wisdom. Ma
called Deepa-Auntie "foolish hen" when she wasn't angry with
her and much worse things when she was.

When Deepa-Auntie corrected Ma about the lice, Ma's face turned purple. I worried she might shave off my hair again just to teach Deepa-Auntie a lesson. Instead she told Deepa-Auntie to mind her own business. I went to school, braids and all.

Ma walked with me but stopped when we were still half a block away.

"You can go on from here," she said.

I looked down the road. Tears pricked the backs of my eyes. I stared straight ahead and made my eyes wide so the air dried my tears before they could jump out. I knew I should be grateful that Ma was sending me to a fee-paying school and not a government school like all the other children in my neighborhood. "Why would I send her to a school where the teachers never show up and there aren't even any toilets?" Ma responded to the many who questioned why she was wasting money on a girl-child.

Ma wanted the best for me, even if it meant I was going to a school where I wouldn't know anyone. Maybe if I thanked her she would walk with me the whole way and not make me go alone.

I started to speak but Ma had already turned away. I didn't even have time to ask her if she would fetch me at the end of the day. I wasn't sure I knew the way home. Ma walked quickly. In seconds she'd created a distance between us that seemed too wide to carry my small voice, though perhaps it was the set of her shoulders that silenced me.

I trudged the final few steps. When I reached the schoolyard, it was already crowded with children and their parents. Some children had not just one parent with them but two.

Papas and mamas held their children's hands and talked to them in soft voices. They didn't shout, even when it was time to go into the classroom and some children cried. I looked at my shiny shoes. They didn't make me feel like laughing anymore. I knew if Ma had been there she would have told me to stand up straight and pay attention, so that's what I did.

Teacher told the parents they needed to leave, so the children could "get settled." This made the crying children cry louder, and some who hadn't been crying joined in. Things got very noisy, and I thought Teacher had made a bad decision sending the parents away because there was no one to hit the children to quiet them. Still, I was relieved to see the parents go. I was the only child without a parent, and several of them had been eyeing me strangely.

Teacher stood at the front of the classroom and held up her hand, just like a traffic cop, so I understood this meant stop what you're doing. It took a bit of time for the crybabies to control themselves. Finally, they took notice as well. Teacher said we'd made a good start to the year. I wondered what a bad start looked like.

Then she said we were going to take our seats according to *the alphabet*. I was frightened because I didn't know what *alphabet* was, so how could I know where to sit? There were so many desks, in perfect straight rows, side by side, from one end of the classroom to the other. Their shiny wood surfaces beckoned, and I imagined if I sat at one I would already be smarter. I was certain the children who came from mama-papa homes would know *alphabet*, and my ignorance would be discovered. Teacher would send me home and tell me not to return.

All the children clustered at the back and I hid behind them.

Teacher called out the name of the first child and pointed to a seat at the front, right next to the window. I was glad I didn't get that seat because the window was very large and looked out on a cement playground with three leafy mango trees on one side. If I sat there I would be tempted to look out the window all day long. We had only two small windows at Binti-Ma'am's and both were enclosed with bars. If you looked out those windows, men in the street shouted rude things. Our street was always crowded, especially at night when the bootleg bars opened, and there was not a single tree in sight. It was never enticing to look out our windows.

An empty playground with three mango trees sparked the imagination. I could picture myself sitting on a wide branch, though I'd never climbed a tree in my life. I'd shimmy along to the plump mangoes and pluck all I could eat. At home I plucked only spoiled mangoes from the trash that had been discarded by the fruit-wallah when they were too rotten to sell. Perhaps I would even see a parrot or a monkey perched in the branches above me. Ma said parrots were common in Mumbai, just not in our neighborhood. Monkeys and even leopards could be found on the outskirts of the city. Ma said I was lucky not to have to worry about leopards but I thought it might be nice to see a leopard. They couldn't be any more frightening than Pran.

Teacher called out the second name and that child took the seat immediately behind the first. By the time she came to Noor Benkatti, I knew exactly where to sit. Before I took my seat I counted rows and desks so I wouldn't forget where it was the next day. I already knew how to count from running errands for the aunties. I was second row from the window, third seat from the front. I felt very proud and grown-up as I walked straight to the desk behind Gajra Bawanvadi. I smiled at her just before I sat down and she smiled back. I still didn't know *alphabet* but I'd learned something even more important. School was not so different from home. I just had to keep quiet, watch carefully and do what everyone else did.

The rest of the morning passed swiftly. I didn't understand much of what Teacher said but Gajra sat with me at lunch and gave me a samosa because her mother had packed not only dahl and a thick, flaky paratha but two samosas as well. I told her I forgot my lunch. I wish I'd told her I always ate so much at breakfast that I never had room for lunch. That would have saved me from having to think up a new lie the next day and the day after that.

But I really wanted that samosa. It had meat in it. I never got meat at home. That morning, like every other, I'd had only a handful of rice for breakfast. My stomach, usually resigned to the meager scraps it received, roiled when confronted with dahl, a paratha and meat samosas as well. If I hadn't filled it with Gajra's samosa I'm quite certain it would have made itself heard in the afternoon lesson.

After the first few days, Gajra didn't bother to ask if I wanted to share her lunch, she just divided it in half as if we were sisters. She even started bringing an extra paratha so I could share her dahl. It was the most wonderful food I'd ever tasted, but my stomach wasn't used to such vast quantities. For almost two weeks I had constant diarrhea. One day Ma followed me into the latrine and watched as I squatted over the hole and did my business.

"What's that?" she demanded, pointing at the foul-smelling pile I'd just expelled.

"It's my shit, Ma," I said. Sweat beaded my forehead. I hoped she wouldn't notice in the tiny, dimly lit confines.

"I know that, stupid girl. Don't try to trick me. What's that in your shit? Have you been stealing food?"

The smell of the room was making me dizzy. I scooped a cup of water out of the bucket and cleaned my bottom, then I scooped a second, planning to wash down the evidence. Ma seized the cup. She held it aloft, not even minding that she was wasting the water that splashed down, soaking the blouse of her sari. She smashed it three, four, five times on my back and shoulders. I bent over, shielding my head. As long as she didn't hit my face none of my new school friends would ever know.

Finally she grew tired. She had a new baby weighing heavily in her belly. She cradled it and panted. "If Pran finds out you've been stealing food you'll get far worse. Do you understand?"

I nodded, keeping my eyes down.

"Answer me, Noor. Do you understand?"

"I understand, Ma." I didn't look up, or let the tears fall, until I heard the door close behind her.

The next day she got up before I left for school. I'd rarely seen Ma awake before noon. She couldn't have had more than an hour of sleep since her last customer left. She handed me a small packet of biscuits as I went out the door.

"For your lunch," she said.

I ate them on the way to school and was already hungry again before the lunchtime bell, but I told Gajra the lie I should have told her in the first place. "I ate so much this morning, four dosas and dahl makhani and eggs. I almost fell asleep in our lesson I was so stuffed." I puffed out my flat stomach and rested my hand on it. "I couldn't eat another bite."

Grace

Dinner that night was an awkward affair. My parents were trying their best to engage me in conversation but fifteen years of being *the quiet one* was a habit that was hard to break. Don't get me wrong, I love my parents. They're great people. But we're as different as strawberries from a lima bean. They're smart, good-looking and athletic. Sound familiar? If I didn't have my dad's hazel eyes, I would have been sure I was adopted.

"How was school?" asked Mom.

"Fine."

"Did anything exciting happen?" asked Dad.

"No."

"What was the most interesting thing you learned?" he persisted.

That Madison hated me. "Nothing."

"So, who are you eating lunch with these days?" My dad's not a quitter.

"Just a bunch of girls."

"It must be hard without Tina," said Mom sympathetically. "Have you heard from her recently?"

This was a sore point. Tina had missed our last two scheduled Skype chats because she was hanging out with new friends. She had a boyfriend now too, which made me feel even more left behind. "A couple of weeks ago. We're both pretty busy."

There was a long silence. My parents exchanged glances. They were debating whether to challenge me. I'd been home directly from school every day since term started and I was home every weekend as well. I was the walking definition of *not* busy.

"I got a message from Kyle," said Mom. "Only that he arrived safely." She couldn't keep the wistfulness out of her voice though she was putting on a brave face. "I imagine there's a lot going on. He'll write more when he settles in."

"Absolutely," agreed Dad. "And he'll start football practice soon. He's going to have to work hard to keep up his grades."

"He'll be fine," said Mom. "He's always been good at managing his time."

"I bet he has a girlfriend before long," said Dad.

"It will be strange not to know his friends," said Mom.

"We can always meet them when we go home on vacation this summer."

"That's true, but I wish we'd taken him to school."

"We can Skype him this weekend."

They continued like this for the next fifteen minutes, talking about the kid who wasn't there, instead of to the one who was. I didn't blame them. Mom and Dad wanted nothing more than to talk to me. I was the one who pushed them away. I always felt bad about it afterwards but I couldn't stop myself. The way they hovered over me, always worried I'd have no friends, or do poorly in school, drove me crazy. I was the sole reason they'd decided to stop moving. It was my academics and social isolation they were concerned about. Even when I had Tina, they went over the top trying to make her feel welcome, like they didn't trust me to hang on to her friendship by myself. Of course, it turned out they were right.

I sat for a few more minutes listening to them talk about Kyle. Finally, using the homework excuse, I retreated to my room. Bosco, the family Bichon, was already asleep on my bed. Someone must have put him there. Bosco was way too lazy to jump up on furniture by himself. I didn't care how he got there; I appreciated it. Kyle was Bosco's favorite, but with Kyle gone I was happy to take his place.

"Shove over, Bosco," I said, flopping down beside him and reaching for the TV remote. Friday used to be my favorite night of the week. Tina and I had a well-established routine. We'd sleep over at my house or hers and watch old Bollywood movies long into the night, then all day Saturday we'd hang out at the club. One of the weird advantages of Mumbai being such an overcrowded city, with few public facilities, was that everyone who could afford it joined expensive health clubs, with everything from swimming pools to tennis courts. Our families were no exception.

My room felt unfamiliar without Tina in it, as if all the furniture had been slightly rearranged to hide a major theft. Even my bed felt wrong. I switched on the TV, a present from my parents two Christmases earlier. It was bigger than the one in the family room. They, too, had loved my Friday night routine—it was more proof that I had a friend and was happy. The TV was a bribe to make Tina enjoy spending time with me. It was one of many. For three straight years our fridge was stocked with fresh sushi, even though Tina was the only one who ate it. And she and I always got first dibs on rides. That used to bug Kyle. Even if he'd asked for the car first, if we decided at the last minute that we wanted to go somewhere, he had to cadge a ride with a friend.

For the next few hours, I watched TV while trying not to think about Madison. It was an epic fail. Our conversation replayed in my mind at least a hundred times. I imagined a million things I should have said to calm her down before she demanded I never sit with them again. Why did I have to go and mention Anoosha? Why didn't I immediately reassure her that she was every bit as hot as Anoosha? Who cared if it would have been a big, fat lie?

"The fact is, I'm not sure anything I said would have helped, Bosco." I know exactly how lame it is that I talked to my dog but it's not like I had anyone else. "I think she was looking for an excuse to get rid of me. She didn't like me." I hated the way my voice cracked when I admitted that out loud. "They never included me, not in conversations, not in weekend plans. It wasn't getting any better."

Bosco lifted his head and dropped it in my lap.

"I don't know what's wrong with me. Kyle says I have to be more outgoing but when I try to join in, it never works out." I buried my hand in his soft white fur and scratched his ear.

"Do you think I should apologize again? I could text her right now. But what if she didn't answer? I wouldn't know if she was ignoring me or just hadn't seen my text."

Bosco stood up and resettled himself on my lap.

"What do you think, Bosco? Time to start on my Asian History paper? I'm pretty sure the Mughal invasion of India isn't going to be any more confusing than Madison." I gently slipped out from under him and scooted to the edge of the bed to take my laptop off the bedside table.

I was doubtful that Mughals were going to distract me, so when my cellphone bleated from my schoolbag several hours later I was almost as shocked by the fact that is was nearly eleven o'clock as I was by receiving a text on a Friday night.

Bosco, who was pressed up against me, raised his head and growled.

"Who do you think it is? Tina's too busy with her new boy-friend to be texting me on the weekend. Do you think they broke up? I don't wish that on her, but we were *both* supposed to get boyfriends this year and I'm not even close."

Bosco gave me a thoughtful stare.

"I know. It's weird, right? Who could it possibly be?"

I had a flutter of anticipation as I slid off the bed and walked to my bag to dig out my phone. I carried it back, clicking through to the message at the same time. It was from an unknown caller. I opened it.

Hi. What u up 2?

Could it be someone I knew? That seemed unlikely. I could probably count on two hands the number of people who even had my number.

"What should I say?" I asked Bosco. "Should I ask who it is? It must be a wrong number. Should I admit I'm chatting with my dog and doing homework on a Friday night? I'm not sure which part of that would sound more pathetic."

Listening to music, I typed. What are you doing?

I waited.

Thinking about u.

I smiled. "That's so cheesy it's sweet. But he's definitely got the wrong girl, if it is a *he.*"

Do u know who you're txting?

The girl I'm crushing on

"The wrong girl all right." I sighed and tried not to feel jealous of the girl who should have been getting these messages. Bosco put his head in my lap again and I stroked his head as I thought about whether to fess up. It was so nice to actually be communicating with another human being. It had been weeks since I'd done anything in the evening other than watch TV and do homework. But it was only going to get more embarrassing if I let it continue.

Its Grace, I texted finally.

McClaren, I added.

I waited again.

Gracie ive waited 2 yrs to tell you I like u. I no who u r!

I stared at the name, Gracie. Only my family called me that.

Who is this?

Don't u no? ☹

I stared at Bosco as if he might have a suggestion. "I have no idea who it is. Do you think I could have a secret admirer?" As unlikely as that was, I couldn't help but feel a warm glow of excitement. In my head I knew it had to be some weird mix-up, but what if it wasn't? What if someone actually did like me? Tina liked me. Could lightning strike twice?

Sorry I really don't know who u r.

Its todd

No freaking way, positively no freaking way! I didn't think there was more than one Todd at our school but it was just too coincidental. I had to be sure.

Todd who?

There was a long pause this time.

Gracie, ur killing me. I w8t 2 yrs till yr brothrs out of the way to finally get up the nerve to ask u out and u say todd who?

I gave this some thought. I'd always thought there was bad blood between Todd and my brother. Could this have been why? Did Todd want to ask me out and Kyle didn't want him to? But why? Kyle wanted me to have a social life. He was always bugging me to be more sociable. He'd even tried to drag me to a couple of his cool-kid parties. I'd chickened out, of course, but that wasn't his fault.

"What do you think, Bosco?" I gave him a questioning look, only to discover he'd dozed off. "Some help you are." I ruffled his ears. He opened an eye and closed it again.

None of it made sense, but what if it was true? Guys can be weird about other guys. Maybe Kyle thought Todd was too old for me. Todd was a jock, and from the little I knew he'd had a number of girlfriends. Maybe Kyle thought he was too experienced for me, or a bit of a player. I felt the tiniest flame of annoyance as I considered the possibility that Kyle was being overprotective. It wouldn't have surprised me. No one in my family trusted me to do anything on my own.

Why would Kyle stop u? I had to ask.

Dunno u hav 2 ask him. What music u listening 2?

Crap! The truth was, I listened to angry indie girl bands. I didn't want to tell him that. It's not that I was trying to impress him. I just didn't want to un-impress him so quickly.

What music do u like? I was pleased with myself that I'd managed to dodge his question without lying.

U listen to indie doncha?

Crap again! Another message came in before I could figure out how to respond.

U want to watch me play sometime? We hav r 1st match nxt Sunday.

I tried to remember what season we were in. Cricket, maybe?

Wat u playin? I decided to be honest. Perhaps he'd find it charming.

Ha! Wat u do for fun?

Read, swim, movies. I was honest again.

Want 2 see a movie sometime?

He couldn't begin to imagine how much I wanted that. Ever since Tina left, the only people I'd gone to movies with were my parents. Even Kyle never wanted to go with just me, and I refused to go with his gang of boisterous friends. I'd had some hope at first that Madison's group might invite me some weekend—they often talked about going to movies right in front of me—but the invitation never came. After today, it wasn't likely it ever would.

Was I doomed to spend the rest of my high school years with no one to hang out with but my parents? Was Todd offering me an alternative? If so, it couldn't have come at a better time. As bad as I'd felt when Tina left, today had been a new low. It was one thing to miss my best friend but quite another to feel like a social pariah.

I wasn't sure if I wanted to date Todd. The fact that Madison was under the impression they were starting something gave me serious qualms. I had no desire for revenge. Quite the contrary, I still clung to the faintest hope we could somehow make up. At the same time, she couldn't have been clearer that she had no interest in being friends. And Todd did. Maybe I didn't have to spend the year lonely and bored.

I needed to clear up a few things though.

R u goin out with anoosha?

No! Not since last year. Why, do u want to go out with me? ☺

R u asking?

I looked at the screen. I wasn't really going to send that, was I? Of course I only meant it as a joke. I added a happy face.

R u asking? ☺ I typed

It still looked like an invitation. From a desperate girl. Who had no friends. I deleted it.

Maybe to a movie sometime . . . I hit send.

U dont like me? ☹

Didnt u just ask Madison out?

Madison who??

Ha! After the grief she'd put me through, he didn't even know who she was! My phone tweeted again.

So u dont like me? ☹

Surely a guy like Todd wasn't really worried that an average-looking, morbidly shy girl wouldn't like him. He had to be fishing for compliments, not reassurance. Despite that, his question stirred something in me. What if he wasn't as confident as he pretended? I'd seen Kyle fake it enough times to know that some guys were good at hiding their insecurities.

It was a relief that Madison's relationship with him was all in her head. That didn't stop me from feeling guilty though. Obviously she had a crush on him. But I couldn't help feeling a glimmer of satisfaction that the very guy Kelsey said would never be interested in me was the guy who was. The symmetry of it was almost poetic. And wildly coincidental. Unfortunately, the wildly coincidental aspect didn't occur to me until later.

I do like u. I typed it and hit send before I could change my mind. I gave a little squeal at my own boldness. Bosco pricked an ear and woofed.

"I don't really know if I like him," I confided to Bosco, "but I think I could. He's really cute, and Kyle said I need to take more risks."

U don't really like me. u r just sayin that

I shot Bosco a guilty look. Bosco flipped onto his back for a belly rub. I laid the phone on the bed so I could text and rub at the same time.

Im not. I don't know u vry well but I want to get to no u. I lik what I do no of u

U don't

I DO!!!

How can I believ u when it took u so long to say it?

I'm shy

2 shy 2 kiss me?

Bosco pawed the hand that had frozen on his stomach. My own stomach was doing somersaults. I'd never kissed a boy in my life. Even the idea made my whole body feel tingly. It wasn't a pleasant sensation, but it wasn't entirely unpleasant either.

"I think this is it, Bosco. I think this is the opportunity Kyle was talking about. My life will never get better if I don't change. I need to take risks."

I could feel the sweat beading on my forehead and collecting under my arms. If Todd had seen me just then, kissing me would have been the last thing on his mind.

"What should I do, Bosco?" He'd rolled over again and was watching me intently. "I have to go for it, don't you agree? Maybe Madison will understand. If Todd likes me, it would never have worked out for her anyway. And it's not like she and I are best friends. I just want a life, Bosco. Imagine what Mom and Dad will say when I come home with a boyfriend. They'll have to stop worrying that I'm a social reject. Kyle might be angry at first, but when he sees how happy I am . . ."

I looked at the clock on my side table: a minute to twelve. I picked up the phone and cradled it in both hands, almost as if it were the boy himself. Just like Cinderella, on the stroke of midnight, my life was about to change.

If I'd only known how much . . .

5

Noor

Ma is a devadasi . . .

Deepa-Auntie and I were in the washing room, doing dishes. It was my job. Even on school days, dirty dishes would be left there, awaiting my arrival. The single bucket of water, which had to last me two days, was also my responsibility. Along with the dirty dishes, I collected money from the aunties to pay for the water.

The space in the washing room was too small for us to crouch side by side so Deepa-Auntie couldn't really help me. That wasn't why she was there. It was a humid Sunday afternoon with not a breath of wind, so there were no customers. The aunties had arisen, as they always did, around one o'clock in the afternoon, to bathe and eat. Most had gone back to sleep. The men would come later that evening, when the temperature dropped, which meant more customers squeezed into fewer hours. Deepa-Auntie wanted to enjoy the temporary respite, so she had to hide where Pran wouldn't find her. He always considered a lull in customers his own chance to take a turn with her.

He could have had any of the aunties. Some would have appreciated the opportunity to win favor with Binti-Ma'am's son—even Ma would have agreed—but Pran's cold eyes always fell on Deepa-Auntie. Ma said Deepa-Auntie's golden skin was both her good fortune and her bad. I wasn't sure it was Deepa-Auntie's skin that held Pran's interest. He didn't have the restless hunger of the men who came at night. Usually he looked tired, even bored. Only if Deepa-Auntie cried and begged him to choose another did he light up, and Deepa-Auntie always cried.

"I grew up on a farm," said Deepa-Auntie. It was the beginning of a story I'd heard variations of many times. I never tired of hearing it, nor she of the telling.

"We were very poor but I didn't know it. When the rain came it was so heavy it dripped through our grass roof. Mama caught it in buckets and joked that it would save me a trip to the river, though in the rainy season I never had to go as far as the river to fetch water. It filled the cistern in our front yard and was so plentiful we'd throw full buckets over ourselves when we bathed.

"I never went to school. Only my younger brothers went. I didn't mind. I was happy to have them out of the house. They were always chasing the chickens and stealing eggs. They never took a turn milking the goat, or helping Daddy hitch the bulls to the plow. The house was peaceful without them. I enjoyed the time alone with Mama and my baby sister, Yangani. I carried Yangani everywhere on my back, even while doing chores. Daddy called me 'little mother,' and I dreamed about the day I would have my own babies. My blood had not yet come when the man took me and brought me here."

Deepa-Auntie always stopped her story at this point, though she arrived there in a slightly different way each time. She never told me what happened between the day a man came to her village with promises of domestic work and the day she ended up in our house. Many times I'd seen the scars on her body. I pretended not to notice. Though I was nine and in the 4th class at school, she thought I was too young to know the truth. We colluded in this, my feigned innocence and her delusion that anyone could remain uncorrupted in that house.

With the dishes done, I sat back on the floor, trying to stay clear of the drain so I didn't get my kameez wet. It would take hours to dry and I didn't own another. I wanted to go outside but I couldn't leave Deepa-Auntie.

"Tell me about Yangani," I said.

Deepa-Auntie smiled at the memory. "She was the most beautiful baby in the village. All the other girls were jealous of me and would beg to hold her. I'd let them, but Yangani would always cry until they gave her back. After I taught her to walk, she followed me everywhere."

We both jumped when the door suddenly opened. It was only Ma, with my sister, Aamaal, who was born three years earlier.

"What are you doing in here, Noor? If you're done with the washing up, you should do your homework."

I was already finished my homework, as Ma well knew. It was the first thing I did when I got home from school every day, such was my pleasure in studying. Ma also took pride in my schoolwork. Every year I won firsts in Math and English. She secreted each medal into the hem of her skirt as if they were made of real gold and not just gold-colored tin. Her real concern was not too little time spent on homework, it was too much with Deepa-Auntie.

"I'm telling her about my farm," said Deepa-Auntie. "Didn't you also grow up on a farm, Ashmita-Auntie?"

"No," said Ma. "I didn't. And if I had I wouldn't waste my time thinking about it since I'd be smart enough to know I would never live there again."

"How can you be sure, Ashmita-Auntie? The voyage of life is very long with many bends in the river. So many things can happen. Who knows what course it might take?"

"It's not so long for us," said Ma.

"Why do we never visit your home anymore, Ma?" My breath quickened to ask.

The last time we'd been to Ma's village was for the birth of Aamaal. Before that we'd gone once a year. On our final visit, Ma and Grandma had argued behind closed doors, and when we left, Grandma didn't walk us to the main road, where we waited in silence for a bus. Ma hadn't spoken of Grandma since. I never asked, but I missed those visits. For those few days, I could laugh as loudly as I wanted and run far and fast. No one shouted at me, or beat me. I risked a beating now, asking Ma about these visits, but she was far less likely to let her anger loose with Aamaal beside her. I didn't begrudge Aamaal her favored status. With her golden skin and thickly fringed eyes, anyone could see she was going to be a beauty. She was my mother's child in a way I could never be.

"You should not waste your time thinking about the past, Noor."

"Please, Ma."

She frowned.

"Please, Ma," Aamaal echoed. For once I was happy that she always copied me.

"They only wanted our money, Noor. In my village the elders pretended it was something else, a sacred duty. Maybe there was a time when that was true but it was many years ago. When my mother dedicated me to the temple, it was for money, not religion, not even tradition."

"I don't understand."

"Grandma felt it was time for you to learn your history, your calling. We didn't agree. She's a devadasi, as am I."

It was the first time I'd heard the word that dropped like a stone from my mother's lips. I understood it was significant. "Am I also a Devadasi?"

Ma laughed mirthlessly. "The foolish hen tells you life is a twisting river like the one in her mountain homeland. Do you see such a river flowing past our house? There is only the open sewer carrying foul waste discharged from bodies too numerous and worthless to count. Perhaps it goes underground when it passes the great mansions of South Bombay, or slinks, like a thief carrying treasures, when it courses through the sleek neighborhoods to our north. It makes no difference. When it empties into the sea it's still shit, and the destination was never in question. You were born into your fate, Noor. I may forestall it but you can't escape it. We can only hope your next incarnation will be more forgiving."

She stroked her belly where another child was already growing inside her, though the bump barely showed. "I'm going to lie down. Look after your sister." She pushed Aamaal through the doorway and closed it behind her.

"What's a Devadasi?" I asked Deepa-Auntie.

"I'm not sure, though I know several women here are also devadasis and they all speak Kannada, like your ma. I don't think we had Devadasis in Nepal."

"If Ma and Grandma were devadasis, am I also one?"

"You are whatever you choose to be, Noor-baby. Someday we'll leave this place. I'll pay off my debt to the fat one and her pig-faced son and we'll go back to my village. We'll climb the hills of my homeland, follow the egret's flight to my father's herd. We'll see him first as we crest the hill overlooking my home. He will be watching for me, as he's done every day since I left, and will run to greet us, shouting the news of my return. Even my worthless brothers will laugh with joy. We'll take them presents like they've never seen—a cooking pot made of the strongest iron for my mother, and bells for each of our goats, so my father will never have to search long for them when they stray. But the greatest gift will be for Yangani."

"What will that be?" I asked. I already knew the answer.

"It will be you, of course. A new sister for her to play with and love. She will follow you as she once followed me, or perhaps she will be grown and you will walk side by side, sharing secrets as sisters do."

I wanted to ask her how she could have such optimism. We knew not one woman who had escaped the trade. The few who had managed to buy their freedom continued to work alongside us. Rejected by their families, who were ashamed of what they'd become, regardless of the circumstances, they survived in the only profession they knew, among the only community that would accept them.

"Do you want me to check if Pran has gone out?" I asked.

"Perhaps we could sit out in the window box for a while. Men won't bother with us on such a hot day."

"Thank you, my love. I'd like that."

The window box was the only outdoor freedom Deepa-Auntie was allowed, and of course that had all the freedom of sitting in a shop window. Unlike the other aunties, not to mention myself, she couldn't come and go from the house as she pleased. She had to ask permission and be escorted by Pran or Binti-Ma'am. Her only outings were infrequent trips to the temple to pray, and she always returned home more disheartened than when she'd left. I often stayed in on the weekends, when I'd have preferred to play in the street, because it cheered her to have my company. I didn't realize until years later that Deepa-Auntie was not so many years older than me and my friends.

Taking Aamaal's hand, I left Deepa-Auntie and went into the hallway, pausing for a moment to listen to the voices of the house. I could hear murmurings from the second floor. One of the aunties barked with laughter, which was enough to confirm that Pran wasn't upstairs. I put my finger to my lips to silence Aamaal and led her down the short, narrow passage to his room. We had to pass Binti-Ma'am's room. There was no danger of awakening her. She slept deeply in the afternoons, knocked out by the heat and her own bootleg booze.

I leaned my ear against Pran's door. Aamaal's hand sweated in my own. How quickly she had learned to fear him. I shook my head to let her know he wasn't there, though I didn't speak, as it was possible he'd heard us come out of the washing room and was deliberately keeping silent, waiting to pounce. Aamaal tugged at my hand and I let her lead me back down the hall to the washing room. I stuck my head in and gestured to Deepa-Auntie to come out. I still didn't dare speak.

The three of us crept as silently as we could to the ladder leading to the second floor. Deepa-Auntie had one foot up when the door to Pran's room flew open and he raced out.

"Where do you think you're going?" he demanded.

Deepa-Auntie started to cry.

6

Grace

I was nervous going to school on Monday but it was happy nerves. I realized it was possible that things wouldn't work out with Todd, but just the fact that he liked me made me feel like a brand-new person, prettier, more confident. As I entered the building, I smiled at kids and said hi to the receptionist, like it was completely normal for me to speak to an adult even when I was not compelled to.

Todd and I had texted all weekend. It turned out we liked a lot of the same music and we shared a passion for Bollywood films. Like me, he was studying Hindi so he could watch them without subtitles. We agreed to a Bollywood movie marathon that coming Friday night, just like I used to have with Tina. It was all I could do not to share my excitement with my parents but I wanted to see their look of amazement when I brought him home. He wasn't only good-looking, he was smart and funny and surprisingly wise, in a teenage boy way. I told him a bit about what happened with Madison, not his part in it of course, but just that I'd said something thoughtless that upset her and she didn't want to be my friend anymore. It felt so good to tell someone. I told him how Madison's group made me wonder if I was even capable of making friends. He said that was ridiculous and I couldn't let other people get inside my head like that. Nothing he said was a revelation, but just hearing it from someone else made me feel stronger.

By Sunday evening the conversation had taken a romantic turn, though perhaps *romantic* isn't quite the right word. At some point we got more playful, flirted, talked about sex and crossed a line. Just thinking about it made my stomach churn. I never would have thought I'd do something like that. I deleted all of his texts immediately and made him promise to do the same. I was horrified that anyone might read them—or worse, see them. I don't even remember what I wrote. It was like I was channeling someone else, someone sexy and fearless.

We'd agreed to meet for lunch and show the whole world we'd become a couple. I'd got up early and dressed carefully. I'd left my hair down, instead of scraping it back into a ponytail the way I usually did. I'd brushed it until it fell in one shiny waterfall almost to my waist. I'd put on makeup, which I almost never did, and wore the dress Tina and I had picked out before she left. She'd insisted on buying it as a going-away present. She'd said to save it for my sixteenth birthday but I knew she'd understand why this occasion was more important. It clung to my body, accentuating what little I had in the way of curves. When I looked at myself in the mirror I felt different, more sharply defined, as if my whole persona had gone from black-and-white to color.

The only thing weighing me down now was Madison. I'd had time to get over my shock that Todd liked me and not her. That knowledge made me feel both invincible and sad. In the first few weeks I'd been having lunch at Madison's table, we had peacefully coexisted. She could've been nasty then, and she wasn't. She'd let me sit with her group when I had nowhere else to go. And this was how I repaid her. If I didn't owe her an apology for my comments last week, there was no question I owed her one now. I'd knowingly taken the boy she wanted. The fact that she'd never had a chance with him was beside the point.

I was so lost in these thoughts that I didn't notice the stares and giggles until I reached my locker. I didn't even feel trepidation when I saw the paper taped to the door—not until I got close enough to see the photo, my photo. It was blown up, in full living color. My heart galloped and my mouth went dry. I was naked from the waist up. I'd never seen myself quite that way. Of course I'd looked in mirrors, but a photo is something different. It's more than a representation of life, it's a retelling.

I can't explain why I did it. I didn't even let other girls see me in public change rooms. I'd always been shy about my body. I'd wait till the room was empty, or I'd duck into a toilet cubicle.

Todd and I had been texting for hours. It was close to one in the morning, barely seven hours ago, when he asked me to prove my feelings for him. What a stupid request. Really, I barely knew him, but at the time I didn't feel that way. I'd confided how I always felt like an outsider. He said he did too, that most of his friends couldn't be trusted. Everyone was always jockeying for status and position, looking to take each other down a peg. We could rely on each other, he said: the two of us against the world. I teased him for being so cliché; we were hardly Romeo and Juliet. He insisted on calling me Juliet for the next hour.

I pulled the paper off my locker and stuffed it in my backpack, as if that was going to change anything. I felt a thousand eyes burning into me from every direction. My face was so hot I'm surprised my head didn't burst into flames. It was all I could do to hold back the tears.

"Hey, Grace, nice tits! Who would have guessed?" I whirled around, expecting to see Todd, but it was a boy I barely knew.

"I don't know," said another boy. "From what I saw—and I saw EVERYTHING—I think she's going to need implants. What do you think, Grace? Time to go up a few cups?"

"She could earn money for the operation by stripping. She obviously enjoys it."

The comments came from all sides, a cacophony. I could no longer distinguish one voice from another. Laughter reverberated off the walls. It seemed like the entire school was there. I tried to push through the mass of bodies but they formed a wall, tight, impermeable. Then one voice rose above the others.

"I feel sorry for her. I always knew she was desperate, but I never realized she was quite that desperate. Imagine sending her photo to everyone. Why would she think any of us were even interested?"

Madison. She'd slithered through the same crowd that had prevented my escape and stood in front of me, her retinue behind her.

"Poor, pathetic *Gracie*," said Kelsey. "It's the only way she could get a boy to look at her."

Gracie? She'd never called me that before. In a flash it occurred to me that I had no idea who I'd been texting with all weekend. It might not have been Todd. Maybe it wasn't even a boy. I could see Todd now on the periphery of the crowd, smirking. Clearly he wasn't the sweet guy I'd been thinking, but there was no reason he'd single me out for this kind of humiliation.

Unlike Madison and her posse.

"It was you," I accused, though my voice was tentative. A part of me couldn't really believe she'd do it either.

"What was me?" demanded Madison.

"You were messaging me."

"I have no idea what you're talking about. All I know is that you're so desperate for attention that you sent your topless photo to the entire school. But I think you've had more than enough of our attention." With that, she collected her minions and the crowd parted to let her leave.

They closed in again before I could make an escape, but I'm not sure I would have been capable of it anyway. I was shaking so badly I felt in danger of collapsing on the spot. I turned my back to the crowd, opened my locker and just stood there, one hand gripping the top shelf for support. I leaned in, under the pretense of looking for books, and took deep breaths, trying to slow my racing heart. The barrage of comments continued but the buzzing in my own head was drowning them out. This couldn't be happening. I'd spent my entire life striving to go unnoticed. How could I have been so reckless?

After an eternity the bell rang and the crowd dissipated. When I was sure the last of them had cleared out, I sank to the floor next to my locker and tried to figure out what to do next. It wasn't like I had a lot of options. I was at the only international school in Mumbai with a North American curriculum. It briefly went through my mind that I could kill myself. Surely this was the kind of thing that drove girls over the edge. At the same time, a small voice of reason told me this would all blow over. I was certain I'd heard of other girls suffering things like this in the past. The fact that I couldn't bring any to mind was probably a good sign. I didn't realize I'd been hyperventilating until my breathing finally slowed to normal. No wonder I felt like I was going to pass out.

I got to my feet. I was going to get through this. The one silver lining was that at least my parents hadn't found out. I couldn't have borne it if they'd had this irrefutable confirmation that I was a loser who clearly didn't fit in to their perfect family. As bad as things were, at least that indignity had been avoided. I shouldered my backpack, closed the locker and made my way to the office for a late pass.

The secretary scrambled to her feet the second I walked through the door. It was odd behavior but I figured she was just keen to get me back to class.

"She's here!" she shrieked.

Something told me things were about to get worse.

Noor

I have a brother . . .

Shami arrived in the early evening of a drizzly monsoon day. The fruit-wallahs who lined our street were packing up their carts, giving way to the bars just starting to open. Men poured out of buses, mostly migrant workers eager to douse their loneliness in cheap liquor before spending their miserable earnings on gambling, or women like Ma. Ma was already inside with a jittery boy who'd been coaxed in by Binti-Ma'am herself.

We all knew Ma's time was close. Though Shami was still little more than a bump—Ma had carried him barely eight months—he'd already dropped low in her belly. Few men wanted her in this condition, but Binti-Ma'am insisted she continue to work.

"You should have got rid of it," Binti-Ma'am scolded. "Is it my fault that you chose to keep it? I'm not running a charity. You must pay for your bed like everyone else."

Ma didn't argue. Everyone knew that too many children was bad for business. One or two were acceptable, even encouraged. Young girls recently forced into sex work would often be forced to have children as well. The need to feed their own child was sometimes the only thing that broke their resistance to the work. Ma didn't state the obvious: she wanted a son. Binti-Ma'am knew as well as anyone. Everyone preferred boys. Why would Ma be any different? *His Father?*

And so it was that I found myself outside with Aamaal, perched on the step of the building next door to ours, which housed our local heroin den. The owner was one of a few in the neighborhood who would allow us to huddle in his doorway. He thought a couple of young girls out front would throw off any police who might be suspicious of his business. For a rupee I promised to tell him if I saw the cops coming, though the regular bribes he paid ensured that was unlikely.

My friend Parvati kept us company with her baby brother, Eka. He was fast asleep in her arms. Parvati could have left him at home under her mother's bed, but she'd heard there was a group of foreigners coming through our neighborhood. This happened periodically. There was a tour company that specialized in showing off the poor areas of Mumbai. My neighborhood, Kamathipura, was an especially popular destination. The tourists gawked at our mothers as if they were Madari monkeys performing for coins. They didn't look at us though, the children of Kamathipura. If they noticed us at all, they quickly turned away.

Parvati was determined to get money from these foreigners. She called it "only fair," though she knew they wouldn't share her sense of justice. It would take some trickery to squeeze it out of them, which was why she'd brought Eka. It was common knowledge that foreigners couldn't resist babies. Professional beggars would borrow or even rent babies to increase their earnings.

Parvati tried to enlist Aamaal as well. "When I spot them, you must start crying, Aamaal, and clutch your tummy like you're hungry."

"I am hungry," grumbled Aamaal. She was cranky because she wanted to watch TV. Our small TV was in the room where Ma and the aunties entertained customers. There would be no TV for either of us that night, or any night. I wasn't allowed to bring Aamaal inside until she was ready to drop from exhaustion so that she'd sleep peacefully under the bed without disrupting business. Many aunties drugged their children at night. Ma only did that when we were too sick to stay outside.

"That's even better," said Parvati. "If you're really hungry, you should have no trouble convincing them. Remember to grab the woman, if there is one, and don't let go until she gives you something. If the amount is too small you must cry louder. Money is nothing to them. They'll forget it in an instant. You, if you're clever, can live off it for a week."

"I'm not so sure," I said. "I think they must love money very much. It's never easy to get them to part with it."

"Perhaps we should undo her braids," said Parvati. "She looks too clean."

"I spent half the morning picking out her lice and oiling her hair. I certainly hope she looks clean."

"There they are!"

We all watched the group making its way toward us.

"Start crying now, Aamaal," urged Parvati. "It will look more natural if your face is already red when they arrive."

"I don't want to," said Aamaal, though her lower lip trembled. Like me, she knew what Ma would do if she caught us begging.

Parvati sighed. "All right, watch me this time. You'll see how easy it is."

Dragging one foot, as if she were lame, Parvati hobbled out to the center of the street. She didn't even try to shelter Eka from the rain. He woke up and screamed his annoyance. Parvati ignored him as she focused intently on the approaching group. Cupping her hand and putting the tips of her fingers together, she gestured toward her mouth, making the motions of eating. She really did look pitiful.

There were six foreigners, three men and three women, with a local guide. A couple of them gave Parvati sidelong looks. The ones nearest shied away, almost tripping over each other in their determination to avoid her. Parvati limped after them.

"Just one rupee," she called out in her heavily accented English. I almost laughed. She would certainly not be satisfied if that was all they gave her.

The foreigners looked at their guide, who glared at Parvati. "Get away. Stop bothering them."

"Please, just one rupee. My brother is hungry." She singled out one of the women, catching up to her and grabbing her shirt. The woman gasped and pulled away, dragging Parvati and Eka with her. The guide raised his hand to Parvati threateningly but she stared him down. The guides were guests in our neighborhood as much as the foreigners. He wouldn't dare hit us. Snorting in disgust, he reached into his pocket, pulled out a small handful of coins and tossed them on the ground. They rolled into the muck at the side of the road. Parvati let go of the woman to dive for the change, leaving the group to hustle away.

Aamaal and I helped Parvati collect the scattered coins. Slime from rotting food, mixed with human and animal waste, coated our fingers by the time we'd collected every coin. There was barely enough for a couple of panipuri, but the vendor knew us. He added a third for free. We got spicy, but I reminded him to hold back on the onions as they gave Aamaal gas. Parvati divided the three small stuffed pastries equally, ripping a little piece off her own for Eka, though he had no teeth. He stopped whimpering as he sucked greedily on the fried dough, and we all settled back on the stoop to enjoy our treat.

We were just finishing when we heard loud voices from our own house next door. I heard my name called. My alarm was reflected on Aamaal's face as we leaped up and tore home. We slowed down as we entered, wary of coming upon Pran, who would surely beat us for coming inside so early.

Lali-didi, a recent addition to our house, practically plowed into us in the narrow hall. "Noor, thank goodness you came. I've been shouting for you. You must go down the street and fetch Sunita-Auntie. Your ma is having the baby right now." I didn't ask why Lali-didi hadn't gone herself. It would be years yet before she was allowed street privileges. She might have secured her freedom sooner if she'd had a baby of her own, but she was still a child herself.

I was happy to go back outside as I could hear Binti-Ma'am just around the corner in a loud argument with a customer. It sounded like the young boy who had gone with Ma.

I left Aamaal with Lali-didi, as she'd only slow me down, and ran as fast as I could to the house where Sunita-Auntie worked. Though she did the same work as Ma, she was no longer a live-in but had a room of her own in a building nearby.

She rented her bed only when she had a customer, and split her profits with her madam. She supplemented her income with her other skill, delivering babies. It was a dwindling business. Even in our community, women preferred to have their babies in a hospital.

I wove through the crowded streets, finally reaching Sunita's Auntie's brothel. Her madam snorted in disgust when I asked for her.

"If you find her, tell her not to bother coming here again. I've plenty of whores who can make better use of my beds."

"Please, Auntie," I said politely. "My ma's in a desperate way."

"Try the Elephant Café," she said, naming a gambling den that was as notorious for murders as for the large amounts of cash that changed hands each night.

I had strict instructions from Ma to stay away, but I was desperate so I continued on.

Half a block farther, I entered a long, narrow corridor not unlike the one at our house and followed the voices up a narrow staircase to the second floor. I didn't get farther than the top of the stairs when I was stopped by a large, muscular man.

"What's your business here, girl?" he said roughly.

"Please help me, Uncle. My ma is having a baby and needs the services of Sunita." I didn't give her last name. If he was from our community he wouldn't need it.

He examined my face, for what trickery I could only imagine. I looked at my feet to show him I understood his power and did not wish to offend.

"She's in there," he said finally, stepping back and gesturing to an open doorway farther down the hall. "But I'd think twice about having her deliver your ma's baby."

"Thank you, Uncle." I slipped past him and ran to the open door.

I heard Sunita-Auntie before I saw her. She was standing at one of the many round tables, arguing with another woman. They were fighting over a man who had a large pile of cash in front of him. The problem was as clear to me as any in my school Math book. In the next few moments they would come to blows if I didn't intervene. I rushed forward and grabbed Sunita-Auntie's arm. She was so absorbed in her dispute that she barely acknowledged me. I pulled at her with a desperation that finally got her attention. She was quick to follow when I explained the situation. Perhaps even she realized that the other woman, many years her junior, would inevitably win the wealthy customer, and give her a sound thrashing as well.

As soon as we got outside I could smell the liquor on her. Still, I was grateful that she followed me, however unsteadily. We tried to creep past Binti-Ma'am, who was now outside our door arguing with the same young man. He was demanding his money back, as I'd earlier suspected. It was impossible to hide from her.

"Tell your ma she owes me for this one," said Binti-Ma'am.

"You should be ashamed making Ashmita work in her condition, you greedy donkey!" snarled Sunita-Auntie.

Binti-Ma'am's chest puffed up as she prepared to explode. I shoved Sunita-Auntie through the open doorway. Sunita-Auntie's blood was still up from before. She was itching to let loose on someone. It wouldn't take much to ignite her long-standing feud with Binti-Ma'am. Many years ago they'd been friends, working alongside each other in the same house, but while Sunita-Auntie's unwillingness to train new girls had kept her forever at the bottom of the trade, Binti-Ma'am's innate viciousness had fueled her rise to the top.

Several aunties and their children waited anxiously in the hallway and directed us to where Ma was giving birth. We were too late to help. Shami was already squalling on Ma's chest when we arrived. It may have been fortunate he hadn't awaited Sunita-Auntie's arrival. In her current state, she may have cut more than his cord, though the scene we came upon was no less horrific.

Binti-Ma'am had sent Ma to the lockup to have her baby. The room itself made my heart race. Everyone who lived in our house had heard the screams from that room when new girls were broken in. Lali-didi had emerged from a prolonged confinement only three weeks ago and still bore the marks of her suffering.

It was more a wooden box than an actual room, standing four feet off the floor and accessed by a rickety stool. It was barely large enough for the single soiled mattress it contained, and the roof was so low it wasn't possible to stand upright, even for me, and I was small for my ten years. A bucket overflowing with filthy rags and watery blood stood underneath the open door. Prita-Auntie, who shared our small four-bed room, stood sentry outside, giving orders to the other aunties to bring fresh water and clean clothes. A bucket arrived just as we did. Whatever rivalries might have existed between the aunties on a daily basis, they were family and would always help each other in a crisis.

"She's going to be fine," said Prita-Auntie. Her eyes told a different story.

I steeled myself to climb into the box. Sunita-Auntie made no move to follow. I didn't blame her. I glanced nervously at the bolt and huge padlock on the door. Binti-Ma'am would have no reason to lock us in, but I'd seen Pran's cruelty extend beyond reason, many times.

The room was stifling. Deepa-Auntie sat on the far side of the mattress, mopping Ma's face with a rag that looked little cleaner than the ones outside. Aamaal crouched beside her, rigid with fear. I tried to smile reassuringly at her. I'm sure it came out more like a grimace. Old Shushila, who'd long ago retired from the trade but stayed on at our house to help, was between Ma's legs trying her best to wash her. Light flickered from a single kerosene lantern that hung barely two feet above Shushila's hunched body. It cast ghastly shadows, making the scene look like a massacre and old Shushila a demon crone. I thought they must have cut the baby out and was surprised to see that Ma's exposed belly, covered in a film of sweat, was unmarked.

Ma looked relieved to see me. "Greet your brother, Shami."

I reached across her and took him in my arms.

"You need to get a box for him to sleep in. There should be some discarded fruit cartons at the garbage dump. Get the cleanest one you can find." Her voice was weak.

"I'll take care of it, Ma. Don't worry."

I was surprised by his lightness. He was much smaller than Aamaal had been. Even at birth she'd had round cheeks and a robust glow. Our brother was frail and wizened like an old man. His eyes fixed on me and his wails, which had reverberated off the walls since my arrival, subsided into a quiet snuffling. It was foolish to think anything of it. Babies couldn't see properly when they were this young. I kissed his forehead and held him close.

Ma fell asleep almost immediately. I took her hand. It felt as cold as death. I quickly dropped it. Shushila, who was continuing to gently bathe her, met my eyes and nodded toward the door. There was nothing more I could do. Aamaal lay down and rested her head in Deepa-Auntie's lap, closing her eyes as Deepa-Auntie stroked her hair. She would soon be asleep as well.

The quietness in the room, rank with the smell of blood, was oppressive. I scooted backwards toward the door and swung my legs out, carefully stepping down onto the footstool and then the floor. I knew Ma's bed would be empty for at least the next few hours. I wasn't ready yet to introduce Shami to our life. I wanted some time alone to get to know him, and privacy was scarce. The curtain around Ma's bed afforded our only hope. One of the aunties made a move to take him from me but I refused to give him up and the aunties seemed to understand. They returned their attention to guarding Ma and passing clean rags in to Shushila.

I was halfway up the ladder to our room, awkwardly holding Shami in one arm, when Sunita-Auntie stopped me with a hand on my thigh. I started and almost fell backwards. I didn't realize she'd followed me.

"Your ma's sick," said Sunita-Auntie.

"Just tired," I said.

"No," said Sunita-Auntie, with the certainty of one who had seen much sickness. "She has the virus, and so does the babe. You'd be doing everyone a favor by smothering him now." She turned away, placing a hand on the wall to steady herself before trudging off down the hall.

I waited until she'd rounded the corner and then looked into the milky, opaque eyes of my brother. "She's an old fool and a drunkard," I told him.

Shami didn't blink.

Grace

One thing I liked about the principal's office was that all his chairs were lined up in a straight row facing him, like he was about to deliver a speech and you were just there to listen. Most of the time I expect that's the way things went. He didn't count on my mom. I don't think she'd stopped talking in the fifteen minutes since she'd sat down. I felt sorry for him. Every so often he'd start to say something like *If I could interject here*, but she would barrel on. Sooner or later he'd realize she wasn't going to let him interject here, there or anywhere. I was grateful to be facing him and not her.

I was already in his office when my parents arrived, farthest seat from the door, closest to the open window. Are you having the same thought I was? In fact, I'd been sitting in that same chair for over an hour. I gathered that Mr. Smiley—that's his name; you can't make that stuff up—had called my parents even before I showed up. He was surprisingly calm about the whole thing. Maybe I wasn't his first student to "disseminate pornographic images to the student body." Yes, that is what he said. Technically, he didn't accuse me of disseminating to everyone, only those with a cellphone. Although apparently there were several images posted around the school, in addition to the one on my locker, so presumably the 1.2 percent of kids at Mumbai International without a cellphone were still exposed to my corrupting influence.

As luck would have it, disseminating pornographic images is an expellable offence. Personally, I think accusing a fifteen-year-old of being the likely culprit of her nude photo going viral should be an expellable offence, but that's just my opinion. Mr. Smiley did let me tell my side of the story, and he took copious notes. Then he had me write everything down and sign it.

I felt both panicked and vindicated when he asked his secretary to make an appointment for him to talk to Todd and Madison. I wasn't sure whether to bring up Madison's name. I didn't accuse her but I did say we'd had a disagreement about Todd the same day he started texting me. I genuinely wanted Mr. Smiley to draw his own conclusions. I didn't know what to think.

Dad was sitting in the seat closest to me. He didn't look at me, which was a relief and hurt at the same time. Only when we were well into the second thirty minutes of the interview did he reach over and take my hand. At that point, I was white-knuckling the hard plastic armrest. Mom had just started talking about getting a lawyer and suing the school.

Dad cleared his throat and Mom stopped talking. This wasn't a strategy they'd worked out ahead of time, unless you count the past twenty-two years as "ahead of time." Mom looked at Dad expectantly. I didn't need to see her expression to know it was a mixture of *Don't interrupt me* and *What took you so long?*

"I think it's obvious Grace has been the victim of a cruel if not criminal attack," said Dad. I couldn't help but notice Mr. Smiley was suddenly way more alert and not trying to interrupt. "She used bad judgment, but her error was a private one, which we'll address with her when we get home."

"I'm sorry, Mr. McClaren," said Smiley, who looked sorry and more than a little nervous. My dad runs a company with over two thousand employees; he can have that effect on people. "But even if Grace only sent the photo to the boy, she still sent a pornographic image to an underage student."

"Really," said Dad. "And have you identified that student?"

Mr. Smiley shifted uncomfortably. "Not as yet, no."

"Have you traced the cellphone number?"

"It doesn't match any we have on record, or the numbers of either of the two students Grace named as possible perpetrators."

"So, as far as we know, Grace could have been in communication with anyone, an adult even?"

"That's highly unlikely," Mr. Smiley objected. "The picture was sent to almost every student in the school."

"And how did that happen?"

"The image went viral. Students were passing it on. But your daughter was the first to send the image, obviously."

"We don't dispute that, but you can't produce a single student who received the image from my daughter, and she doesn't know who was play-acting as the teenage boy.

We're in complete agreement that Grace needs consequences for her actions, but the humiliation of having her
image disseminated is already a severe consequence. We'll take
her home for the rest of the day. It will give her time to reflect
on her actions and we'll talk to her. However, Grace cannot
afford to miss school. She'll be back in class tomorrow."

My father stood up. Mr. Smiley, no longer living up to his
name, stood as well. Mom and I followed suit.

"My colleagues and I will need to discuss appropriate sanc-
tions," said Mr. Smiley.

"We will not accept any consequence that jeopardizes her
education," said Dad firmly.

"At the very least she'll have to do community service to
atone for what she's done," said Mr. Smiley, equally firm.

"Grace already does community service as a requirement of
her International Baccalaureate diploma," said Dad. I could
tell he didn't like letting the school decide my punishment, but
he was wrong on the community service front. I wasn't involved
in anything. In fact, I'd invested considerable energy into dodging the community service requirement.

"According to our records, Grace is not yet involved in any
activity that will contribute to her required hours."

I stared at my feet.

"Thank you for letting us know," said Dad, without missing
a beat. "Of course, we support any effort to help Grace find a
suitable activity."

Dad held out his hand and Smiley shook it.

"I trust you'll keep us informed if you get any information
on who's responsible for this attack on my daughter." Dad
sounded every bit like the captain of industry that he was.

We walked out of the office. Dad only dropped my hand when it was necessary to pass through doors. He took it again when we were out of the building. I couldn't remember him ever holding my hand before. It felt nice, though weird. Mom stalked ahead of us to the parking lot.

"I'm sorry," I said quietly, daring to glance at Dad's face for the first time.

He gave me a wry smile. "Everyone makes mistakes, Gracie, but this sure was a doozy."

I couldn't help but grin. Only my dad would use a dorky word like *doozy*. Who says that anymore?

"I guess you were missing your brother," he said, as if he was trying to work it out for himself.

"And Tina," I said.

"But still."

"I know it was stupid but I never expected anything like this would happen."

We reached the car. Our driver, Vitu, opened the door for me. Mom was already in the front seat. She never sat there. Obviously, she didn't want to sit with me.

It was a silent ride home. She didn't speak in the elevator either, but I could feel the pressure rising with each passing floor. I tried to plan what I was going to say when we were finally alone. I felt mortified, apologetic, betrayed, frightened; I couldn't formulate a single sentence that would capture the depths of my regret. As it turned out, I didn't need to. The second we were inside the apartment Mom burst into tears and Dad wrapped his arms around her. No one acknowledged Bosco, who rushed to greet us and was jumping around, yipping with delight.

"Why don't you go to your room," said Dad. "We'll talk later."

"No," said Mom, pulling away from him. "We'll talk now. Grace, how could you do this?"

The abrupt shift from tears to anger left me speechless.

"You're a smart girl. How could you be so unbelievably stupid? Do you realize your image is out there in the public domain forever? Universities, future employers . . . someday your own children could see this. How are you going to explain to your own fifteen-year-old that you sent a topless photo of yourself to who knows how many people?"

"I didn't do it, Mom." I felt like I was going to throw up. As bad as I thought it was, it was so much worse. I hadn't even begun to think of all the ways this could come back to haunt me.

"Of course you did it, Grace!"

"She means she didn't send the picture to anyone but the one boy," said Dad. "Or whoever it was," he added under his breath.

"Exactly," Mom pounced. "She sent a photo to someone without even knowing who it was. What were you thinking, Grace?"

"This isn't getting us anywhere, Jen. What we need to do now is help Grace figure out how she can move on."

"She can't move on!" Mom roared. "This will never go away."

Dad frowned worriedly. Maybe he hadn't thought through the implications either.

"Go to your room, Gracie. Your mom and I need to talk."

I didn't need to be told twice. I scurried to my room, Bosco hot on my heels. Once inside, I shut my door, dropped my bag on the floor and threw myself on the bed, though I immediately had to get up again to lift Bosco up beside me.

I lay on my back, staring at the ceiling, clutching Bosco to my heaving chest. I'd wanted to be alone since I first saw the picture, so I could finally let the tears fall. Now that I was, I found myself dry-eyed. It was like I was wrapped in gauze; everything I'd done seemed like the actions of someone else. Maybe this was what people meant when they talked about being in shock. Certainly what I'd done was shocking, and the fallout was cataclysmic. But it didn't feel as though I was part of it. I could almost believe that I'd go to school tomorrow and be the same invisible nonentity I'd always been.

And then it occurred to me . . .

Trembling, I slid off the bed and walked over to my pack, knelt down and unzipped the front pouch where I kept my cell-phone. It had already caused so much trouble. I would have been smart to smash it. Instead I pulled it out and brushed the screen. There, on the opening page, was my message icon showing fifty-two new messages.

Fifty-two.

I shouldn't have read them. I stopped after the first dozen or so.

Mom was right. This was so much bigger than I could ever have imagined, and the worst part was that I'd done it to myself. I wasn't the victim of random bullying. I was the one who'd sent my half-naked picture out into the world. The only thing Mom had wrong was saying I was a smart girl. She had it right when she told me I was stupid. I shuffled back to my bed and flopped down.

Dad popped his head in before he left for work.

"How are you doing?" he asked from the doorway.

"Is Mom still angry?"

"Give her some time, Gracie."

"Would you tell her I want to speak to her?"

"I think it's best to wait till she's ready. Why don't you message Tina?"

"I don't want to tell her what I did. I don't want anyone else to know. You haven't told Kyle, have you?"

"No, but you might consider telling him yourself. Your brother's always had your back."

"I just want to talk to Mom."

"I'm sure she'll come talk to you later in the day. She's getting ready to go out now. I think she's meeting some of her friends for lunch."

"Today?" I tried to hide the shock and hurt I felt that Mom could even think of going out when my whole world was falling apart.

Dad walked over to the bed and sat down next to me. I sat up and leaned into him. He put an arm around my shoulder. "I encouraged her to go. It will be good to take her mind off things. I'm sure she'll come back feeling much better, and then you two can talk this all through."

"Do you think she'll forgive me?"

"You will never do anything we can't forgive, Doodlebug."

"Dad, I'm fifteen! You have to stop calling me that." I was grinning though. My dad may be a dork but he's a smart dork. If he said Mom would forgive me, I was ready to believe him.

He kissed the top of my head and stood up. "Are you going to be okay here today? Have you got some work you can do?"

"Sure, I'll be fine." I wanted to ask him to spend the day with me. I knew he would if I asked, but as much as I loved my dad, my mom was the one I went to in a crisis.

I waited all day for her. I tried to do schoolwork but I couldn't concentrate. At least half the day I just paced the room. I checked my phone and Facebook a dozen times an hour. Each time there were new, hateful messages. I was only making myself feel worse, but it was like picking at a scab; I couldn't stop.

When Mom finally came home, she must have been deliberately quiet. Even though I'd been listening for her, I wouldn't have heard her if Bosco hadn't started yipping and jumping around on the bed. I lifted him down to the ground and opened the bedroom door so he could run to greet her. Leaving it slightly ajar, I hovered behind it. My plan was to dash to my computer when I heard her coming down the hall and pretend I'd been studiously doing homework.

She was murmuring to Bosco but I couldn't make out what she was saying. What I could hear was that her voice was getting fainter. She wasn't coming to my room. She was headed in the opposite direction.

As quietly as I could I pushed the door closed and walked over to my bed. I was trembling just as I had when I first saw the photo, as I had when Mom was shouting at me, as I had when I saw the hate messages. I lay down and stared at the ceiling. This wasn't going to get better. Mom wasn't going to forgive me.

I don't know how much time passed before I heard a light knock on the door. I was on my feet in seconds.

"Come in."

It had to be her. Please, let it be her.

Dad walked in carrying a tray, Bosco right behind him. "Vanita said you haven't eaten all day."

It's true. The few times our maid had stuck her head in the

door I'd shooed her away. I couldn't have gotten food past the knot in my stomach.

"It's tomato soup. I made it myself."

I attempted a smile. It was a joke between us. Dad was a hopeless cook. Canned soup was the extent of his expertise. He put the tray on my desk and stood uncertainly in the middle of the room. I too was still standing, my anxiety growing with each passing minute. Mom was the unseen presence between us. I waited for him to speak.

He cleared his throat. "Here's the thing, your mom feels it would be better if you two spoke in the morning. She's taking this pretty hard. She feels she's somehow responsible—"

"She's not!" I cut in, aghast. "How could she think that? This has nothing to do with her!"

"I know, but you have to see it from her perspective. She's invested so much of herself into raising you two. She gave up her career. She's always been so involved in your lives. She just needs some time to make sense of all this."

"Tell her I'm sorry," I said stiffly. I wanted him to leave so I could cry in private. I took a step back and sat on the bed so he'd take the hint.

"Eat something and try to get some sleep. Things will look brighter in the morning."

I leaned down and picked up Bosco, who was agitating to join me, and buried my face in his fur.

"Night, sweetie," Dad said from the door before shutting it quietly behind him.

I didn't know whether things would look brighter in the morning. I only knew that on the very worst day of my life, when I needed her the most, my mother couldn't even look at me. It's not like I blamed her. Mom had done everything right. What Dad had said was true. She had always been there for me, active at every school we'd gone to, home in the evenings every night, helping with my homework, making valiant efforts to get me to talk more. Before Tina, Mom had been my only friend. We did everything together, and still she was nothing but happy for me when Tina came along and I didn't want to hang out with her so much anymore.

I stood up and started pacing again. Nervous energy coursed through me. I felt as if I was going to explode. I reached for my phone; more new messages. I threw it at the wall. The sound was loud in the stillness, but it wasn't enough. I could still hear my mom calling me stupid. She'd never said anything like that before, to me or my brother. Mom wasn't a woman to toss words around. She'd been a successful lawyer before she had Kyle. If she said something, she meant it.

Stupid.

I could hear her voice saying it, the shock, the disappointment . . . the contempt.

STUPID.

The word went round and round in my head. It grew in volume. It reverberated off the walls.

I picked up a pen from the desk and took it to my bed, an idea already forming. I had to get rid of the word, but only after I'd taken control of it.

I dropped down, sitting cross-legged. Bosco immediately tried to crawl into my lap, but I pushed him away and hitched up my skirt, carefully choosing a spot on my inner thigh. I wrote the word, *STUPID*, pressing down until it hurt. Bosco whimpered. The imprint of black ink left angry welts. My leg ached.

It wasn't enough.

Tomorrow the ink would be washed away. A week from now, maybe sooner, the welts would disappear. The indictment of my stupidity would still exist. Outside of me, its power would only grow stronger. I needed to own it.

Taking the pen, I pressed down as hard as I could and went back and forth over the first letter. The pain was intense, yet strangely liberating. I felt only satisfaction when the first bubble of blood broke through my skin. As I set to work on the second letter, the intensity of my anxiety slowly drained away. Each letter brought with it more peace. By the end I felt calm. The pain of disappointing my mother was no longer an unbearable burden. It still hurt, but it had lost its power to consume me.

My scars, spanning the inside of my thigh, were my insurance that I'd never again be carelessly intimate with a stranger. My mother would never again have reason to call me stupid. I might not be able to take back what I'd done but I could contain it. All I needed to do, if my resolve ever weakened, was look at my scars. I was in control now, with my own private message to myself.

9

Noor

Devadasi is explained . . .

I was good at making up games. It was necessary in a life where there were always younger children who needed to be entertained, so they didn't get under the customers' feet. In school this earned me a reputation as lighthearted and creative. As my schoolmates and I milled around the schoolyard during breaks they would often turn to me. "What shall we play, Noor? Let's have some fun."

Toppling Towers was a game I invented one evening when Aamaal was being particularly difficult. She'd had an ear infection for days and Ma refused to buy medicine. A waste of money, said Ma, who had more faith in charms and homemade remedies. She was using both to treat Aamaal's infection. Like the many others she'd used before, they didn't work.

I finished flushing the ooze from Aamaal's ear for the third time that afternoon and slathered on Ma's concoction. I checked to make sure she still wore the amulet Ma had tied round her neck that morning. It was Ma's most precious possession, with a potency she swore could cure any ailment. Years ago Ma had made the dusty two-day journey to Saundatti, in northern Karnataka, to have it blessed at the Yallamma Gudi temple. The goddess Yallamma was revered by many women in our community, and Ma was no exception.

Aamaal complained that the amulet was too heavy. She'd removed it twice that day already—further proof of how sick she felt. Normally she loved Ma's charms, and though she was only five years old, she'd long coveted this one. Night was falling, but despite her discomfort I needed to take her outside and tire her before I could let her crawl under Ma's bed. I'd begged Ma to give Aamaal sleeping drugs but they also cost money, and since the birth of Shami we were always short.

Shami, now six months old, was constantly sick. Twice we thought we'd lost him to pneumonia but both times he pulled through. That night he'd sprouted sores all over his body. They'd appeared as simple scabies only a day before, but no sickness was ever simple with Shami. Disease courted him like a jealous lover, never far from his body and always fierce in its attentions. Ma covered him in charms to ward off the evil eye: a black string around his waist, black plastic bangles on each wrist and even black henna spots to mar his beautiful face.

Despite her efforts, Shami had suffered restlessly all day, so while other babies throughout Kamathipura were sleeping peacefully under beds, I wrapped Shami in a sari and hitched it over my shoulder. The warmth of our bodies pressed together should have irritated his rash further but, unlike my sister, he kept any misery he felt to himself, and even seemed comforted by our closeness. I took him outside, Aamaal grudgingly in tow.

"I don't want to go out," whined Aamaal.

I hardly heard her. My attention was drawn to the foot of our street where a noisy throng of men was spilling out of a bus, the night's customers arriving. I reached for Aamaal's hand. She resolutely stuck both behind her back.

"Stay close to me, Aamaal." I wanted to put some distance between us and the approaching mob. We couldn't go far. One of the aunties had asked me to watch her children that night and they were still loitering inside.

Someone hooted from within the ranks of men as they made their approach. I swallowed down my anxiety and stepped in front of Aamaal, blocking her from their view. The ones who came to Kamathipura regularly knew that the young girls roaming the streets were not part of the night's offerings, but every day there were men newly arrived from the villages. They didn't understand that the underage girls they desired were never allowed on the streets, where they might be rescued by the NGOs, private charities scattered throughout Kamathipura that attempted to prevent young girls from being forced into sex work. The determination of the NGO workers who patrolled our fifteen lanes looking for vulnerable girls was equaled only by the pimps.

Fortunately, just as I was thinking we would have to venture back inside in search of the other children, they tumbled out of the doorway, engaged in a spirited but good-natured fight. Adit, the older of the two, was dangling a paratha just out of reach of his brother, who had clambered onto his back. Bibek was clinging to Adit's neck with one hand, while trying to reach round and snatch the bread with the other.

"He's trying to kill me!" Nine-year-old Adit appealed for my help but couldn't hide his smirk. I took the paratha out of his hand and handed it to little Bibek.

"That was mine!" Adit objected.

"Not anymore."

I shrank back as several men reached our doorway and squeezed past us to go in. At the last minute one leaned toward me and squeezed my breast. I drew in a sharp breath.

Adit rounded on him. "Hey, don't touch what you haven't paid for!"

The man paused and stared at him, as if he couldn't figure out whether to be offended or amused. Suddenly he cuffed Adit on the side of the head, knocking him off balance.

Bibek launched himself at the man but I caught him in midair.

"Stop," I said. Grabbing a boy in each hand, I pushed them behind me as well.

"You need to teach those little bastards some respect," the man said. He raised his fist again, but one of his companions threw an arm around him and made a crude joke about the far greater entertainment awaiting them inside. They pushed *them* past us, laughing. Degrade + humilate to *that* male selvs

Aamaal looked at me wide-eyed after they'd disappeared. *feel* She didn't say a word when I ordered her across the street. *better*

"You should have let me fight him," said Adit, catching up.

"He would have killed you."

"Not before I got in a few good licks." Adit took out a tattered, hand-rolled cigarette to complete the picture of his bravado. His hands shook as he lit up.

The road was crowded, as it always was at this time of night. Snack carts and paan-sellers had rolled in, crowding into every inch of space on the sidewalk and lane that wasn't already inhabited by something more permanent. I yanked Aamaal back just in time as a bullock cart, laden with jerry cans of kerosene, rattled toward her.

"Pay attention, Aamaal," I said, though there were many things in our life I wished she were less aware of.

We crossed the road at an angle to give wide berth to Imran-Uncle, the old fruit-wallah. He used to let us pick from his spoiled fruit at the end of the day in return for the occasional favor from Ma, but after he began parking immediately across from our doorway Ma told us to avoid him. He still called to her whenever she came outside to talk to a customer. Ma acted like she didn't hear.

I wished she would let him be our father. I'd heard he had a small room a few streets away and lived there all alone. I couldn't imagine the luxury of a room just for our family and away from Ma's work. I knew the time was fast approaching when I'd be considered too old to sleep under her bed. Many children my age were already living on the streets. Each night they fought for patches of pavement. Parvati had been doing it for years.

Imran-Uncle's rheumy eyes followed us as we reached the curb on his side of the street. We paused so Aamaal could pet Lucky, her favorite goat. I caught Imran-Uncle's gaze and smiled. I was disobeying Ma's wishes, if not her direct orders, but I liked Imran-Uncle. He said he gave us only fruit he was going to throw away, but more than once lush strawberries and unblemished bananas had found their way into his offerings. I liked his appearance as well. His wizened skin and long white hair made him look more animal than man, not so different from Lucky, now nuzzling Aamaal's pockets looking for sweets. I imagined Imran-Uncle would be an undemanding father, content with Ma's attentions and not chasing after Aamaal and me as well. He might even let Ma stop working and look after all of us on his fruit earnings. It was a future almost too bright to contemplate. Damn.

Aamaal and Bibek were arguing over the half-paratha Bibek still had left.

"Lucky is hungry," Aamaal insisted. She gave Bibek an imploring look.

"Lucky is already too fat," I said seriously. Lucky was a huge beast. A full-grown man couldn't wrap his arms around the goat's middle, and he stood a good foot taller than Aamaal. Aamaal continued to plead with Bibek, who finally and very reluctantly gave in. No one could say no to Aamaal.

She carefully ripped the bread into bite-size pieces, despite the fact that we'd both seen Lucky eat entire shoes in one gulp. While she fed him, two more goats meandered over and tried to nose Lucky aside. Aamaal gave each of them a piece but reserved the bulk of it for Lucky. I looked on with mixed feelings. I was happy to see her distracted, but it wasn't wise to get attached to a goat. Lucky had been around as long as I could remember, but every Eid I feared would be his last. He could feed many families at the feast.

"I'm not sure it's such a good idea to fatten him up," I said quietly to Adit.

He took a last drag on his cigarette and flicked it to the side of the road. "Don't worry. The milk-wallah treats that goat better than his wife."

With the feeding finished, Aamaal's attention quickly returned to her sore ear. She cupped it with her hand.

"I want to go home, Noor-didi," she begged, her eyes filling with tears.

"I have a new game," I said. In that moment it wasn't true but I would think of one in the seconds it took to get them all a safe distance from the house. I nudged them to start walking again.

"What?" asked Adit eagerly.

Aamaal only sighed as she swiped her hand over her eyes.

"I can't explain it here. I have to show you."

"Come on, Aamaal," said Adit. "It will make you feel better."

Aamaal let me take her hand and we walked down the road to the nearest rubbish heap. I examined it hopefully. It often contained the equipment for some of my more inspired games. Discarded syringes, for example, were a versatile favorite. I briefly considered the piles of sheep and cattle dung. We'd created quite a blaze one night, setting those alight. Aamaal had loved it, but we'd got into trouble when flying sparks singed a passerby.

"We need to collect mango pits," I said, an idea forming, "the more the better."

As always, Adit and Bibek threw themselves into the task. "Be careful of needles and broken glass," I reminded them.

Aamaal stood by watching and I put my arm around her. It was unlike her not to join in. We waited for several minutes while the boys collected a large pile of pits. Some were still slimy and many covered in filth. I separated out the worst of them and divided the rest into two mounds, then explained the rules.

"Aamaal, Shami and I are one team and you two are on the other. We need to stand ten paces apart and stack our pits into towers, as high as we can get them. Each team keeps three pits back to use as missiles. When I say go, you throw your three and try to knock down our tower, and we do the same. As soon as we've thrown all the missiles we quickly rebuild. The first to rebuild their tower wins."

The most challenging part of the game turned out to be getting ten paces apart without having multiple obstacles between us. We lined up along the side of the road but the concept of roadside was fluid in Kamathipura, where sidewalks and roads alike brimmed with food stalls, livestock, vehicles and throngs of people. Lucky and his goat friends showed up and became particularly problematic as they were convinced we were throwing the pits for them and kept trying to eat them. Eventually, I got the idea to incorporate them into the game, and outrunning a goat to retrieve a pit earned extra points. Aamaal was reluctant to play at first, but by the time the goats had become a third team she was well into it and cheered gleefully every time the goats bested the boys. Shami fussed a couple of times when the game got too boisterous. I took periodic breaks, swaying my hips to rock him back to sleep.

It was late when the boys' mother finally stuck her head out the window and called them home to bed. I decided it would be a good time for me to slip in and put Aamaal and Shami to bed as well. We were all tired. Aamaal refused to go in until we gave awards to Lucky and his two accomplices, the clear champions of our new game. I dug through the stinking pile of refuse until I came up with a wilted flower for each of them. Aamaal presented them with great flourish and was delighted when the goats ate them. Then we all headed inside.

We skirted a pile of vomit just inside the door, the effects of Binti-Ma'am's homemade alcohol. The stench of urine in the hallway was particularly strong, as it always was in the evening. The customers rarely bothered to walk a few steps farther and use the latrine.

We approached the open doorway of the lounge, which buzzed with the loud voices of drunken men and the aunties trying to tempt them upstairs. Snack vendors calling out their wares as they circulated the room added to the din. Betel nuts were a particular favorite. Old Shushila would spend the next morning, as she always did, cleaning up the red spit that would coat the floor by night's end. By this point in the evening many aunties would be as drunk as the men, or high on drugs. I sped up, pushing my charges in front of me. We needed to pass quickly to avoid unwanted attention.

In my hurry, I didn't see the man coming out of the lounge until he was upon us. He bumped into Aamaal, grabbing her shoulder to steady himself.

"What have we here?" he said, pinching one of her soft round cheeks.

"Just the little ones going to bed," I said, prodding them forward. The boys slipped past but he still had hold of Aamaal, so I stayed where I was.

"You're a pretty one, and already with a baby."

I was relieved to see his attention diverted from Aamaal.

"I need to get them to bed," I repeated.

"How much do you charge?"

"I don't work, Uncle-ji." I deliberately used the term of respect. "I'm just a schoolgirl."

"I won't hurt you. We could have fun."

Aamaal whimpered.

"Go to bed, Aamaal. Tell Ma I'll be along soon." She stared at me with big eyes. I hoped she took my meaning. I untied the sari from my shoulder, gently shifting Shami into Aamaal's arms. The man let her pull away from him, his attention completely on me now. Aamaal ran, Shami's head bobbing on her shoulder as she rounded the corner.

"I'll make it worth your while," he said.

"I'm only eleven, Uncle."

"Don't be coy, girl. What's your price?" He put one hand on the wall behind my back and leaned toward me. I shrank away.

"Noor, what are you doing here?" It was the first time in my life I was happy to see Pran.

"I'm just going to bed," I said and tried to push past the man. He grabbed my arm.

"How much for the girl?" he demanded.

"She's not yet working."

"I'd pay a lot for a fresh girl."

"You don't want this one. She's too dark."

"I don't care. Name your price."

"Let go of my daughter!" Ma charged up behind Pran and stepped into the glow of the fluorescent lamp, grabbing my other arm.

The man laughed harshly. "She's your daughter? But you're a devadasi. Why delay the inevitable? How old were you when your parents sold you?"

"We'll sell her in good time." Pran put a hand on the man's shoulder and steered him back into the lounge. "Come, I'll show you a prettier one."

Ma and I stood alone in the hallway. Her face looked pale in the stark light, her cheeks deeply hollowed.

"What was he talking about, Ma? What does it mean to be a devadasi?"

"It's late, Noor. I need to get back to work, and you have school tomorrow."

I stood my ground. "Tell me."

She hesitated.

"It's the tradition of our community. It goes back hundreds of years. One daughter, usually the oldest, is dedicated to serve the temple."

"Serve in what way?"

Ma sighed.

"In what way, Ma?"

"In the old days we were courtesans to the priests and sometimes the wealthy landowners."

"And now?"

"The history has been lost. Now we're sold to the highest bidder. It's how we support our families. The practice has been outlawed but it remains our tradition."

"And I am also a Devadasi." I wanted her to disagree. There had to be a way out.

"No one can escape their fate, Noor."

I knocked her aside as I bolted past her, down the hallway, up the ladder, across our small, shared room and under her bed. Aamaal was already there. She was curled around a sleeping Shami but her eyes shone brightly from the shadows.

I pulled her into my arms with Shami sandwiched between us and massaged her knotted shoulders. "I'm all right, Aamaal. You did well."

Closing my eyes, I breathed in Shami's sour milk smell and the coconut oil I'd smeared on Aamaal's hair that morning. Gradually her coiled limbs relaxed and her breathing became deep and regular. When Ma came in I pretended I was asleep. All through the night I listened to the noises of her customers. They took on new meaning. For the first time I associated them with my own future. When the last one had finally departed I was still wide awake.

I crawled out from under the bed before dawn and spent longer than usual scrubbing myself in the washing room. I packed my schoolbag and went to school without speaking to anyone. Gajra was at the fence waiting for me when I arrived. Together we walked over to a cluster of girls from my class.

"It's not fair," said one. "The boys always have games at recess. They can play cricket and football. There's never anything fun for us. We just stand here on the sidelines watching."

"I have a game," I said, thinking quickly. "It's called Toppling Towers. You all need to get out your erasers, as many as you have, and perhaps pencil sharpeners as well, if they're flat and we can stack them."

"Trust you to think of something fun for us to do. I bet someday you'll be a games mistress at some posh girls' school."

"You forget she always takes first in Math and English," said Gajra, forever ready to point out my achievements. "Our Noor will become something far more important than a games mistress. A doctor is more likely, or perhaps an inventor."

"India's own Steve Jobs," crowed another girl. "What do you think, Noor? Will you one day be rich and famous?"

I forced a smile. "No one can escape their fate."

10

Grace

The ride to school was as silent as the trip home the day before. Dad held my hand again as we crossed the parking lot. Mom walked on the other side of me. I was grateful for the show of solidarity but it wasn't the same as forgiveness. Her back was rigid as we entered the school. Her eyes betrayed her anxiety, flitting from side to side as though she expected to see the walls plastered with my half-naked image. I wondered if she was thinking about her plan to run for school council president that year. Was it another disappointment I should apologize for?

When we reached the office, we were asked to take seats. We probably waited less than five minutes. It seemed much longer.

Mr. Smiley came out to greet us, shaking both of my parents' hands. They made some small talk about the heavy traffic as he ushered us into a large meeting room off his own office. I was alarmed to see not only the vice principal but my home-room teacher, the coordinator of the International Baccalaureate program, my community service advisor and the school coun-selor. For a fleeting moment, I registered horror that now *everyone* knew, which was silly when you think about it. Who on earth did I think *didn't* know?

As we took our seats, my parents insisted I sit between them. It made me feel marginally better to know that they were both claiming me as their own. Mr. Smiley looked as though he'd regained some of his trademark good humor. He opened the meeting by asking if we'd managed to talk things through as a family.

"We still have a few things to settle," said Dad.

Mom held the same tight expression she'd had yesterday in the elevator. I fervently hoped she didn't start bawling again.

"Well, we've had some very useful discussions on our end," said Mr. Smiley. "Mr. Donleavy, Grace's community service advisor, thinks he has the perfect program to help Grace make amends for what she's done and gain some insight into the risks of this kind of behavior."

"Well, let's hear it," said Mom in a voice that sounded like she wanted to do anything but.

"Mr. Donleavy, why don't you explain," said Mr. Smiley.

Mr. Donleavy immediately produced multiple copies of a package of information, which he slid across the table. He gave me an encouraging smile as I took mine and I did my best to smile back. Everyone liked Mr. Donleavy. If it's possible for a teacher to be hot—and let's be honest, some of them are—Mr. Donleavy was our school's number-one hottie. Before all this happened he'd even started to make me feel guilty because

I'd so resolutely vetoed his various suggestions for community involvement. I guess he got the last laugh.

I looked at the pamphlet clipped to the top of my pile. It had pictures of girls of various ages doing everything from yoga to studying. I really hoped he wasn't going to suggest I work with little kids. My single experience doing that was when I'd agreed to help one of my cousins babysit one summer. She left me alone on a beach with her three-year-old charge for ten minutes while she went back to the cottage to get us drinks. I got so distracted building the kid a sand castle that I didn't notice him wander away. We eventually found him, but after that my cousin and I both agreed I was not babysitter material.

"This is an NGO that works to prevent second-generation trafficking," said Mr. Donleavy. "They have a variety of programs for the girls, including after-school tutoring, life skills, sex education—"

"Wait a minute," Dad interrupted. "Who did you say these girls were?"

"The daughters of sex workers," said Mr. Donleavy, without a second's hesitation. The poor guy had no idea the beast he was about to awaken.

"SEX WORKERS!" Mom shrieked. "My daughter makes one tiny mistake and you think she's fit to work with sex workers?!"

"It's not a punishment—" started Mr. Donleavy.

"Well, actually—" cut in Mr. Smiley.

"She'd work with the daughters, not the actual—" the counselor interrupted, trying to bring things down a notch.

"She sure as hell won't!" said Mom, jumping to her feet. "I've heard enough. If you people can't come up with a better plan than this, this . . ." No one cut Mom off; she was just too angry to finish her sentence.

"What kind of work would it be?" I asked in a small voice.

Dad put a hand on Mom's arm. She sat down again.

"There are several activities, Grace," said Mr. Donleavy, "but I had a particular one in mind. If I may . . . ?" He looked at Mom, who gave a grudging grunt.

"The NGO wants to start a new teen-to-teen program. The girls would be a little younger than you, probably thirteen or fourteen. They'd like to pair students one by one, so you'd mentor one girl, sort of like a big sister." *Grace ✱ needs to be mentored*

"What would we do together?"

"Well, to some extent that would be up to you. You might help with homework. But, as you got to know each other better, you might plan outings. A lot of these girls never leave their own neighborhood, and it's a very poor neighborhood they live in."

"Will she know what I've done?"

"She'll know you're volunteering for school credit. What you tell her beyond that is up to you. But these girls grow up in brothels, Grace. I think you'll find they're pretty difficult to shock."

I nodded.

"I think I could do that. What do you think, Mom?" I was determined not to do anything else to disappoint her.

She gave me a long, steady look. Not taking her eyes off me, she answered, "I think any girl would be lucky to have Grace for a sister."

My relief was so intense tears sprang to my eyes. I didn't kid myself that my mom was over her anger but it was a start.

Mom and Dad left shortly after that and I spent another hour with the counselor talking about how to handle potential bullying at school. She made me promise to tell her if anyone gave me a hard time. All I had to do was show her my phone. Messages were coming in so fast I had to keep deleting them for fear they'd consume my message space. As tempting as it would have been to turn in my tormentors, I didn't know who they were. The last I'd heard, Todd and Madison were denying involvement, though I'd had a brief text exchange with Kyle, who confirmed his antipathy toward Todd. He refused to elaborate, just saying Todd had messed things up with him and Anoosha. Of course, I didn't tell him my own problem.

I walked into my third-period class feeling like everyone was whispering about me. It was probably the first and last time in my life I was happy to be in a Math class; the lesson was at least sufficiently challenging to hold everyone's attention. The class passed slowly but without incident.

The next period was lunch. I'd already resolved to spend that in the library and went back to my locker to drop my books.

I saw the word, scrawled on my locker, from ten feet away. I didn't let my steps falter, though other kids stopped walking to watch my reaction.

Conversations ground to a halt.

I unlocked my locker.

Someone tittered. It was an odd sound in the stillness, like birdsong at the scene of a crime. I piled my books onto the single shelf and shut the door.

"She doesn't even care," said a voice. I knew who it was. "She knows she's a slut."

I turned around and surveyed the group. It was a mix of

kids, some I knew better than others. I'd been in school with most of them for three years, shared classes with a few, worked on assignments with others, cheered alongside many at assemblies. I didn't cry or rage. I wouldn't give them that satisfaction. I just shook my head. Every one of them, whether bully or bystander, was enjoying my humiliation. They didn't care that I'd had thoughts of suicide, or felt so ashamed I'd carved into my own flesh. I was nothing more than a moment's entertainment. I'd never felt so alone.

"Who do you think you are?" asked Madison.

"Well, by all accounts . . ." I let the words trail off.

"You tried to blame me."

I didn't deny it.

"Why don't you just leave? No one wants you here."

Leaving was exactly what I wanted to do, but she and her group were only the front line in a thick circle of kids forming a solid ring around me. I was on the point of saying that when a ripple went through the crowd and it parted to let a boy step forward. Everyone in the school knew him, by reputation if nothing else. He had a following of his own, the school's beautiful people.

"Speak for yourself, darling," he said to Madison in a mocking tone. "I for one am positively delighted she's here. She's the first interesting person we've had at this school since, well, since I arrived."

Drop-dead-gorgeous VJ Patel, son of Bollywood icon Sanjay Patel and a rising film star himself, held out his hand.

"What do you say, Slut? Would you join me for lunch?" He shot me a saucy grin guaranteed to make any female not already in her grave swoon.

I'd never spoken to him before, and would have said he didn't know of my existence, but I did the only sensible thing I could do. I took his hand.

11

Noor

Sleeping on the street . . .

"It's easy," boasted Parvati when I told her I would have to join her sleeping on the street.

It had been two weeks since the man had tried to buy me, and Ma was a bundle of nerves. She acted like it was the first time a man had spoken to me in that way. Admittedly, I'd never told her about the bad things men said to me or the many times they'd tried to touch me, even her own customers. I always assumed she knew. In the same way I knew what men did to her. I thought it was our secret language. We kept our eyes open but our mouths sealed shut. After that night, I began to wonder.

She paced our small room for days. No one could calm her. Deepa-Auntie was the only one who dared try and Ma bit her head off. Prita-Auntie, who'd known Ma the longest and was the closest thing she had to a friend, made herself scarce. Lali-didi, who'd recently been moved into our room, sat nervously on her own bed, watching us both because suddenly we were always together. Ma wouldn't let me out of her sight. She even walked me to school and was waiting at the gate at the end of each day.

At first the novelty of her attention was gratifying. It was the first time I'd felt like I was more than a servant, perhaps even loved, but Ma's restless anger quickly wore on me. I created excuses to steal time away from her. One day I deliberately spoke out of turn in class to get kept after school. That was a mistake though. When my teacher finally let me go, Ma was a hissing cobra, barely able to contain herself until we got home, where she beat me.

I was the one who suggested I was too old to sleep in our house. "The men look at me differently now," I told her. "It will be safer if I sleep elsewhere."

I didn't say that men had looked at me this way as long as I could remember. Was there any other way for a man to look at a girl?

"But where will you sleep?" asked Ma.

It was a stupid question. How many people did we know who slept in the street every night? Did she think I could give her the coordinates of the patch of pavement I would claim as my own?

"I'll go with Parvati," I said. "She knows someone with a small room we can share."

This was a lie and Ma knew it. If she'd believed me she would have asked for more details. To have a room was sufficiently extraordinary that it bore investigation. Perhaps there would be space for Aamaal and Shami as well. But Ma said nothing.

She crinkled her already deeply lined brow and gave me a hollow-eyed stare. It went through my head that she used to be pretty and I wondered if her horror that men were noticing me was in part because she struggled now to get their attention. What would happen if men no longer paid to be with her? How would she support us? I didn't know how old Ma was. Like most people, myself included, her birth wasn't registered and the date was long forgotten. She didn't even have a fake birth certificate, like the one I got to register for school. She'd once said she was barely in her teens when she had me, so she had to be in her twenties still, but time moved faster in our community. Many women, their bodies wasted by disease and addiction, didn't live to see thirty.

"I don't want you begging," Ma said. "I don't send you to school to have you end up a beggar."

I wanted to ask why she did send me to school. What was her plan for me? Did she have one? "I'll only sleep with Parvati. That's all."

She sighed and sank down on the edge of Lali-didi's bed. Lali-didi practically left behind her own skin in her haste to scuttle away.

"I don't like Parvati. She's a bad influence."

I suppressed a smile. As if anyone could be a bad influence in our neighborhood. What did she think I might learn from Parvati that I didn't already know?

"She doesn't even go to school," Ma continued.

"That's not Parvati's choice," I said indignantly, though Parvati always pretended she was glad she didn't have to go to school. "Her ma won't pay for the uniform and books."

"You'll need to be back first thing to wash the dishes. You know what Pran will do if he wakes up and finds the dishes haven't been cleared up."

I nodded, though no one ever knew what Pran would do.

I stood outside our building that evening, discussing sleep-ing options with Parvati. Although it was late, I still had Shami strapped to my back. He had a cough that made it hard for him to sleep lying flat. Sticky yellow goo collected in his lungs so he woke up gasping for breath. It was another reason I didn't mind sleeping outside. Keeping him quiet and breathing at the same time was becoming an impossible task. He would breathe easier if I could keep him upright.

"I told Hussein there would only be two of us," said Parvati for at least the third time. "Why can't you leave Shami with your ma? Aamaal can watch him."

I looked across the street to where a fight was brewing between two men outside a bar. We needed to get moving. It wasn't safe for us to be hanging around this time of night.

"We can sleep under the bridge," I said.

Parvati often worked with the beggars who'd built a shanty community under the railway bridge near Grant Road Station. It wasn't far from Kamathipura. We could make it there on foot in thirty minutes. I'd suggested it earlier but Parvati refused. I couldn't figure out why. I thought the beggars were her friends.

Parvati put her hands on her hips and gave me a look, like I was being unreasonable. Maybe she wanted to show off her "boyfriend," Hussein, who sold T-shirts outside Central Station. He claimed he owned the stall where he worked and we could sleep under the table when he shut down for the night. I had my doubts on both counts. He was too young to own a stall, and I didn't want to risk being discovered by his boss and chased away in the middle of the night. If it had been closer I might have agreed to try it out, but it was more than an hour's walk.

"Why would he let us sleep there for nothing?" The boy's ulterior motive was the other thing worrying me. We couldn't afford to pay him, not in cash anyway, and I didn't want to contemplate what other form of payment he might expect.

Parvati shrugged. "He said he loves me. He gave me this T-shirt and he didn't ask for anything." She puffed out her chest in case I'd failed to notice she was wearing a T-shirt emblazoned with *I'm a Princess* in gold lettering. She was also wearing new blue jeans. It was the first time I'd seen her out of traditional clothes. The difference was startling, as if she were one of those girls who advertised toothpaste on television, with a life as perfect as her teeth.

"Did he give you the jeans too?"

"No, I bought them myself." She looked way too smug.

I suspected she'd stolen them. I just hoped she'd been smart enough not to steal from a stall near the T-shirt shop. The vendor was bound to notice if she sashayed past wearing them. Parvati scared me sometimes. She was much too bold for a girl. It would get her into trouble one day.

Two men walked by and gave us a speculative look. Even after they were beyond us, they turned back for a last gawk. Parvati winked at me.

"Those clothes reveal too much," I said, grateful Ma had already been inside with a customer when Parvati showed up.

"You're just jealous." Parvati arched her back and squeezed her arms on either side of her tiny boobs.

"You can't make melons out of cherries," I said grumpily.

Parvati sighed. "When I get rich I'm going to buy boobs the size of melons!"

"They'll grow on their own, Paru," I relented. "Your ma has the biggest boobs on the street."

Parvati smiled happily. "That's true, isn't it? But I'm a teenager. They should be bigger by now."

"You're twelve. That's not a teenager."

"You don't know how old I am."

"Neither do you."

"That's the problem with being the oldest. Do you remember the exact date Aamaal and Shami were born?"

"Of course."

"Never forget that. When Eka starts school he won't have a fake date on his birth certificate like you and I did. My ma couldn't tell you when he was born but I remember."

"Your ma didn't register his birth so you'll still have to fake the certificate." I didn't have to ask why she knew her ma would let Eka go to school when she'd pulled Parvati out after third standard. Even a goat knew education was more important for boys than for girls. I also didn't suggest that Eka might not be the best candidate for school. Parvati's ma had a serious drug problem. It didn't seem to have affected Parvati but I wasn't so sure about Eka. He wasn't sick as often as Shami, but Shami was already talking, while Eka, though eight months older, was still babbling.

"It's getting late, Paru. We need to decide where we're going."

"Fine," she huffed, "let's go to Grant Road. But leave Shami at home tomorrow night."

I started walking. Parvati fell in step, taking my hand. We both knew that tomorrow night I'd show up again with Shami. We'd have the same argument, and Shami would come along. Parvati may not have loved Shami as much as I did but she did love him, the same way I loved Eka. They were family. And Parvati understood that in the nearly two years since Shami's birth he'd become a vital part of me. I was so used to looking after him that sometimes at school I felt his absence as if the air had been emptied of oxygen and I couldn't breathe. All I could think about was rushing home to make sure he was still okay.

As if he knew what I was thinking, Shami stirred and wrapped his fingers around a strand of my hair. I craned my face around and kissed his tiny fist.

"Do you want me to carry him for a bit?" asked Parvati.

"No, he's not heavy." The truth of that statement made my stomach twist.

"He'll grow, Noor. He's like my boobs. We're late bloomers, right, Shami?" She briefly dropped my hand to reach up and ruffle his hair.

"Right, Shami," agreed Shami.

We laughed.

Leaving our crowded street, we hit the bright lights of Bapty Road. Food stalls on carts gave way to proper restaurants, open at the front so their fluorescent lighting lit up the whole street. You could tell we were coming into a richer neighborhood because bright lights shone from upstairs windows as well, as if the whole street were one big carnival. In our neighborhood, electricity was scarce and not so frivolously wasted.

"Are you hungry?" asked Parvati. She always seemed to have money these days. That also worried me. dark

"Are you buying?"

"Sure, why not?"

I almost asked her where the money came from but she beamed at me so full of pride that the words shriveled on my tongue and I swallowed them down again. "I'm not hungry," I lied, and immediately felt guilty. Even if I didn't want to take her money, I couldn't deny Shami. "Maybe just a samosa for Shami."

"We'll all have samosas," she said magnanimously, like an NGO worker who could produce food as easily as spit.

We stopped at a café that had tables spilling onto the sidewalk. That was another thing you didn't find in our neighborhood: space was too precious to waste it on the luxury of tables and chairs on sidewalks. People ate as they walked along or took their food home. We approached the counter. There was already a crowd of men waiting to be served but Parvati pushed her way to the front and shouted her order. The server tried to ignore her, looking over her head to the men who now engulfed her. She put her hands on the countertop, which was almost as high as her shoulders, and peered over the top, continuing to bellow. I chuckled at the foolish man who thought Parvati could be ignored. Giving her a foul look, he took her order, snatched the cash she held up and practically threw a bag of samosas at her.

Parvati returned, grinning all over her face. She handed me one samosa and broke off a small piece from another, holding it up to Shami. I felt rather than saw him turn his head away.

"Keep trying," I said. "He'll take it eventually."

We started walking again and Parvati did her best to get Shami to eat, in between tucking into her own samosa. In the end he didn't have more than a few bites but I still felt a measure of satisfaction. Every bit of food that went into him felt like a victory.

It was close to midnight by the time we reached the shanties under the bridge. I was ready to drop from exhaustion and wondered if we were really going to have to make this trek every night. Lots of girls didn't. They just slept in doorways or on the sidewalk in our own neighborhood. Lots of them got attacked as well though. It was worth the walk to sleep surrounded by people we knew, even if they were Parvati's friends more than mine.

Several people greeted her as we wove our way through the corrugated metal and tarpaulin structures looking for a few feet of empty pavement. Finally we came to a patch large enough for all three of us to stretch out. Parvati helped me ease Shami off my back. He'd fallen asleep after his small meal and we didn't want to wake him. She held him while I spread the sari on the ground and then gently laid him on it. Without discussion, we settled ourselves on either side.

Kidnapping was another hazard of life on the street, though baby girls were more often stolen than boys. Boys could be sold to beggars, who used them as props to get bigger handouts, but girls could be sold to brothels. They were far more lucrative. Babies sometimes disappeared from the brothels themselves. No baby had ever been stolen from our home but I knew several aunties whose babies had gone missing. Everyone knew it was the brothel owners. They sold them to traffickers who resold them in distant cities far from the protection of their families. The brothel owners made money, and it was a powerful way to punish mothers who'd resisted allowing their children to follow them into the trade.

I was almost asleep when I was aroused by a thud, quickly followed by a shriek. I sat up to discover Parvati rubbing her shoulder and recoiling from the raised foot of a young man.

The stubble on his face was as patchy as grass in the dry season. He couldn't have been more than sixteen.

"Get up, thief," he snarled.

Parvati scrambled to her feet, planting herself firmly between the boy and Shami. I jumped up too and reached down to pick up Shami, taking in our situation at the same time. There were half a dozen of them. The boy who kicked her was the oldest. The youngest looked to be about Adit's age. I stepped closer to Parvati so our bodies were touching.

"Where's my money," demanded their leader. He seemed genuinely furious, but that didn't impress me. From what I'd seen of life many people spent every moment of every day simmering with anger.

"I haven't been working." Parvati glared back at him defiantly.

Parvati never understood the value of pretending humility. I cast my eyes downward, trying to communicate my own respect.

He backhanded her across the face. Her head cracked sideways with the force of the blow. Blood spurted from her lip and hit my cheek. I caught her as she staggered into me, but she righted herself quickly and again met his gaze.

"Have you seen me begging?" she demanded. "I haven't been working."

I silently willed her to be quiet.

"We've all seen you throwing your money around. If you're not begging for it, you must be stealing. Either way, you owe me my cut."

What had Parvati done? Surely she wouldn't steal from her fellow beggars. There was a hierarchy in every begging community, just as there was for sex workers. Beggars worked in teams under the supervision of middle-level lieutenants who reported to gang lords. Whatever beggars earned on the street had to be turned over to those they worked for. Parvati knew that. It suddenly occurred to me that maybe she had bought her jeans. Was that the meaning of her sly smile?

"What if I do have money? What's it to you? I didn't earn it begging. You have no claim to it."

Why couldn't she have just lied?

"I own you. That means I own everything you earn. What do I care how you earned it? It's still mine. In fact, you should be grateful your money is all I take from you."

"You would have to force a girl, wouldn't you, Suresh? No girl would let you touch her voluntarily."

We reached for her at the same time, me to pull her back and him perhaps to kill her. We met halfway and he knocked Shami from my arms. I leaned over to pick up Shami, who was already struggling to his feet, stunned.

Parvati dove for the boy's neck, wrapping her hands around it. Shami headed unsteadily toward them but I caught him and wrapped my arms around him. Several more boys joined the fray. Parvati was knocked to the ground. I left Shami to go to her. Kicks connected with my back and sides as I shielded her. Suddenly Shami was beside me, taking blows meant for me. Tears streamed down my face as I beseeched them all to stop.

When we were all three on the ground bleeding and inert, they stood back to savor their victory.

Suresh leaned down to Parvati, shoving his hands into every one of her pockets until he found her money.

"Don't ever try to cheat me again," he warned.

Parvati's unflinching stare said it all. He laughed, but it was a reed-thin imitation.

We were silent after they left. I carefully examined every inch of Shami. He'd have some bruises in the morning but there was nothing broken and only minor cuts. It was still agony to see him hurt. He winced when I held him close and buried my face in his hair.

Parvati reached over and stroked Shami's head. "Don't worry, Noor. One day I will make Suresh pay for that beating." Her beautiful new T-shirt was smeared with dirt, the *I'm a Princess* obscured.

If anyone else had made the threat, I would have put it down to bravado, but it was Parvati. I didn't doubt her.

"Be careful, Paru. Suresh is protected. If you defy him, he'll only do worse to you."

Neither of us knew how right I was.

Grace

I didn't know where VJ normally sat, but I noticed that he chose a table in the epicenter of the cafeteria, guaranteed to ensure we could be seen from every direction.

"Can you give us a moment?" He looked around at the girls who'd followed him in. "Grace and I need to have a private talk."

A couple of the girls shot me hostile looks but they melted away at his request.

"What do you want to eat? I'm buying."

Still reeling from the last five minutes of my life, I had no idea what to say. I'd never spoken to this boy before and he was offering to buy me lunch. Would it be more rude to refuse or accept?

"Chips?" I suggested hesitantly.

"Not going to happen, my nubile nymph." He pursed lips that any girl would kill to have—kissing her, or just stuck on her own face. "I'm not going to be the one to destroy your perfect feline physique, so let me rephrase: Do you want a veggie wrap or a salad?"

"Salad?"

"Perfect choice! Aren't you clever." With that he sauntered off, pausing at least a half dozen times on his way to the food line to chat with people, all of who seemed utterly charmed by him.

As surreal as the last twenty-four hours of my life had been, this took bizarre to a whole new level. VJ Patel was the local version of royalty. There wasn't anyone in the school richer or more famous. Everyone knew he drove around in an armored car with a personal bodyguard, though apparently school regulations required the bodyguard to wait in the parking lot. The stories of his lavish parties and excessive drinking were legendary. In fact, legendary pretty much summed up VJ Patel. So . . . what was he doing with me?

It was possible he felt sorry for me, but I wouldn't have pegged him for a particularly altruistic guy. The numerous times I'd seen him on the front of the lifestyle section of the newspaper it was never in connection with anything charitable, unless he was attending a fundraising art auction or gala.

I wasn't thrilled about being his latest charity until a more hideous thought occurred to me. He was concerned about me gaining weight. A wave of nausea swept over me. Did he believe the hype that I was a slut? Given the photographic evidence, it was hardly surprising. The only question was, did he want me for himself or was he planning to follow his dad into the film industry, perhaps starting with a porn flick? As shocking as my behavior was to the average westerner, it had to seem worse to the Indian students. Their own films had only recently allowed kissing. Even imported western films were heavily censored.

VJ appeared with a large Greek salad, placed it in front of me and dropped into the chair across the table. I stared at the salad. With the knot in my stomach I wouldn't be able to force down a single bite. I cleared my throat. He grinned.

"What's on your mind?" he said. "Spit it out."

I tried to think of a tactful opener. "I really appreciate you rescuing me," I started. "But, you should know I'm not . . . I'm not . . ."

He arched his perfectly shaped brow. He was so good-looking he was pretty. "You're not what?" he prompted.

"Available."

"Available for what?"

I blinked and made the mistake of shoving a forkful of salad into my mouth with the hope that it would give me time to think.

"Sex?" he asked, leaning forward across the table. "Are we not going to have sex?"

I couldn't chew. His face was inches from my own and he was talking about sex. My face was suffused with heat.

VJ leaned back in his chair and sighed heavily. I quickly chewed, swallowed and resolved to give up vegetables for the foreseeable future.

"Well, Gracie," he said, "I'm going to tell you something, but you have to swear it won't go any further."

"Who would I tell? Everyone hates me."

"This secret you could probably sell to the press."

"The last thing I want is more attention."

His tone was so dramatically earnest that I wasn't sure if he was serious, but his dark eyes searched my face as though he really was trying to decide if he could trust me.

"Okay." He took a deep breath. "I like boys, Gracie. That's the truth of it. I like you too, obviously. As a person, I think you're very interesting . . . but not in *that* way."

My mind was reeling. In all the stories I'd read and heard, not one said VJ Patel was gay. I was never obsessed with him or anything, but I was a major Bollywood film fan. I felt this was something I should have known. I'd seen him in at least three films playing a teen heartthrob, and I'd read countless articles detailing his latest romances. I had to hand it to him: if he was telling me the truth he was a better actor than I'd given him credit for. At another time I might have been disappointed—like every other girl in the school, I'd harbored a small crush on him—but recent events had decidedly dampened my romantic inclinations.

Still, it was hard to reconcile the boy before me, claiming his lack of interest in girls, with all the stories. "I don't understand," I said.

"You don't understand?" A smile played about his lips. "How shall I explain?" He thought for a moment. "As much as I hope we can be friends, at no point are you going to get any. I hope you're not too disappointed."

I laughed.

VJ frowned. "That's a little harsh, pet."

"I'm sorry." I tried to stop grinning but I couldn't help it. I was just so massively relieved. "So, if you aren't interested in me, why'd you bail me out?"

"Who said I wasn't interested in you? You're the school slut. I think that's positively delicious."

"I'm not really a slut."

"Don't be so quick to give away your power. Remember, there's no such thing as bad press."

"Look at that, she's already got her claws into another guy." Madison's voice rose above the usual cafeteria babble. I looked over to discover that she wasn't at her usual table. She, too, had chosen to sit in a central spot. But it was who she was with that took my breath away. Flanked by her usual entourage, she sat directly across the table from none other than Todd.

"I don't believe it," I said, more to myself than to VJ.

He followed my gaze. "Ah, an alliance of your enemies. What can it mean? The intrigue of it all! This just keeps getting better!"

I gave him a cool look. "I'm glad you find my life so entertaining."

"Of course I do. I wouldn't hang out with you otherwise."

"Is nothing serious with you?" I knew I didn't have enough friends to risk losing the only person willing to speak to me, but I was starting to wonder if VJ was really friend material.

He straightened his face and looked so determinedly solemn that I found myself smiling.

"There are many things I find serious. Declining achievement levels in rural schools, female infanticide and my mother's suicide attempt after my father's affair are all things I consider very serious. A bunch of children displaying their pack mentality by attacking a vulnerable girl is distasteful but hardly catastrophic."

"Did you say your mother's suicide attempt?"

"I shouldn't have said that. I don't want to talk about it."

"I'm sorry."

"Me too. It destroyed my family. But it also put a lot of things in perspective."

"So what I did, you don't think that's serious?"

"You showed off your boobs. I'm no connoisseur but it didn't seem to me you have anything to be ashamed of. You're very thin but you know what they say about wealth and thinness."

"Don't you think my behavior was a little . . ." I found I couldn't bring myself to say the word, though I'd been called it so many times in the past twenty-four hours I was surprised it still stung.

"Avant-garde, bold, even, gasp, sexy?"

"Slutty. You have to admit, what I did was slutty."

"Grace," said VJ, looking me straight in the eye without a hint of humor. "My forty-two-year-old father encouraging every young ingénue in Mumbai to think sex with him will further her career is slutty. What you did may not have been your wisest decision, but it wasn't slutty. In fact, it was so naive it was kind of sweet. Seriously, Grace, didn't your parents teach you anything?"

"Apparently not," I said wryly.

"Well, Bambi, you've come to the right place. As someone who's spent a lifetime in the public eye, who's had his every debacle documented, I'm going to teach you how to deal with the hunters."

"If you've had every debacle documented, are you sure you're the best person to advise me? It doesn't sound like you know how to avoid publicity."

"Avoid it?" VJ made big eyes. "Baby, why would you want to avoid it? What you want to do is control it."

"Like you do?" I didn't even try to hide my skepticism.

"Absolutely. Let me ask you one question. Did you know I was gay?"

I paused. He had me there. Everything I'd ever read about him told the same story. He was a womanizing bad boy, in sharp contrast to his father, invariably portrayed as a dignified family man. How could the press have got it so backwards?

"Exactly." VJ read my mind. "The trick is to take control of your image. Don't let it control you. Now finish your salad. You're going to need your strength for the days ahead."

"Why do you even want to help me?"

"Did your brother Kyle ever mention me?"

"No, I don't think so."

"He was on my cricket team. Last year we played a tournament in Singapore. He never mentioned that?"

"I knew he went, but so what?"

"I met someone at the tournament. It was the first and last time I've had the freedom to act on my feelings. We got a little physical and your brother walked in on us. He never told you about that?"

"No, he didn't say a thing."

"I'm not surprised. He never told anyone. He could have destroyed me, but he didn't, and he never made me feel awkward about it either. He didn't treat me any differently than before."

"You know it really isn't a big deal, right? It's perfectly normal."

"Not in my world. If the press got wind of my inclinations, my career would be over. It's not okay for a regular Indian boy to be gay, much less a teen idol. And take a good look at my friends, wannabe starlets and sycophants. Not one of them would stick by me if my star plummeted."

"You don't know that. Maybe you just need to give people a chance." I suddenly realized I'd just parroted the same advice Kyle had given me not so long ago.

"Has that been your experience, Grace?"

My silence was sufficient response.

"Do your parents know?" I couldn't imagine how hard it would be to keep a secret like that.

"I told my mother last year. She slapped me and said we wouldn't speak of it again." He kept his voice level but his eyes clouded at the memory.

"What are you going to do?"

"I'll do what my parents expect of me—get married, produce at least one child, ideally a boy, and never under any circumstances let anyone outside the family find out what I am."

I only had time for one more bite of my salad before the bell rang, but it wasn't going down so well anyway. As I picked up what was left of it and headed for the bin, I found myself worrying about the most popular guy in school, which probably explains why I didn't see her coming. She crashed into me, tipping salad down my shirt. The whole oily mess crashed to the floor. A crowd quickly formed, her minions already on the scene.

"Get your cameras ready, boys. She's probably going to whip off her shirt and start rubbing that oil on herself."

I stared at the mess on the floor. "Why don't you give it a rest, Madison?" I was more sad than angry.

"Why, what are you going to do about it?"

"Oh, good!" exclaimed VJ. I didn't realize he'd pushed his

way through the crowd to stand beside me. "Look, Grace, it's the wicked witch and her flying monkeys!"

Madison glowered, but even surrounded by her supporters she didn't have the nerve to take on the famous VJ Patel.

"You drag me into your sordid little drama again and you're dead," she snarled, but she scuttled away before I could respond.

"Hey, man, what are you doing?" asked Todd, perhaps emboldened by his own role in my downfall. "You can do better than her."

"Actually, *man*, I've convinced Grace that she can do better than you. Strangely enough, that wasn't hard."

There were a few giggles from the crowd.

"I'd certainly take VJ over Todd," said a senior I didn't know but instantly liked. This was followed by general murmurs of assent.

Todd looked around at his faithless friends.

"Do you know what I can't figure out, McClaren?" Todd demanded. "How you could have believed even for a minute that I'd be interested in you. Don't you know what a total loser you are?"

VJ stepped up to Todd so their faces were inches apart. "You're the only loser I see."

"Whatever, man." Todd shot me a final contemptuous look before stalking off.

I waited for the crowd to disperse before I turned to VJ. "Are you sure you want to hang out with me? People are going to wonder why you're sticking up for me. They might even think we're a couple."

"Exactly, darling. Now you're getting the hang of it."

13

Noor

The doctor . . .

I rehearsed what I was going to say when my name was called. I'd tell them Ma was too sick to come but gave me permission to bring my brother. I'd admit he'd been coughing for several weeks but I'd lie about the blood in his spit, claiming it was a new symptom. To admit the truth would have raised questions I didn't want to answer.

We took two buses across town to visit a hospital where we weren't known. I hoped there wasn't a central registry of hospital visits. We'd been to more than a dozen throughout the city. Ma had no idea we'd visited any. She would have beaten me senseless if she'd known.

It was the only way I could get enough medicine for Shami. Each new clinic would give him only a single injection and medicine for a week or two at most. I was handed prescriptions for the rest, which I hadn't the money to fill. Traveling to a new clinic was half the cost of filling the prescription and had the added benefit that if his condition worsened, a doctor would catch it.

Each new doctor had given me a stern lecture on how to administer the drugs, writing it all down so I could pass the information to my mother. Each time, I'd listened intently, folded the instructions and made a show of zipping them into my bag. Never once did I say my mother couldn't read or that she believed doctors were tricksters and thieves. Ma said free clinics were like the fruit-wallah who gave you a slice of mango and then tried to sell you a whole one at twice its value.

Fortunately, like every other morning, Ma was sleeping off the effects of alcohol and her night's work. If things went according to plan, I'd have Shami back under her bed before she noticed he was missing, with another dose of drugs in his system and a small supply to keep him going.

That day, the trip to the clinic had taken longer than I'd expected and it was already full of people when we arrived. I checked in at the front counter and was given a number in the hundreds. I could only hope that they didn't start with number one each day but carried numbers over from one day to the next.

The clinic was in a small section of a much larger hospital. The designated waiting area, on the second floor, was little more than a widening of the corridor with several dozen hard, molded chairs bolted together and to the floor. Every one of them was already filled, as was most of the available floor space. In some cases whole families were camped out. It was a roll call of diseases, every one present and accounted for. Running noses and hacking coughs were the most obvious symptoms, but Shami wasn't the only child with a glassy-eyed stare.

He'd fussed on the trip over, trying to convince me with his few words not to take him. Barely two years old, he knew where we were bound whenever we boarded a bus in the early hours of the morning. The excitement of the first time had long since passed. For him it meant poking and prodding, a painful injection and foul-tasting medicine. He didn't understand that it was to make him better, and truthfully I was losing faith in that myself. This bout of bloody coughing was only his latest affliction. He was visited by one symptom after another, each gnawing at him, stealing the light from his eyes, so it seemed as he got older that he'd skipped childhood altogether and gone straight to old age.

"Shami want 'nana," said Shami. I held him in one arm with his own draped around my neck. He watched me as I scanned the room for a place to sit down.

I turned my attention to him skeptically. Shami rarely expressed hunger, even less so in the past weeks. The cough had drained his desire for food, along with the energy to eat it.

"If we leave, we'll lose our place."

"Shami want 'nana," he repeated earnestly.

I spotted a corner for us at the end of the waiting area farthest from the doctor's office. I took him over and settled us on the floor. I laid Shami out beside me with his head in my lap and stroked his hair. It was a relief to sit down, though I kept a vigilant eye on the doctor's door. Shami fell into a fitful sleep despite his frequent fits of coughing.

Two hours passed with fewer than a dozen people going in and out of the office. I looked at the other invalids and was reminded of the herd of goats that filled our street every Eid. They were petted and overfed, yet their darting eyes showed too much white. Somehow they understood death was upon them. How many of these patients knew they would never recover? A doctor's visit was just one more item crossed off their list of chores and had less purpose than cleaning a toilet.

Shami started another deep bout of coughing. My rag was already wet with his blood but I held it to his lips anyway so it didn't splatter on the floor. It oozed between my fingers. I rummaged in my bag for our water carafe with my free hand. When his coughing slowed, I held it to his lips.

"Take him outside before he makes us all sick," scolded a woman who was seated on the floor a short distance away.

She was round like a tomato, as were her husband and even her two young children. I wasn't surprised at her order, though she knew very well I wouldn't obey. Picking fights made the waiting pass more quickly. A schoolgirl alone with her baby brother was an easy target. Who would speak up for me? I looked at her gold necklace. It was only gold-plated, and the inlaid jewels were fake. Did she think she was fooling anyone?

"So sorry, Auntie, but I must let the doctor see him. My mother is also sick or she would have come." I kept my eyes down, my tone respectful. There was nothing to be gained by fighting. She was a married woman, a mother and wife. Shami and I were nothing, less than nothing. Whether she'd started it or not, if I allowed myself to get drawn in, we would be the ones tossed out on the street like trash.

"Go sit farther away." She didn't sound any friendlier but she was no longer demanding we leave. I looked around us. Every inch of space was taken.

"Shami want 'nana." Shami regarded the woman hopefully.

"I'll get you a banana after we see the doctor," I said hastily. Shami sighed.

The woman murmured something to her husband and he handed her a large bag. She opened it up and rifled through, pulling out a metal tiffin box. Shami watched in fascination. She opened the top level, revealing a dish of fresh-cut fruit— mangoes, papaya and pineapple. She handed the dish to Shami, who snatched it greedily and began tucking in. Since Ma's brief affair with the fruit-wallah ended, we rarely got fresh fruit.

"Thank you, Auntie," I said.

"Your mother should be here," she said gruffly, watching the fruit rapidly disappearing into Shami as though he was worried she might snatch it back if he weren't quick.

In my head I made a promise that I would talk to Ma about giving Shami more fruit. In school they taught us about eating a balanced diet. But they never taught us how to do that when you lived in a house with two dozen other families and everyone, all the mothers and children, shared a tiny kitchen with a single element for cooking. Like most residents of Kamathipura, we lived on street food, fried dough, sometimes stuffed with potatoes and onions. The closest we came to fresh fruit was the occasional dollop of tamarind chutney.

I'd have to make up a story about why I thought it likely Shami would even eat fruit. That didn't worry me. Most of what I said to Ma was lies or half-truths, as was most of what she said to me. Sometimes, if Ma lied hard enough, I could make myself believe her. I don't think Ma ever believed my lies, though. I think when you get bigger your imagination gets smaller, or maybe Ma just didn't have the energy for pretending.

Shami finished the dish and began noisily sucking juice

off his fingers. I handed the dish back to Fat-auntie. Shami smiled at her. She fought a losing battle to hold back her own smile, which flooded her face like a monsoon rain.

"He's a beautiful child," she said.

"Yes," I agreed without embarrassment, because it was true, yet counted for so little. A boy needed only to be strong, and Shami wasn't that.

"Shami strong," said Shami, reading my thoughts as he so often did.

"Of course you are," said the woman, exchanging a look with me.

"Shami strong," Shami repeated firmly.

"Do you know what time it is, Auntie?"

She nodded to a clock on the wall.

It was later than I'd hoped. Ma rarely got up before one, but when she did, she'd expect to find Shami at home, either asleep under the bed or playing with Deepa-Auntie. No matter where Shami and I spent the night, I always took him home before leaving for school. I'd told Deepa-Auntie where we were going. I gave her instructions to tell Ma I'd taken Shami for a walk because his cough had made him restless. Ma would see through the deception in an instant. I would never willingly miss school. If we weren't back by one she'd try her best to beat the truth out of me. She wouldn't succeed. It had worked when I was a child but I was more stubborn now.

Parvati had agreed to walk Aamaal to school, which was kind of her, considering we'd both had another restless night. She had a new boyfriend who pumped gas at a station not far from our street. He'd told us we could sleep behind the station building, but halfway through the night his supervisor, alerted by Shami's coughing, had discovered us and chased us off. It was getting harder and harder to find a safe place. If Shami were not so sick I'd have asked Ma for money to rent space in a room. Lots of families did that, several families together in a room not ten feet square. The rooms were cramped and un-ventilated but it was better than sleeping on the street. Instead I hoarded every rupee I could squeeze out of her for trips to the doctor and herb-filled poultices for his chest. Ma didn't even seem to care about him anymore. She never suggested he stay with her at night. Aamaal was the only one she noticed.

"Shami pee pee," said Shami, interrupting my thoughts.

"All right." I'd seen a washroom near the entrance down-stairs. I stood up and took his hand. Just then a nurse poked her head out of the office door and called our number.

"It will have to wait, baby. Can you hold it in?"

Shami furrowed his brow. I took that for an affirmative and led him through the crowd to the doctor's office. We entered a tiny waiting room with two vinyl-cushioned chairs and one metal-and-plastic one. The nurse sat in the metal chair and reached for a clipboard. She directed us to sit as well. I pulled Shami onto my lap but he wiggled off and climbed onto his own chair. It was covered in bright red fabric that looked like leather but wasn't. Shami pressed his finger into the cushion and giggled in wonderment when it regained its shape.

"Why are you here?" asked the nurse.

As if on cue, Shami started to cough violently. The nurse looked alarmed, though she must have dealt with this kind of sickness many times.

"How old is he?" she asked.

"Two and four months."

She looked surprised. "He looks younger. I thought under a year. And what is the patient's name?"

"Shami," said Shami.

I added our family name and answered her other questions with the lies I'd rehearsed.

She had him stand on a scale and weighed him. His weight had dropped since our last visit to a doctor two weeks ago. I bowed my head in shame, though the nurse couldn't have known. Finally she told us to wait and disappeared through an inner door, where I knew from experience the doctor would be finishing up with another patient.

Ten minutes later the nurse reappeared and ushered us into the examining room. The doctor was a woman. She looked around the same age as Ma but years younger at the same time. Her glossy black hair hung loose around her shoulders. Her back was straight, her eyes clear. The first time I'd encountered a woman doctor, I was surprised to discover women could be doctors, but now I knew they were as common as men, at least at the free clinics.

Familiar with the routine, I lifted Shami onto her examination table and took the wooden chair next to it. She sat on a rolling chair that allowed her to roam the empty space between her desk on the far wall and us. She slid up next to me and grinned. It made me nervous to have her so close.

"So, who have we here?" she asked, reading the chart.

"This is Shami. He has a cough with blood. My name is Noor. I'm his sister." While she'd asked her question in Hindi, I'd answered her in English, for the same reason I'd put on my school uniform that day. She might know my caste from my family name, if not my too-dark skin, but I would do everything I could to give her the impression I was from a respectable family.

"Where are your parents, Noor?"

"My father is dead. My mother is sick. She wanted to come today but she was too weak."

"I'm sorry to hear that. When did your father die?"

I didn't hesitate. I'd told this lie many times. "Three years ago. He had a heart attack."

"I see. And what's wrong with your mother?"

"She has a fever. It's probably just a virus." I blanched, realizing what I'd just said. In our neighborhood a virus meant only one thing. "Like the flu," I added, "or a bacterial infection."

"A bacterial infection?" She had a mischievous gleam in her eye. It made me feel even more jittery. "Or a virus. Well, that covers it, doesn't it? How old are you, Noor?"

"Fifteen," I lied again. I'm not even sure why I told that lie. Fifteen was no better than my real age, twelve and a half. Either way, I was still a minor with no right to make any decisions for myself, much less my brother.

"And you go to school. What standard?"

"Nine." This was only a minor lie. I was in eight, which was correct for my real age. I couldn't say that though because nine was already a year behind for my fake age.

The doctor gave me an appraising look. "Your English is very good. You must study hard."

I didn't know how to answer this as my lie suggested the opposite.

"I'm trying to catch up," I finally said. "I got sick last year and had to repeat."

"Hmmm, a lot of sickness in your family. What were you sick with?"

I stalled again. She asked more questions than most free clinic doctors. Usually they were too busy. No wonder she had such a crowd waiting outside. I considered pointing that out.

"Pneumonia." Shami had had pneumonia several times, so I was familiar with the symptoms. If she wanted to continue the interrogation, I was well prepared.

She just gave me a long look before standing up and moving over to Shami.

Taking the stethoscope from around her neck, she began the all-too familiar routine of checking him out. Even Shami knew what to do, taking deep breaths, which brought on another fit of coughing, leaning forward and back, opening his mouth, tilting his head. He followed every instruction almost before she asked.

She turned to me. "How long did you say he's been coughing up blood?"

"It started yesterday."

She pinned me with penetrating eyes. I felt myself sweat. I reassured myself that my anxiety didn't show on my face. I was a master at hiding my feelings. Her loud exhale told me she knew I was lying. My gaze didn't waver.

"He's significantly underweight," she said.

"He's a picky eater." I felt guilty, remembering the fruit.

"Is that true, Shami?" she asked in Hindi. Her voice was light but I saw through her act. "Don't you like to eat?"

"Shami eat manga an' napple," said Shami.

"Oh, I love manga an' napple!" the doctor exclaimed.

"Shami like 'nana," said Shami.

"Me too!" said the doctor. "You and I must go out for lunch sometime, Shami. I can see we have the same culinary tastes. You relax now. I'm going to talk to Noor."

"Where do you live?" She sat down again and picked up the chart and her pen.

"I told the nurse."

"It says here you live in Bandra." She named the upper-middle-class neighborhood I'd laid claim to. It was nowhere near Kamathipura, but familiar to everyone in the city for the number of Bollywood stars who lived there. It was also close to this clinic. I didn't want to raise the slightest suspicion that I'd traveled halfway across town because I'd already been to every free clinic near my own neighborhood.

Her pencil stayed poised above the chart. "You live in Bandra?" Her distrust was badly concealed. The rich were so often poor liars. It made me wonder how they were so successful.

Though I was lying, I felt angry to be disbelieved. I didn't answer. She glanced up. Her lips twitched as she tried to maintain a serious expression. Suddenly I was reminded of Parvati.

"Reclamation," I amended my story. It was a mixed neighborhood on the edge of Bandra, mostly squatters' shacks. I could have lived there. Despite my worn, too-tight uniform and scuffed shoes, I was still a school-going girl.

She put down the pen. What did she think she knew? Was my mother's profession printed on my forehead? It wasn't her business anyway. Her job was to give me the medicine. No wonder her line of patients moved so slowly. Did she think we had all day to pour out our life stories so she could spice up her boring life with our desperation?

"And you're fifteen, you said?"

I stared at my feet. I could feel her watching me with the intensity of a raven, as if my words were morsels of food and she was just waiting for me to drop one. I hoped I looked humble, like a beggar. I didn't want her to see the tiger inside me.

There was a long pause as she waited for me to say something.

"What do you say we try this again, Noor," she said gently.

I didn't know if it was her tone, or the stress of too many doctors, too many close calls with Shami's life. A tear slid down my nose and dropped on my knee, and then another. I wiped them away as quickly as they fell but they wouldn't stop coming. It was not worth it, all this trouble for a few days' worth of medicine. I was so tired of it all. Shami's sickness consumed us both. I could have no life while I watched his slip away.

I heard her chair roll toward me and suddenly her arms were around me, hugging me tight. The shock of it made me freeze; my belly seized, trapping my breath inside.

"Let's see if we can't help Shami together," she said. Her face was close to my hair. I'd oiled it only yesterday but still I feared lice would leap from my head to hers. She rubbed my back and gradually my breath returned.

"I don't know how to help him," I said truthfully.

She slid back and lifted my chin so she could see my face. "An accurate medical history is a good place to start. How long has he been sick?"

I swiped my hand across my eyes and took a deep breath, trying to regain control. A million lies flooded my brain. I could have told any one of them.

"From the day he was born."

We talked for a long time after that. I told her everything, or most things, anyway. I didn't tell her about Parvati, or my dream of becoming a doctor myself, or being a Devadasi. But I told her what Ma did. She asked many questions about Shami's birth. I said only that it was a home birth but I did my best to remember every illness he'd had since then and gave a faithful account. I told her we didn't have any place to cook proper meals. I was grateful when she accepted that and didn't ask for details. I told her Shami slept on the floor and let her figure out the significance of that. I'm not sure she could have imagined it, even if I'd explained. I didn't tell her we slept on the street, wherever I could find a place. I think she knew. Her raven eyes glistened with unshed tears. She seemed shocked by what I told her, as if she didn't live in Mumbai and drive by people living under bridges every day and see others digging through garbage to survive. She was like the people who took guided tours through our neighborhood, capturing our images with their cameras while failing to actually see us. We were no more real than a Bollywood film. Still, I was amazed by how stupid smart people could be.

Finally, she asked if she could test Shami's blood. I knew what she wanted to test it for. I told her what I'd told all the previous doctors: I had no money for the test, and it wouldn't matter anyway because we couldn't afford the drugs. She said there were ways to cover the cost if Shami was registered with an NGO. I'd heard about these NGOs that took children like Shami away from their families. They shoved all the sick children in big homes together, separated from everyone who loved them. How was that a better life for my brother? I agreed to talk it over with my mother. It was yet another lie.

I was on the point of leaving when a male doctor poked his head in the door. It startled me, not just because of the intrusion. I had the unsettling feeling that I knew him. I kept my back to him and crossed my arms over my chest so he couldn't see the school crest on my shirt. Was it possible I'd taken Shami to him in the past?

"Are you just about done here, Karuna? Our meeting has started."

"I'll be along shortly. You're on the board of Mercy House, aren't you? Do you know if there's any space for a new admission?"

I felt the doctor's eyes on my back but didn't turn.

"How old is he?" There was a pause. The question was directed at me.

"Almost two and a half," said the lady doctor.

"I'll look into it."

They were discussing putting Shami away as if it were as routine as prescribing a pill. The male doctor left, but a yawning gorge had opened inside me. The lady doctor and I were not on the same side.

She gave me another hug and for an instant I allowed myself to picture a life totally different from my own. But it wasn't my life.

As I stepped out into the heat and bustle of the swarming masses and joined a sweaty crush of people shoving each other for space on a bus, I was already planning which hospital we'd go to the next time Shami needed drugs.

Grace

I was not a maverick.

Whatever VJ thought, no amount of telling me it was good to be different could change nearly sixteen years of wanting to fit in. Alone in my bedroom that night I couldn't get Todd's comment out of my head. As much as I didn't like being called a slut, being called a loser was so much worse. *Slut* only described my recent behavior; it didn't define me. *Loser* was something else again. A loser was a person who couldn't make friends. Losers screwed up all the time and hurt those around them.

Until Todd said it, I'd never realized that, as insecure as I was, I didn't think of myself that way. I knew I was shy and had trouble making friends, was lousy at sports and was just an average student. But lots of kids are like that. Even my recent debacle had seemed like poor judgment, not a defining moment. I'd already taken steps to make sure I didn't screw up like that again.

So why was the word *loser* going around and around in my head? My nerves jangled as I stood up and walked to the window. I stared at the world below without seeing it. Was that what everyone thought of me? It had the ring of truth. I was the main reason my parents had stopped moving around. Kyle flourished no matter where we went. It was my social isolation they worried about.

I sat down on my bed and pulled up my leg to look at the word I'd carved into it the day before. I remembered the peace I'd felt when the task was finished. Though the wound still hurt, the word itself had lost a lot of its power. It didn't change Mom's disappointment in me, or my disappointment in myself, but it did make me feel more in control. I didn't want to do it again though—that would be crazy. Nevertheless my body vibrated with the effort of keeping still.

I pulled up my legs and wrapped my arms tightly around them, willing myself to calm down. Suddenly my phone beeped. I tried to ignore it. It had to be another hater. There was nothing to be gained from reading another cruel message but not reading it only made me dwell on it even more.

Finally, curiosity got the best of me. I got up to fetch my phone, hoping that at the very least, it would take my mind off cutting. I flipped to the message as I walked back to the bed.

U been quiet lately. Everything ok?

It was my brother.

I sat back down. Why was he texting me now? Had Dad told Kyle what I did?

U there grace?

Dad said you were having friend problems.

I knew it! I seethed.

Bosco stood up on the bed madly wagging his tail.

"How did you know it was Kyle?" I demanded. "I know you miss him but you're going to have to get used to the fact that it's just you and me now. He deserted us." It was an unfair thing to say. I felt guilty when Bosco sat down and cocked his head like he'd actually understood.

"I'm sure he's missing you too, Bosco," I said, scratching his ear before turning my attention back to the phone.

Im fine, I texted. Was asleep. Will call u tomorrow.

Would I call him tomorrow? And say what? If I told him about what was happening to me, I'd have to tell him what I'd done to provoke it. There was no way I could tell him that.

Ok, call anytime. Luv u sis.

I furiously wiped away the tears that had started streaming down my face. I'd managed not to cry today, up till now. I knew Kyle was just trying to be supportive, but reminding me how much I missed him wasn't helpful. If he'd been here maybe I would have found the courage to tell him everything. Though if he'd been here, probably none of this would have happened. I might have had a lot of years of feeling lonely and different but I'd never been bullied before, because no one would have dared mess with Kyle McClaren's little sister. Who knew how many kids over the years had wanted to tell me I was a loser but had only been deterred because of my perfect brother? Even VJ had said he was only being my friend to pay back Kyle's kindness. If it wasn't for Kyle, I would have been labeled a loser years ago. Kyle had been the only thing standing between me and the truth. I really was a loser.

I got up and went down the hall to the kitchen. Vanita was there doing the dishes. She eyed me curiously when I went straight to the cutlery drawer and pulled out the sharpest knife I could find.

"What are you looking for?" She came and stood next to me. "Do you want me to cut some fruit for you?"

"No, thanks." I liked Vanita but, like everyone, she treated me as if I were helpless. "I'm just working on a school project."

I returned to my bedroom and closed the door behind me. Bosco was sitting up on my bed giving me "the stare." It usually meant he wanted food, but if I didn't know better I'd have sworn he knew what I was planning.

"You can stare all you want but you're not going to stop me," I told him firmly. "I have to do this, Bosco. I promise it will be the last time."

He looked at the knife.

"I know what I'm doing. It will make me feel better."

The minute I sat on the bed and crossed my legs he leaped into my lap.

"Stop it, Bosco!"

I pushed him off and lined the knife up neatly under the first word. Bosco knocked the knife out of my hand as he clambered into my lap again.

"NO! Bad dog! I could have hurt you."

I got off the bed and fetched the knife from the floor. Dropping down to sit there, I was for once grateful that Bosco was too cowardly to jump down from the bed by himself. I felt the same sense of relief when I made the first cut. I owned the word now. It didn't own me.

When I was finished, I lay down on the bed and pulled Bosco into my arms, closing my eyes. Like meditative chanting, my leg throbbed with every beat of my heart. I fell asleep to the steady pulse of my own blood.

The next morning, I arrived at school to find a fresh coat of paint on my locker. Where *SLUT* had been the day before was a bright orange Post-it note telling me to go to Mr. Donleavy's room. I sighed as I pulled off the note and shoved it in my jeans pocket. I liked Mr. Donleavy, and I did want a chance to redeem myself, but I was the school loser. Did he really think I could provide any guidance to a younger girl?

Mr. Donleavy was standing at his whiteboard writing his quote for the day. He was that kind of teacher. You could tell he didn't teach because it was the only thing he could do. He really believed he was inspiring the world's future leaders.

Today his quote was: "Everyone thinks of changing the world, but no one thinks of changing himself." He added the author's name, Leo Tolstoy.

"Did you choose that one just for me, Mr. Donleavy?"

"Grace!" He gave me a huge smile. "Trust me, there are plenty of people who need to remember Tolstoy's wisdom, myself included. Have a seat and let's go over our plan for today."

I was pretty sure *our* plan meant *his* plan, but I was in no position to claim that I didn't need help in the planning department. The desks in Mr. Donleavy's classroom were arranged in a semicircle. I sat where I always did, nearest the door. Mr. Donleavy came over and perched on a desk nearby.

"I've made arrangements for us to go to the NGO this afternoon."

My heart started to pound. "That fast?"

"We're already almost four weeks into the term, Grace, and you still haven't earned any community service hours."

Fair point.

"Your parents have agreed that I'll take you today after school. I've had another student volunteer so you'll have some company. You need to be in the east parking lot by three forty-five."

There wasn't much left to say so I headed to class wondering who else had been roped into volunteering.

The rest of the day was relatively uneventful. I had only a few new hate messages on my phone, no doubt because I'd blocked virtually everyone. Unfortunately, it was a small school, and Madison was in most of my classes. I kept a low profile, something I used to be good at. Once, I accidentally caught her eye when I was leaving a class. She gave me a contemptuous look and whispered something to the girl next to her, but I kept walking as their laughter followed me.

In English, our teacher told us to get into groups to discuss a novel. As desks were shuffled and groups formed I found myself facing closed circles. It wasn't the first time I'd been left out that year, but it was the first time it felt deliberate. The teacher, perhaps because she knew about my problems with Madison and Kelsey, directed me to join three boys. This occasioned a round of "slut" coughing. I'm not sure which one of us was most embarrassed. In any case, the boys ignored me and I stared out the window. I spent some time wondering how everyone would react if they came to school the next day to discover I'd killed myself. No matter how hard I tried, I couldn't imagine anyone would care.

VJ turned up at my locker at the beginning of the lunch period. He was definitely committed to the ruse that we were a couple, though he spent the next forty minutes talking about Luca D'Silva, the hottest boy in school if you took VJ out of the running. I must have repeated one hundred times that I didn't think Luca was gay but, as VJ pointed out, I would have said the same thing about him not so long ago.

As the end of the day approached I felt more and more apprehensive. I wasn't good with new people at the best of times. The idea of going into the red-light district of Mumbai and trying to make friends with kids whose life experiences were beyond my imagination was terrifying. The fact that our only common link was that their mothers took their shirts off for money and I did it because I was spectacularly stupid seemed like a tenuous basis for a friendship. By the time I'd loaded my books into my locker, I'd concocted so many reasons why this was a bad idea that I actually felt ill.

I dragged myself to the back of the school, walking as slowly as I possibly could. I didn't think Mr. Donleavy would leave without me but it was worth a try. When I reached the parking lot he was waiting for me. I was only mildly surprised by the person he was with.

"Gracie," VJ called out, "what kept you?"

I didn't like to admit to myself how relieved I was to see him. I smiled.

"The stars must be aligned." VJ beamed back warmly. "She's smiling!"

"All right, troops, let's saddle up," said Mr. Donleavy.

"I'm sorry, Mr. D.," said VJ, mock-serious, "this just isn't going to work if you're going to impose your imperialist American culture. We are not conquering the Wild West but the Wild East!"

"VJ, don't make me regret letting you tag along."

"Not a chance, sir. I'm the only one who speaks Hindi and

Marathi, not to mention a bit of Kannada and Gujarati. You people would be lost without me. And I have an armed guard . . ."

"Who we agreed will follow in his own car."

"I wouldn't have it any other way. When the tires get slashed on this heap, we're going to need my ride."

Mr. Donleavy climbed into the front of the van, next to the driver, while VJ and I sat behind. The drive took close to an hour but VJ had no trouble keeping us entertained the entire trip with Bollywood gossip.

I wouldn't have noticed when we left the wide streets behind and entered the narrow laneways of Kamathipura except that we had to slow down to a crawl. There were so many motorcycles, beat-up old cars, snack carts, bullock carts, various huge wooden wagons, and such an assortment of cows, goats and the ubiquitous stray dogs and cats—not to mention people—filling every inch of space that we had to force them aside with our vehicle. At times we were defeated and we were the ones standing still, waiting for some room to inch into. Finally, the driver decided he'd driven us as close as we were going to get and pulled off to one side. In any other part of the city people would have honked at him. Where I lived the van might even have been towed. But in that neighborhood it was now just one more obstacle in a lane that was full of them.

The first thing that assaulted me on stepping out of the car was the awful smell. Though the source wasn't immediately clear, an open sewage canal on one side of the road could certainly have been part of it. Equally possible was the garbage strewed everywhere, and the occasional piles of goat and cow dung. We hadn't been walking two minutes before I noticed a child squatting at the side of the road relieving himself.

Mr. Donleavy must have caught the look on my face. "A lot of these people are homeless. They have no access to running water, electricity or toilets. Some of the girls you meet today will sleep on the street tonight."

"It's so congested. Why's it more crowded than the rest of Mumbai?"

"Kamathipura's a draw for the most impoverished. Migrant workers, beggars, thieves, drug addicts, gamblers, sex workers all make a home here and are accepted in a way they might not be in other parts of the city."

I looked around and for the first time noticed how many people had stopped what they were doing to stare at us. It must have been hard for them to be confronted by our evident wealth. How could they not feel resentful? I was glad I'd followed Mr. Donleavy's advice and left my schoolbag and phone in the car; though, come to think of it, if my phone got ripped off it wouldn't be a disaster.

Mr. Donleavy was already weaving his way around a cart selling some kind of greasy fried dough and heading for an open doorway.

"Ready?" I asked VJ.

"Always," he said.

15

Noor

Crocodile arms . . .

I waited for Parvati for over an hour outside our usual café at the train station. I'd come late and was worried I'd missed her. Our house was in an uproar because Lali-didi had disappeared. The night trade had just started and, as usual, Lali-didi was in great demand. Every night she had enough regular customers to meet her quota, but Pran forced her to take as many as turned up. They waited their turn in the lounge like passengers waiting for a train. No one knew how many customers she had each night. Only Binti-Ma'am saw the money that changed hands. She promised Lali-didi that one day soon her debt would be cleared, but everyone knew Binti-Ma'am was a liar. No one in our house cleared their debt while they were still young enough to fetch a high price.

Everyone in the house said Lali-didi was too young for the work. Prita-Auntie was particularly vocal. Lali-didi herself said little. Ma said she was resigned to her situation but I wasn't so sure. I saw the scars that snaked up her arm, horizontal lines, like the belly of a crocodile, and only on her left arm. Lali-didi was right-handed.

Her last day with us had seemed no different from the others. I'd been at school, so I didn't see her until the early evening. She sat on her bed making preparations for the night, lining her eyes with kohl and painting her lips. As always I felt a stab of anxiety as I watched the transformation from the girl that she was, little older than me, to the object that she became. For weeks I'd seen something die in her each time she went through this process, and every day less of her returned. She rarely spoke, never laughed; it was as if she was dead already.

Pran discovered her bed empty only when he was ushering in yet another man. They'd passed Shami and me in the downstairs hallway as we were leaving for the night. Pran's outcry drew me back. Her few possessions were in their usual place, as if she'd just stepped out to the latrine. Lali-didi didn't have the freedom to step out anywhere—and yet she had. Like a bird slipping through the bars of her cage, Lali-didi was gone without so much as a whisper. Of course, someone must have helped her. That much was undeniable, though no one was admitting to it.

Pran flew into a rage. Deepa-Auntie was his first suspect, not because she was the most likely but because he wanted her to be guilty. "I'll kill you!" he screamed, beating her until she was no longer able to rise from the ground. "Tell me where she's gone!"

Ma ordered me out of the house. I wanted to leave—I didn't want to witness any more—but I couldn't. I feared Pran would kill Deepa-Auntie. Finally Ma gave up trying to shoo me out and turned on Pran.

"Stop it, Pran," Ma commanded.

He raised his fist to her too but she didn't quail.

"That's enough," she said. "Deepa's too stupid to have planned a betrayal like this. What do you think she did, squeeze Lali through the window bars? Deepa was with a customer. She couldn't have helped."

"Keep out of it, Ashmita. This is none of your business."

"Isn't it? How do you know I didn't do it?"

"Because you're not a fool. You understand how things work, and you have too much to lose. You're already splitting your profits with my mother. In another year or two you'll have enough money to rent a room for your family."

"If I live that long," said Ma, giving him a steely look.

Ma talked more and more of her own death these days. I wished she would stop. She ate little, even when I skipped my own dinner so I could afford her favorite biryani.

"Deepa knows something," Pran insisted.

"She would have told you if she did. She's little more than a child. Do you really think she could hold out against a man like you?"

I almost laughed. Behind his back, Ma called Pran "the little brown monkey" because he danced to Binti-Ma'am's bidding.

"There will be trouble from this," Pran threatened.

He didn't say that the worst trouble would be for him. His ma was the brothel-keeper but they both worked for another man. Nishikar-Sir, the owner of our brothel, was the overlord of our world. Some say he owned twenty brothels in Kamathipura. We rarely saw him. The arrival of his black Mercedes was an event greeted with equal measures of awe and dread. Stories of his temper were exceeded only by those of his violence. He wouldn't let the loss of one of his most valuable girls go unpunished. As the enforcer in our home, Pran would be held accountable. I felt a shiver of anticipation and hoped I was around when the confrontation took place.

"Look what you've done to her face," said Ma, gesturing to Deepa-Auntie, who was lying on the floor quietly moaning. "How is it going to help you to damage the girl who is now your top earner?" Ma must have been really frightened for Deepa-Auntie. Otherwise she'd never have admitted Deepa-Auntie was more desired than herself.

"Clean her up and get her back to work," Pran snarled. "Everyone meets their quota tonight." He turned on his heel and disappeared down the ladder.

Ma and I rushed to Deepa-Auntie, who was struggling to sit up.

"Help her wash," ordered Ma.

"But what happened to Lali-didi?" I asked.

"Who can say?" said Ma, but a look passed between her and Deepa-Auntie. "The girl wouldn't have lasted much longer. We're well rid of her."

Deepa-Auntie leaned heavily on me as I got her to her feet and over to the ladder. I went down ahead of her and was relieved to find Shami exactly where I'd left him, sitting against the wall near the bottom rung. Deepa-Auntie moved slowly. She was favoring one foot and hunched over, cradling her chest. I hoped nothing was broken. I helped her hobble to the washroom.

As soon as the door was closed she quickly filled me in on the basics. "The customer I was with had really come to rescue

Lali. He's fallen in love with her and agreed to help her escape. She's going to live with him now."

"Did Ma help?" I was incredulous.

"Your ma planned the whole thing, Noor-baby. Lali wasn't strong enough for this life."

I helped her wash as quickly as I could but her pain was extreme. She must have had cracked ribs at the very least. I begged her to let me take her to a hospital but she refused. Her fear of Pran was far greater than her fear of a rib puncturing her lungs. It was more than an hour later before Shami and I were on our way again.

Standing outside the café, waiting for Parvati, I felt spent. The nervous energy that had seen me through the last hour had left me feeling hollow and weak. I just wanted to sleep but I didn't want to bed down without Parvati. Pran's recent viciousness was still vivid in my mind. The streets felt even more dangerous than usual. Without Parvati's reassuring bravado I felt exposed and vulnerable. I tried to think where she might have gone. We'd recently found a quiet spot behind the train station but I'd checked there before I came to the café. There was no sign of her.

"What do you think, Shami?" I looked down at Shami, who was sitting on the pavement at my feet. He was too little to have an opinion but his presence comforted me. "Where's Parvati? Should we try the bridge?"

"I want Par-di," said Shami.

"Me too," I said.

I hitched him up on my hip. His arms circled my neck and he rested his head against my chest. It didn't make sense to me that she'd go back to the shantytown where we were attacked, but it was the only place, other than our own street, where I knew she had friends. I was on the point of setting off when I heard a noise that froze me in place.

"Did you hear that, Shami?"

He cocked his head, his face scrunched with the effort of listening.

"Paru," he confirmed.

It certainly sounded like someone calling my name, but the sound was so faint it might have been buzzing from the fluorescent streetlamp above us.

"Noor," called the voice again. That time it was unmistakable.

I looked past the café to the narrow alley that separated it from the pawnshop next door. I wanted to run but my legs had gained twenty pounds in an instant. I was terrified of what I'd find. I put Shami down and took his hand. We followed the sound, running as quickly as we could. It felt as if we were moving in slow motion.

Rounding the corner of the building, we stepped into a dimly lit passageway. It was barely wide enough for the two of us to walk side by side, and it got darker with every step. Broken glass crunched under my sandals, and I almost slid on something with the distinctly foul smell of human waste. We moved cautiously, jumping at every shadow. Finally, we saw a mound on the ground that moved ever so slightly. We'd found her.

I cursed the darkness as I knelt beside her and tried to assess the damage. Curled up on her side, she raised one hand and touched my face, feeling my features like a blind person. That terrified me. Her blouse was ripped, exposing one shoulder. She had no other clothes on. I gagged at the metallic smell of blood.

"Noor." Her voice cracked. I could hear rather than see that she was crying. I took her hand and held it.

"Paru," I said. "Were you . . . ?" I couldn't finish my question. I didn't want to hear her answer.

"Yes. It was Suresh," she said. "And he wasn't alone."

"We need to get you to a doctor."

"No."

For just a moment I felt a searing flash of anger toward Lali. If I hadn't been delayed by her escape, I would have been on time to meet Parvati and this wouldn't have happened. Deepa-Auntie and now Parvati; how many more victims would Lali claim with her selfish flight? I immediately felt guilty. Lali couldn't have lasted much longer. But what could I do now for Parvati?

I pulled Parvati's head and shoulders onto my lap and scanned the dark alley for her clothes. I could see a pile of something some distance off.

Shami crouched beside me and touched Parvati's face.

"Is Par-di sick?" asked Shami, his voice etched with worry.

"She'll be fine," I said. "Go find her clothes, Shami."

He set off with the resolve of a three-year-old on a mission. He crouched down at the pile then straightened up and kept going. My heart stopped for a minute when he disappeared around a huge heap of refuse. Seconds later he reappeared with something in his hands and ran back to us.

"Don't run," I scolded. The damp, uneven ground was littered with all manner of dangerous things. I felt a surge of hatred for Parvati's attackers, who had discarded her in a dumping ground.

Shami handed me her clothing. Her pants were ripped as well. I wasn't sure they would cover her. For the moment I laid them on top of her. She moaned at even that light pressure. Shami crouched down beside us and patted Parvati's hair.

"It's okay, Par-di. Me and Noor-di are here."

She closed her eyes and gave the smallest of smiles, wincing with the effort.

"I know, baby," she said. "I'm okay now. Don't worry."

After a time her breathing became deep and regular and I realized she'd fallen asleep. Only then did Shami settle himself on the other side of me, curling against my side, with one arm draped around my waist. He too fell asleep. If I'd only had Aamaal, my world would have been complete, surrounded by the people I loved. Then I thought of Ma and felt bad because I'd so easily forgotten her. And what of Deepa-Auntie?

Though it was now the early hours of the morning, the noise from the street beyond our alley still echoed inside our narrow refuge—a refuge where my best friend had been thrown away like trash. In my head, I made a list of all the people I would take with me if I could disappear like Lali had. I'd start over someplace clean and safe, where young girls slept without fear, and children never went hungry or were wasted by sickness.

Finally the events of the night caught up with me. My determination to remain on guard faltered. I too gave in to sleep.

Not many hours later I awoke to the coldness of Parvati's absence. She hadn't gone far. She'd pulled on her pants and was several feet away, near the garbage where Shami had found them. She didn't notice I was awake, too intent on what she was doing. It was seconds before I realized what that was.

I leaped to my feet, startling Shami awake, and ran down the passageway, dropping to the ground beside her. I grabbed the fist that was doing the slashing and wrenched the broken glass from her hand. There was so much blood it was hard to tell how many gashes she'd already made.

She gaped at me wordlessly as if she shared my horror at her handiwork.

"No, Paru," I sobbed. I took off my dupatta and wrapped it tightly around her crocodile arm.

16

Grace

We entered the open doorway of a narrow, nondescript, two-story wooden building. The single thing that set it apart was a small hand-painted sign above the door that read "Sisters Helping Sisters." I was glad to leave behind the heat and chaos of the street outside, until I discovered the temperature inside was easily several degrees hotter, and the cacophony of voices was ear splitting. Even more overwhelming was being immediately swallowed up by a pack of street urchins.

Altogether, there were perhaps thirty children. From their clothes, I thought they were all girls, though it was hard to tell. Several had shaved heads. Most of them were dressed in salwar kameez, though a few wore bright frilly frocks and still others were in school uniform. Their clothes looked worn but relatively clean. They ranged in age from three or four years old to perhaps ten or eleven. They were desperately thin in the arms and legs; many had protruding bellies. I knew enough to understand this was a sign of malnutrition and not good health. It took me several minutes to realize that, amid the cacophony, several were shouting in English: *How are you?* and *What is your name?* I glanced at VJ, who was removing his shoes while carrying on multiple conversations at the same time. I recognized a bit of the Hindi, but he must have been speaking other languages as well because sometimes I couldn't pick up a single word. Mr. Donleavy, who'd preceded us inside, was nowhere to be seen.

VJ carried his shoes to a large pile of sandals, mostly little ones, on one side of the entrance, so I took off my own sandals and did the same. We walked farther into the room, dimly lit by a single fluorescent bulb, and paused to allow our eyes time to adjust. There wasn't a single window or any source of ventilation but the open doorway.

The children led, or more accurately dragged, us over to a metal ladder that went straight up to an open hatch in the ceiling. Since it was the only place Mr. Donleavy could have gone, we started climbing. I went first, eager to get away from the noise. I hoped the children wouldn't follow. I already felt overwhelmed.

I saw Mr. Donleavy as soon as I emerged through the hatch. He was sitting on a chair, talking to three women, all Indian, in a tiny office partitioned off from the rest of the room by a half-wall. One of the women was sitting in the only other chair. The other two were awkwardly hunched over behind her. The ceiling was too low for them to stand upright.

"Grace, there you are," said Mr. Donleavy.

I stepped through the hatch and kept moving to allow VJ to follow. I was dismayed to see he wasn't alone; the children were right behind him. The upstairs room quickly became even more crowded than the downstairs had been.

Since the only other option was crouching, VJ and I plopped down on the cement floor in the room outside the office. Though the floor was stained, it was spotlessly swept. The children seemed to have some sense of what was happening. After much shoving to establish who would have the privilege of sitting next to us, they all sat down as well. I had one on either side, and they pressed up against me, even though there was room for them to have a bit of space. One grabbed my hand and held on to it. The other reached up and stroked my ponytail. My hair has always been a mousy brown, definitely not worthy of the admiration she was according it.

The upstairs room was at least ten degrees hotter than it had been downstairs, and again there was no ventilation. The sweat poured off me. VJ, on the other hand, was as fresh and dry as when we'd arrived, and happily chatting with the children.

"I wouldn't have pegged you for a kid-lover," I said, trying not to sound as jealous as I was feeling.

"Come on, Gracie, in a world full of conspiracies, malice and deceit, how can you possibly not like children? They're the only honest creatures on the planet."

I had to admit I'd never thought about it that way. I gave the little girls now leaning against me a tentative smile and was rewarded with two exuberant gap-toothed grins in return.

Mr. Donleavy came out of the office with the women and they joined us on the floor. I wouldn't have believed there was space for close to thirty children, two teenagers and four adults.

"This is Miss Chanda," said Mr. Donleavy, introducing one

of the women. "She's going to tell us a little bit about their concept for the program."

Miss Chanda didn't look much older than a teenager. She wasn't beautiful, but every time she smiled, every single kid in the room smiled back. You could tell they worshiped her.

"I want to thank you so much for volunteering," she began. "I'd like to introduce you to one of the girls who will explain what we do." She looked across the room at an older girl. "Fatima, can you tell us a little bit about yourself?"

"My name is Fatima," said the girl, and laughed nervously when she realized she'd just told us the one thing we already knew. "I'm fourteen years old and I like school very much." I was shocked to discover she was that old, and I looked more closely at the other girls. They were all so small. Perhaps I'd misjudged their ages.

"My mother says I should be going to school but sometimes we don't have money for books and . . ." She hesitated and looked at Miss Chanda, as though she wasn't sure how much detail she should go into. I was willing to bet the list of what her family didn't have money for was a long one.

"One of the things we provide here is funds to cover any school-related costs the girls have, as well as meals and sometimes night shelter," said Miss Chanda. "Why don't you tell them how long you've been coming to SHS?"

"I am coming to Sisters Helping Sisters since I am three years old. My mother didn't to let me sleeping in the . . . the . . ." She looked at Miss Chanda again.

I was shocked at how good her English was, though I suspected that was why she'd been chosen to be spokesperson.

"Do all the children speak English?" I asked Miss Chanda.

"They all speak a little. Some, like Fatima, study in English-language schools, so they speak more. We'll only match you up with girls you can communicate with." She gave VJ a worried look. "I'm afraid we won't be able to give you a girl to mentor. Many of our girls have already been molested, so we're careful not to put them in vulnerable situations. But you're more than welcome to work here at the center in our after-school tutoring program."

"I'd be happy to do that," said VJ smoothly, not mentioning that the girls were in no danger of sexual advances from him. "If it's all right, I can help Grace with whoever she's paired with."

Miss Chanda looked relieved to have that settled. "Great. Then let's talk about how this will be structured. Today I'm going to introduce you to a few girls and give you a chance to get to know each other. At the end of the session, I'll ask you if there was a particular girl you felt you could help."

"This sounds just like speed dating," said VJ. "What fun! I've always wanted to try that!"

Miss Chanda gave him a stern look. "We're going to get out some paper and pencils. Our girls love to draw. It will help them relax and give you a chance to chat at the same time."

"What happens when we've found the girl we want to be paired with?" I asked.

"We ask for a minimum of two hours a week. Our girls have had little experience of life outside the brothel. Most of their mothers were sold against their will, and in spite of that, many have been disowned by their families. For the girls who grow up here, the brothel life is all they know, and there's often pressure to follow their mothers into the trade."

I looked at the sweet faces of the girls surrounding me. I

could tell Mr. Donleavy was watching me carefully. If he was wondering whether it had been a good idea to bring me here, he had reason to be concerned. There was no question these girls and their mothers needed help, but what could VJ and I do? We were just kids ourselves.

"Well, I don't know about the rest of you," said VJ, "but I can't wait to get started. Where are the art supplies?"

Noor

Coming first . . .

In the months after Parvati's rape I threw myself into my studies. Only at school could I pretend everything was the way it had been before. Parvati had become a ghost. Suresh hadn't stopped with the single rape; he took her every night he could find her. Together we hid from him, constantly changing where we slept. Still, there were days I got home from school and Parvati was nowhere to be found. On those days, I knew he'd found her first.

In the middle of September every year, regular classes ceased and we wrote our first-semester exams. Just before we broke for the holiday, the grades were posted. My friends and I always met at school to look at our grades together. For many children, this was a time of great anxiety and disappointment. For me, it was a rare time when I didn't feel like a fake. I always took firsts in English, Math, and Biology. Several times I'd taken firsts in Chemistry as well.

None of my schoolmates knew where I came from. Over the years I'd created a family history of such complexity, with so many embellishments, that to them it had the familiarity of truth. I retold the lies so often that at times I almost believed them myself. My classmates knew all about my father, the mid-level civil servant, my mother, the former actress who gave up fame to marry him, and of course my siblings. It was my one disappointment that I couldn't enhance their attributes, but Aamaal already went to the same school, and I had every hope that someday Shami would as well. Aamaal had been coached to maintain our fiction. With her sweet face and enormous, thickly fringed eyes, people were always inclined to believe her. They never suspected that in addition to being beautiful she was a skilled liar.

The one time I felt closest to my fictionalized self was when I looked at my exam results. No one would have believed that the girl who was awarded so many prizes came from a brothel in Kamathipura. Even I found it hard to reconcile. My two selves—the school-going girl and the daughter of a sex worker—felt like two separate people, awkwardly inhabiting one body. I was like a *hijra*, not one thing and not the other, but a third thing entirely, unique and not happily so.

Gajra and I stood with a group of our friends near the school gate discussing our results.

"I knew you'd sweep the awards," said Gajra, squeezing my arm excitedly. Her pleasure was so complete you might have thought she'd achieved the results herself. Gajra had never taken a first in anything in her life, though her kindness outshone all my achievements. I could never understand why being a truly good person was overlooked when it came to handing out medals. It seemed to me it must be much more challenging, considering how few people managed it.

"Of course she did well," said Sapna, whose scores were never far behind mine. "Her father does nothing but sit at home and coach her. My father's a doctor. He can't be spending every minute helping me."

"Which is why you have hours of paid tutoring every evening," said Kiran, Sapna's best friend and fiercest competitor. I actually think their friendship survived only because I so often snatched the wins from both of them.

"Well, it appears to have paid off. You beat me in only one subject this year," said Sapna.

"The year's not over yet," Gajra intervened. "There's still plenty of time for everyone to get good results. The important thing is to improve our own scores."

"Tell that to my father," said Sapna darkly.

"I think you're going to have to tell him yourself," said Kiran, forgetting their recent fight and slinging her arm around Sapna's shoulder. She nodded to the other side of the street, where Sapna's father was just emerging from a parked car.

I recognized him the minute I saw him, though it had been well over a year since he'd come into Shami's examining room. That was why he'd looked so familiar. It wasn't because I'd already taken Shami to him before.

I looked away, hoping he hadn't noticed me. The danger of my identity being discovered was far worse than just being caught in a lie. Ours was a fee-paying school, and a good one. I would be expelled if it was discovered that my mother was a sex worker. If he remembered that I had an HIV-infected baby brother he'd make the connection in an instant, especially considering we were only blocks from my red-light neighbor-hood. I said a fervent prayer that he wouldn't recognize me in my school uniform. Then it occurred to me that I'd been in uniform the last time he'd seen me. I started to sweat.

"Come on, Gaj. Let's see if any of our teachers are in their classrooms so we can wish them a happy midyear break." I took Gajra's hand.

"Okay, but we must say hello to Sapna's father first," she said.

I reluctantly let her hold me back. It would have drawn more attention if I'd insisted on rushing off, now that she'd made the point that we must greet him.

I toyed with the books I was holding and told myself I was being ridiculous. To the best of my knowledge I'd never spoken to Sapna's father before, or since, the hospital visit. He must have seen hundreds, even thousands of kids like Shami and me. But how many of them went to his daughter's school?

I knew from Sapna that her parents' expectations of her were high. They came from more modest backgrounds than many of the girls at our school. Ironically, her real-life story wasn't so different from the fake life I'd created. Her father had raised her family's status through his own determination and hard work, but it had taken them only so far. His greatest ambition was to see his children marry into the wealthy, more established families who were happy to call on him when their health was poor but would never welcome him at their dinner tables. Getting his children into the top universities was his only hope of further elevating their status.

"Darling," he shouted grandly when he was still several feet from the gate. "How did you do? How many firsts?"

I feigned absorption in my Biology text. For once, I felt sorry for Sapna. She wasn't the nicest girl, often bossy and opinionated, but it couldn't have been easy living up to such high expectations. Being fatherless had its advantages. At least there was no one to embarrass me in front of my friends.

Sapna didn't answer. I snuck a peek at her and was horrified to see she was hanging her head, close to tears. Kiran had both arms around her now and Gajra had stepped closer, supporting her from the other side.

I tried to think of something I could say that would take the spotlight off her, though the last thing I wanted was to draw attention to myself. I felt a pang of guilt at my own role in her humiliation and scowled at the ground, willing her father to go away. He stood on his side of the gate, waiting for her reply.

"I only took first in Geography," Sapna mumbled, her voice so low I wouldn't have been able to understand her if I hadn't already known her results.

"What was that? Speak up, Sapna."

I shot her a sympathetic look.

"You didn't get firsts in any of the sciences? After all the money we spent on tutors?" She didn't answer. What could she say?

"Aniket Bihar took the first in Physics," I said, louder than I'd intended. "His father is Dilip Bihar. Perhaps you've heard of him?" I added the last comment knowing full well it was provocative. Aniket came from probably the richest family in our school, just the kind of connection Sapna's father hoped to secure.

"I see." He scrutinized me as he might a perplexing rash. "I've forgotten your name."

"Noor Benkatti."

"And how well did you do, Noor Benkatti?"

Was it only my imagination that his tone held a subtle threat? My heart pounded, certain I'd been found out.

"She took firsts in everything," said Sapna. I understood that, though she was exaggerating, she wasn't trying to make things worse. In the subjects that mattered to her father, I had taken firsts.

"Ah," said her father. He unhooked the gate and stepped through. There was now less than a foot separating us. My stomach roiled.

"I believe we've met." He let that sink in before he continued. "I believe your mother works in the neighborhood, isn't that correct?"

My skin went hot and cold in quick succession as bile gushed up my throat. It was as bad as I'd feared. The lady doctor had told him everything.

"No, sir," I said, "you've mistaken me for someone else. My mother is a housewife."

"You have a little brother," he continued, ignoring my denial. "He's very sick."

I turned away just in time to fall to my knees and vomit in a patch of grass. I was surrounded immediately by solicitous friends. I was fortunate that they liked nothing better than a bit of drama, and I was certainly giving it to them. Hands reached for me and practically lifted me off the ground. I was relieved to see Sapna's father had stepped back. He watched through narrowed eyes as I was hustled away. We were almost at the school building before I realized it was not just Gajra but Sapna supporting me.

"Thanks." She smiled. "That was a tad dramatic. Still, if you're ever in a jam, I promise I'll do my best to fake an emergency to get you out of it."

I gave her a weak grin. "Anything for a friend."

The next hour was a blur. I was taken to the nurse's office. She tried to make me lie down but I was more jittery than I'd ever been on exam day. I knew who he was and he knew me. The only question was what he would do about it. I tried to calm myself with the idea that he was a doctor. Surely, he wouldn't be so unkind as to get me expelled. But Sapna had made no secret of her father's ambitions. He'd clawed his way out of the muck and demanded only the best for his children and from them. The last thing he'd want was to have his daughter associating with the low-caste daughter of a sex worker. The fact that I also surpassed her academically only added to my peril.

I walked home on shaky legs. As soon as I reached my street I went looking for Parvati. It never occurred to me to talk to Ma. I knew that somehow she'd blame me, and there was always the chance she'd pull me out of school. My fear that my school days were numbered had intensified since Parvati had fallen under Suresh's control. So many of my neighborhood friends were already doing sex work; how could I be far behind?

I didn't even bother to change out of my uniform. I searched for close to an hour. Other than hearing multiple reports that she'd last been seen heading for Bhatti Road, no one had a clue where she was.

Tired and grimy, I finally went home. I wasn't looking forward to the fight I was bound to have. I was late for my chores and Ma would be furious I hadn't at least come home to change out of my school clothes. Her pride in my uniform, visible proof of which school I attended, was almost as great as her pride in my medals. I reluctantly clambered up the ladder to our room, only to find Ma wasn't there. Deepa-Auntie was sitting on her bed braiding Aamaal's hair. Prita-Auntie was asleep on her own bed, an open movie magazine draped over her face. The small black-and-white TV, perched on a high shelf in one corner of the room, was on as usual, though no one was watching it. Shami played in the corner with Deepa-Auntie's basket of hair clips.

"Where's Ma?" I whispered, after greeting Deepa-Auntie and giving my siblings a hug. Prita-Auntie could get riled up almost as fast as Ma if you disturbed her "beauty rest," as she called it, though she was about as beautiful as a plucked chicken, even on her best day.

"She got called to your school," said Deepa-Auntie. A worried frown creased her unlined face. "Did something happen today? Weren't you getting your exam results?"

My heart plummeted as I sank down on Ma's bed. I didn't know what to say. I wanted to tell her the whole story so she could reassure me there was nothing to worry about but I knew that wasn't true. The coincidence was too great. What other possible reason could Ma have for going to the school if it wasn't provoked by Sapna's horrible father? Ma never went to my school, not when I won medals, not when there were parent meetings, not ever.

"Did she say why she was going to school?" I asked.

Deepa-Auntie shook her head. "Do you know why?"

I nodded and told her the whole story.

"We can't be certain. Maybe your ma went to school for another reason," said Deep-Auntie.

Prita-Auntie rolled over. Her dupatta slid to the floor as she fastened me with a death stare.

"Aamaal, go get Prita-Auntie some tea," I ordered quickly, pulling some coins from my pocket.

Deepa-Auntie had only finished one braid but Aamaal scrambled off the bed. She had no more desire to see Prita-Auntie's temper than we did.

"Wait," growled Prita-Auntie before Aamaal could make it to the hatch. "Take some money out of my box and buy me some masala kheema. Make sure you get it from Basheer on the corner, the old Muslim. Don't buy it from that young donkey that's set up next to him. He'd cheat you as soon as look at you, and he drips his snotty nose right in his mix. You can tell him I said that."

She barked out a few more directives as Aamaal crawled under her bed to rummage in the tin box where Prita-Auntie kept all her worldly possessions, and at least one dead baby, if local gossip was to be believed. Finally Aamaal emerged, triumphantly clutching a hundred-rupee note.

"Make sure you bring back the change" was Prita-Auntie's parting shot.

"Now, what's this nonsense I'm hearing about Ashmita being called in to school?" Prita-Auntie moved to the head of her bed and heaved her bulk heavily into a sitting position, leaning back against the wall. She closed her eyes again. "I can feel you staring at me, mutton-breath. When you've done this work for as many years as I have, you'll enjoy a drink or two as well, even if you do suffer for it the next day."

It wasn't clear if she was talking to Deepa-Auntie or me. We exchanged nervous looks.

"Noor-baby has run into some problems with a doctor she met on one of Shami's hospital visits," said Deepa-Auntie. "He may have told the school who she is. Ashmita's been called in to speak with the principal. We don't know for sure that was why they called her in though."

"Of course the doctor has told on her, turnip-brain. She's a bright child, a good deal brighter than his own children, I'll wager. He won't be able to stand it. A prostitute's daughter, and a dark one at that. It's against the whole order of the universe." She opened her eyes and fixed her glare on Deepa-Auntie. "Get me a drink, a real drink. I need to figure this out."

"But we don't know yet what the school will do, Prita-ji," said Deepa-Auntie.

Prita-Auntie snorted in disgust. "How long have you lived in this country, Deepa? And you still haven't figured out the first thing about it! A rich doctor exposes the school's top student as the daughter of a sex worker. What do think the school is going to do? If Noor were a stupid child she might have some hope of being allowed to stay. All those rich parents would smile their pitying smiles and pat themselves on the back for being so broad-minded. But our Noor is the top student. They won't be able to get rid of her fast enough."

Deepa-Auntie hung her head. I hopped off Ma's bed and went over to sit with her on hers. Shami, catching the mood of the room, came over and crawled into my lap.

"They'll ask Noor to leave school," predicted Prita-Auntie. "Just you wait."

"Isn't there something we can do?" asked Deepa-Auntie.

"There's nothing you can do. You're not even from this country," said Prita-Auntie sternly. Though she didn't mean to be unkind, Deepa-Auntie looked stricken. "I will take care of it. You can be sure our Noor isn't going to get kicked out of school until her mother decides it's time for her to leave."

With that, she resolutely stood up and reached for her kurta, pulling it over her head. "Get up, Noor, you're coming with me."

"Should I could come too?" asked Deepa-Auntie hopefully.

"Just because you're allowed out of the house now, that doesn't mean you're of any use to us," said Prita-Auntie. "Stay with the children."

"Good luck, Noor," Deepa-Auntie said as I followed Prita-Auntie to the hatch.

I waited while Prita-Auntie lowered herself through. If she'd been out of earshot, I would have reminded Deepa-Auntie that being Nepali hadn't stopped her from helping Lali-didi escape. She was far from the useless creature everyone made her out to be. Then it occurred to me that being thought useless was probably the only thing that had stopped Pran from killing her.

I ran back and gave her a quick hug before leaving.

18

Grace

I don't know what we would have done without VJ. I tried to talk to the few girls who spoke English but the conversation remained stilted and limited. I wasn't sure if it was the cultural difference or the language. I just knew they didn't want to speak to me. With him they were voluble and uninhibited. It surprised me, given what Miss Chanda had said about their bad experiences with men. Clearly they could overcome that in the presence of a cute, not to mention famous, boy.

Mr. Donleavy had just told us our time was almost up when we heard loud voices from the floor below. Someone sounded angry. Too late, it occurred to me that we were trapped in that tiny windowless room, in a neighborhood that most Mumbaikars would never dare venture into.

Miss Chanda crouch-walked double time to the ladder. All of the other adults, including Mr. Donleavy, followed.

"Do you think we should stay up here?" I asked VJ.

"If there's trouble, we'd be safer down there, where we can slip out the door."

He went first and I followed, though a couple of kids squeezed in ahead of me.

The room at the bottom of the ladder was packed. I had to push myself between several unfamiliar women to get off the ladder.

A fleshy woman with a fierce look about her was shouting loudly at one of the NGO staff. There was a palpable feeling of discontent among the audience she'd brought with her. The NGO staff were looking nervous. I almost didn't notice the young girl standing next to her. She was making every effort to back away from the argument, but there was nowhere for her to go. Her obvious desire to melt into the background was such a familiar emotion that I felt immediate empathy. In fact, her look of embarrassment and distress was so painfully reminiscent of the way I'd been feeling almost constantly for the past few days that I wanted to go to her. Slowly I worked my way through the crowd.

I couldn't understand what the argument was about. They weren't speaking English. The big woman was doing most of the talking. She seemed to be demanding something that Miss Chanda wouldn't agree to.

I reached the girl and tried to catch her eye. She was staring resolutely at her feet. I doubted she spoke English, but she was in a school uniform and looked a little older than most of the girls upstairs, so I figured it was worth a try.

"Is that your mom?" I asked.

She looked up in surprise.

"No," she said gruffly, and looked down again. Though it

wasn't a response that encouraged conversation, I'd just spent the past hour feeling expendable, and here was a girl who seemed as uncomfortable as I was.

"What's she shouting about?" I persisted.

She glanced up again and away. I wasn't sure if she was considering her answer or ignoring me. She was very thin, like most of the girls, with watchful, intelligent eyes.

"Why are you here?" she finally asked.

It was my turn to hesitate. The truth was, I wasn't sure myself. The past hour had reinforced my skepticism that I could be helpful to these girls. While the little ones were friendly, the older ones, the girls I was supposed to connect with, had no interest in talking to me. I couldn't imagine mentoring any of them.

"I have no idea," I said honestly.

She smiled sympathetically and nodded in the direction of the angry woman. "She is asking them to help me stay in school."

"Well, I guess we have that in common." I smiled back.

"Your school is saying you must leave? What did you do?" She sounded genuinely intrigued.

Having started down this path of honesty, I found myself stuck. As much as I didn't want to admit the truth, I didn't want to lie to her.

"I took a picture of myself without my shirt on and sent it to someone I thought was a boy I knew, and he, or someone, sent it to every kid in the school. They even printed up a few hard copies and posted them around the halls."

She giggled.

"It really wasn't funny."

She giggled again.

"Still not funny." I tried to sound stern but fell short, mainly because I was shocked to discover my own spirits had lifted at her reaction. Maybe someday even I would see the humor in what I'd done.

"Okay," I said, "fair is fair. I told you mine. Now you have to tell me what you did."

"I got first in all my subjects."

"Wow, your school is tough. In my school, the worst you'd get for good grades is a suspension."

She laughed outright. Her English was excellent and I'd made her laugh. My spirits rose higher.

Together, we watched the adults for a few minutes. Their discussion wasn't showing any signs of calming down. The angry woman was practically spitting she was so mad, and several of her friends were throwing in their own comments. I was worried for Miss Chanda.

"What did you really do?" I asked.

"My ma is a sex worker."

"I figured that."

She looked offended.

"Only because you're here," I said quickly.

She nodded. "The school found out about my ma."

"So?"

"They do not want the daughter of a sex worker in their school."

"Too bad. Just refuse to leave."

"It is not like that. They can make trouble. My ma does not have an identity card. She does not have a birth certificate. And my birth certificate is fake. I have no right to be in the school."

"That's crazy."

She shrugged.

"Well, then the rules need to change," I said stoutly.

She gave me a look like I'd just suggested we should throw up a high-rise across the road to solve homelessness.

"Hello," said VJ, suddenly materializing beside us. He extended his hand to the girl. "I'm VJ Patel. Yes, that VJ Patel. And who might you be?" He gave her his best magazine-cover smile.

I thought, even in her current circumstances, her heart must have skipped just a little. If so, she hid it well. In fact, she looked at his hand as if it were a dead rat. After a delay that would have embarrassed most people, though it did nothing to shake VJ's confidence, she took it for about a second.

"Noor," she said. She added her surname after an extended deliberation. "Benkatti."

"Noor Benkatti," said VJ warmly. "It's a pleasure to meet you!"

"So why have you come to Sisters Helping Sisters?" I asked when it was clear that Noor wasn't going to respond to VJ. "Are you a member?"

She cut a look at VJ and crossed her arms. I wished he'd leave us alone. Instead, he shot her another winning smile. She glowered back but finally answered.

"I am not a member, but sometimes the NGOs can stop the schools from making us leave."

"Her school's going to kick her out," I explained to VJ.

"Really?" exclaimed VJ cheerfully. "I go for years not meeting a single interesting person and then I meet two rebels in one week. Isn't life unexpected?"

"So, if the NGO speaks to the school they'll let you stay?" I asked, elbowing VJ in the ribs.

"I said *sometimes*."

"We don't need the NGO," said VJ. "Just tell me who to pay off."

"My ma does not know I am here," said Noor.

I could tell by the way she said this that it was significant information. I'd actually forgotten that the woman with her wasn't her mom.

"Is your mom sick?" I asked hesitantly.

"I could pay the medical bills as well," said VJ.

"My ma hates the NGOs," said Noor.

"Oh." I didn't really understand. Even if her mom didn't like NGOs, surely she'd make use of them under the circumstances. "So . . . ?" I prompted.

"The NGO lady says they cannot help me because I am not in their program."

"Can't you join?"

"My ma would never allow it. Prita-Auntie, the lady who brought me, wants the NGO to talk to my school anyway."

"Do you want to be in the program?" asked VJ. I could tell he was hatching something.

"I want to be in school. If I have to be in a program for them to talk to my school . . ." She trailed off. "Ma will never agree. She will take me out of school before she will allow me to come here. Ma says the NGOs think they are better than us. They waste our time teaching useless things like sewing and Mehndi."

"Mehndi?" I asked.

"Henna design," said VJ. "Noor, if you take Mehndi, can I sign up with you?" he added.

I glared at him, while Noor looked at him curiously. Even I knew that only girls did Mehndi.

"Ma is proud," Noor continued, as if she was explaining to herself as much as me. "She comes from a tradition where sex work was part of a religious duty."

I tried not to let the shock show on my face but that had to be one of the strangest things I'd ever heard. "Religious?"

"Devadasi," said VJ. "I'll explain it to you later. It's positively medieval."

Noor scowled at VJ. "It goes back a long time to when women like my ma were given to the temple to serve the priest. At that time, it was not only for sex. Devadasi women had many talents. Ma is not proud of being a sex worker but she is not ashamed."

"So, let's just recap, if I may," said VJ, holding up his fingers as he itemized his points. "Noor has to join the program but can't actually darken the door of this building as someone in the neighborhood is bound to see her and spill the beans. Gracie has to find a teen she can mentor, which isn't going to be easy since the girls here aren't keen on her."

I started to object but he raised his hand and continued. "Sorry, darling, but you know it's true. So, I have the solution."

VJ stepped away from us and raised both hands in the air. "Ladies, attention, please," he shouted over the babble of voices. "We've solved the problem."

Shockingly, everyone actually did quiet down.

"Grace and Noor have discovered a budding kinship. They give true meaning to the idea of sisters helping sisters . . ."

"Get to the point," I groused.

He gave me a wounded look before continuing. "They're going to meet at least once a week, for the requisite bonding experiences, but they will never meet here, so there's no need to get Noor's mom's permission. Should anyone ask, we say only that Grace is Noor's new friend. Are we all in agreement? Can I have a show of hands?"

There were several minutes of stunned silence. VJ repeated his suggestion in Hindi.

"Is this what you want to do, Grace?" asked Mr. Donleavy.

I didn't even have to think about it. "If Noor agrees."

I looked down in surprise when I felt Noor slip her hand into mine.

19

Noor

The foreigners . . .

Parvati and I waited on the corner, at the end of our lane, for the foreigners. Shami was asleep in my arms. As usual he had a fever. It wasn't too high, though his breathing was raspy and labored. I'd stolen some of Binti-Ma'am's alcohol that morning. An alcohol-soaked rag was wrapped tightly around his chest.

Aamaal picked through a rubbish heap across the street from us. I scolded her whenever she accidentally picked up broken glass or syringes, though she rarely did. Aamaal had learned quickly how to avoid the dangers of our world. Most days she amassed a small bag of recyclables, carefully sorted, to sell to the rag picker when his cart rattled by. I let her keep what she earned. We could have used the money but she wouldn't have stuck with it if she'd had to share. It was worth it just to keep her busy.

"Are you sure they can be trusted?" asked Parvati, for perhaps the tenth time.

A lot had changed in the months since Parvati's rape, not the least of which was Parvati herself. She'd always been distrustful of strangers; that was just common sense in a community where most of the girls and women we knew had been forced into sex work. But her spark of mischief had withered.

"You can't count on them to help you. Foreigners are as different from us as elephants." Parvati rhythmically thumped Shami's back as she talked. She was as familiar with the tricks for loosening the mucus in his lungs as I was. "Elephants act tame for years and then one day they crush their masters to death. People think the attacks are unprovoked but elephants have long memories. They take revenge for things that happened long ago, sometimes in a previous life. Foreigners are like that—unpredictable."

I squeezed Parvati's shoulder. I knew what was really troubling her. "We'll find a way to get you away from Suresh. We don't need the foreigners for that."

Parvati self-consciously put her left arm behind her back, as if I hadn't already noticed the fresh cuts. I had tried to talk Parvati into asking Chanda-Teacher for help but I couldn't convince her she wouldn't be arrested for prostitution. We'd both heard stories about the prisons where they incarcerated underage sex workers who'd been "rescued." The conditions were so bad that only last year a group of girls had scaled the thirty-foot fence surrounding their "rescue home" and broken their legs in the long, desperate drop to freedom.

"What if the foreigners try to kidnap you?" asked Parvati.

I had explained the deal I'd struck with the NGO, but Parvati refused to believe that friendship with a foreigner was necessary to prevent my being expelled from my own school. I still felt raw when I thought of the teachers I'd loved who'd tried to get rid of me. I wondered if any of them had argued to let me stay before Chanda-Teacher spoke to them.

Chanda-Teacher tried to comfort me by saying that many of my teachers were even more impressed with my academic success when they learned of my background, but that made me feel worse. It was like everyone expected me to be stupid or lazy just because my mother was a sex worker. Didn't they know it was because of my mother that I studied so hard? Ma suffered to send me to school. The teachers had things completely backwards.

"I have to do this, Paru."

"I still don't understand what the foreigners want."

I didn't have time to answer as just then a gleaming silver SUV turned into our lane and stopped. I glanced back at our house to where Adit was leaning on the wall out front. He'd followed me outside. In the old days I would have invited him along but we weren't friends anymore. Adit said he had no time to waste with girls. I'd heard he was working in one of the gambling houses, running errands. I prayed he wouldn't tell Ma what I was up to. It made me nervous, the way he watched me.

"I'll let you do the talking," said Parvati.

I hid a smile. I doubted Parvati's English would have been up to doing the talking and it was me the foreigners were coming to meet, not her.

"If I nudge you," she continued, "it means there's something suspicious going on and we must make an excuse and leave."

I gave her a solemn nod. I couldn't admit that secretly I hoped the white girl was serious about being my friend. Parvati would have said I was foolish. Even worse would have been to share my hope that perhaps the foreigner understood, even more than Parvati, that my too-dark skin and my mother's work weren't the whole story of who I was. The white girl didn't come from a world where people were judged by the caste they were born into.

The car doors opened and suddenly she was there in front of me. Vijender Patel climbed out on the other side. Parvati gasped. I hadn't told her about Vijender. There was no way she would have agreed to spend the day with him. The only people Parvati mistrusted more than foreigners were film stars. Every once in a while they showed up in our neighborhood, taking photos of themselves handing out cheap toys to the poor children, which was us. They always promised they were going to make our lives better but the promises were broken as quickly as the toys.

Vijender came round the car and again held out his hand to me. This time I didn't let my nerves show. I shook it and politely introduced him to Parvati.

"Pleased to meet you, Parvati," he said. "Will you be joining us today?"

I wasn't sure what he meant by *joining him*, since we were just going to sit in a local café.

"Hi, Noor," said Grace. "It's nice to see you again."

I was reassured to have the same good feeling about her as before.

Aamaal raced over from the rubbish heap and leaped on VJ Patel. She must have recognized him from billboards or TV commercials. I would have smacked her for her boldness if we'd been alone.

"Hello," laughed VJ, pretending he liked nothing better

than little girls leaping onto his back. He pranced around in a circle for a moment and whinnied like a horse. It was funny and got us through the awkwardness, but she was still going to get a scolding later.

"And who might you be, young sir?" asked VJ, speaking in Hindi to Shami, who had just woken up.

"Shami," said Shami. He wasn't impressed by film stars.

"Would you like to climb aboard as well?" asked VJ, leaning toward us.

Shami shook his head and stuck his thumb in his mouth. I pulled it out and kept hold of his hand as I knew he'd just stick it back in.

"So, shall we be off?" VJ gestured toward the gleaming car.

"Off where?" asked Parvati suspiciously.

"Bollywood, of course. We were told to expose Noor to new experiences, so what better place to start than the epicenter of this great city of ours?"

"He wants to show you where his dad works," said Grace. "Don't worry. If it's boring we'll do something else."

"Of course," agreed VJ grandly. "Your wishes are my command."

"I cannot go," I said. "I must look after my brother and sister."

"Bring them along. Don't tell me they wouldn't like to see a real Bollywood soundstage."

"I want to go to Bollywood," said Aamaal, pounding VJ on the back.

"Feisty," said VJ. "I like that in a girl."

I gave him a look, which meant *Don't try anything with my sister.* He smiled innocently. Normally that would only have deepened my suspicions, but I felt strangely reassured. VJ might be a foolish boy but he didn't look at us the way I was used to men staring in Kamathipura, like they wanted to eat us up.

"We could go, Noor," said Parvati in Kannada, so even Vijender was excluded from our discussion. "Your ma won't miss you for hours."

I tried to hide my surprise. It was the first thing she'd shown interest in since the attack.

"Someone might tell." I glanced down the street. Adit was still watching. If he told Ma I'd gone off with foreigners there'd be no end of trouble.

Parvati looked away, but I caught the flash of disappointment.

"Can you meet us on Bhatti Road?" I asked Vijender. The main road was far enough away that at least Adit wouldn't see us getting into the car.

"No problem," he said.

The car was cold when we climbed in a few minutes later. I pulled Shami onto my lap, though there was space for him to have his own seat, and wrapped my arms around him. He seemed more tired these days. He was often asleep when I got home from school and had no interest in playing. Every evening, he fell asleep right after dinner and rarely stirred till morning, even if I was having a disrupted night finding us a safe place to sleep. Sometimes, when I was holding him like this, it felt as though his chest wasn't rising at all. At times like that I squeezed him hard, until he squirmed, so I could go back to knowing he was alive.

At every traffic light, beggars tapped at our windows. For the first few lights I looked closely to see if it was someone I knew. After a while I realized we were too far from Kamathipura, so I did what the foreigners did and tried not to look at them at all. I still heard them though—*tap, tap, tap*. They must have thought I was rich, riding in a car like that. I wanted to lower my window and explain. I had a few rupees in my pocket for lunch. I was tempted to hand it over, which would have been foolish. It would only have gone to their gang boss, and then how would I have fed Shami and Aamaal? The foreigners talked the whole trip, as if the beggars were just part of the landscape, like garbage and stray dogs.

Gradually, we left the heavily populated part of the city and entered an area that was a mix of small settlements and open spaces. Whistling Wind Studios was on the very edge of Mumbai, in the forested foothills. As we passed through ornate iron gates and headed down a long, winding road, I watched intently for leopards and monkeys. All I saw was what must have been movie sets. There were huge mansions, covered in scaffolding and platforms; a town that was only storefronts; an arid patch of sand, with a few bristly plants that had arm-like branches sticking straight up. Scattered throughout were large, square, windowless buildings pasted with gigantic movie posters. It was interesting, but I would have preferred to see a leopard.

We pulled up to another gate and were waved through by a guard. He saluted to us, as if we were important. Parvati clutched my arm. I think she was regretting our decision to come.

We stopped outside a long, two-story, sparkling white building. It didn't have any paint missing at all, and there were lots of windows with glass in them and no shutters or metal bars. The windows were so clean and so much light poured into the building that you could see the people inside going about their business.

Shami slept during the drive but woke up when I lifted him out of the car. Two women were standing in front of the building. They rushed forward and hugged VJ. One called him

"Darling." He put his arm around her but his eyes were cold when he turned to us and introduced her.

"You all recognize Vanita Kapoor, don't you? Rising starlet and the leading lady in my father's new movie."

"Not the leading lady, darling," she purred in a sex-me voice that sounded as false as any I'd heard at home. "Your wicked father only gave me a tiny part."

We heard the approach of VJ's father even before he came into view. Sanjay Patel was surrounded by a crowd of people, all competing to be noticed, yet he strode along as though he didn't even see them. It was the same way the foreigners had acted with the beggars outside the car window. I wondered if rich people all had this ability of not seeing.

VJ's father had his eyes fixed on the beautiful young film star clinging to his son. He seemed far more interested in her than VJ, who stood rigidly, making no pretense of enjoying her attention. I wondered if it was just this girl VJ didn't like, despite her beauty, or if perhaps girls were not his preference.

There were plenty of boys in our neighborhood, working alongside Ma and the Aunties, who served the men who preferred other men. VJ had been friendly to us, without being the least bit aggressive, just like these boys always were. It would be rash to let down my guard but I didn't feel threatened around VJ like I did around most boys.

"Welcome, welcome," he said, clapping one hand on VJ's shoulder and the other on the starlet's back. "On the set barely a minute and already he's in the arms of a beautiful woman. Be careful of him, girls. My boy's a heartbreaker."

"You've broken more than a few hearts yourself," said VJ.

20

Grace

VJ's father loaded all of us, including the starlet, into a bus, saying he had a surprise waiting on a neighboring set. VJ was uncharacteristically grim-faced and subdued. He clearly wasn't a fan of his father's surprises.

We drove a few minutes back down the road and turned into a parking lot in front of a building that looked every bit like a palace out of the Raj era. A dozen or so people waiting in the lot surged forward, surrounding us the second we alighted from the bus.

"Stop," said VJ's father. "I haven't told them the surprise yet." He turned to us. "You're all going to be in my movie. These people will take you to costume and makeup."

He paused for a response. I glanced nervously at Noor, not sure how she'd feel about all this attention.

"They're a little shy," said VJ. "Being in a movie is a bit much for their first outing."

"Nonsense," said his father. "Wait till they see the costumes." He said something in Hindi to Noor and Parvati.

It was Aamaal who answered. I wasn't sure what she said but everyone laughed.

"I guess we're making a movie, then," said VJ, ruffling Aamaal's hair. Noor immediately stepped between them and put a hand on Aamaal's shoulder.

We were led away by a group of women to a large dressing room. There was a rack of gowns in the center, couches along one wall and mirrored dressing tables along the other. One of our entourage directed us to the couches while they searched for our sizes.

I sat next to Noor, with the little ones on her other side and Parvati at the far end. A woman approached with a shimmering length of fabric over her arm and a gold-sequined blouse.

"This would be perfect for you, darling," she said, holding it out to me. "We just need to get you out of those clothes."

I was so busy sweating over the possibility that we might be required to say lines that getting undressed hadn't even occurred to me. I felt as though my wounds were suddenly giving off heat. I cupped one hand over my thigh.

"Thanks," I said, my voice barely more than a whisper, "but I'd rather just watch."

"We can't have that," said the woman firmly. "Mr. Patel will be disappointed."

"I don't want to," I said more forcefully.

"Don't be shy. We're all girls here."

"I'll try it." Noor stood up and reached for the blouse.

"It's too big for you," said the woman, holding the ensemble just out of Noor's reach.

She didn't count on Parvati, who leaped up and snatched it out of her hands. The woman made a dive to retrieve it but she was no match for Parvati, who easily ducked away, a triumphant gleam in her eye.

"Grace is feeling sick," Noor said firmly.

She couldn't have known how accurate her assertion was.

Costumes were brought for the others, including the cutest little maharaja suit for Shami, complete with turban and golden dagger.

Makeup followed. Only Aamaal reveled in the attention, insisting on false eyelashes in addition to the mascara and eyeliner. She chortled with delight at sparkly green eye shadow and everyone joined in when she demanded Shami must wear it as well.

"She's going to be a star when she grows up," commented one of the makeup artists, admiring Aamaal in the mirror as she brushed her hair.

"Is your mum a model, hon?" asked the makeup artist who was working on Noor. Obviously, VJ's father hadn't told them anything.

"She's a housewife," Noor said, "but she's also a great beauty."

"You should tell her to get a screen test for your sister."

Finally they brought out the jewelry. The chief costume lady held up an ornate necklace that she said had been designed by a famous jeweler to match a genuine period piece. Though the emeralds and rubies were fake and it was only gold plate, she claimed it had cost well over eight hundred dollars to commission and would sell for a good deal more. Parvati, who'd shown little interest in the clothing and makeup, perked up considerably at the sight of the necklace and listened carefully as the woman described its value. She squabbled with Aamaal over which of them should wear it. Noor stepped in and decided in Parvati's favor.

In the end, with all the preparations complete, the four of them looked as though they'd fit right into a maharaja's court. I followed as they walked confidently down the long hall, built to look like a throne room. Mr. Patel, sumptuously costumed, was seated on a throne at the far end. VJ stood off to one side looking decidedly out of place. It wasn't just that he was still in his jeans and T-shirt, it was his angry expression as he watched his father chat with a gaggle of women simpering around him. He raced over as soon as he caught sight of us and scooped Shami up into his arms.

"You look great, little man," he said. "He should have come in riding a horse though. Where are the horses, Papa?" he shouted back to his father.

His father got up and came over to join us. "They're tethered out back where they always are. When VJ was little he always begged to come to work with me. I was never sure if it was me or the horses he really loved." He chuckled as he clapped a hand on VJ's shoulder. VJ casually slipped out of his grasp and walked away, carrying Shami.

Mr. Patel watched his son take Shami to the throne and set him down. "He was always a kind little boy," he said. A look of infinite sadness crossed his face. He quickly replaced it with a mask of good humor.

"So, let's get started, shall we?" VJ's father said. "My word." He bent down to Aamaal. "Don't you look lovely."

A director materialized and the next hour sped by as they shot several takes of a crowd scene. Aamaal loved all the pageantry, and her excitement was infectious. Shami made everyone laugh as he trundled around in his finery earnestly saying the lines he was fed. He was, without a doubt, the best-natured four-year-old I'd ever met. I was almost sorry when the director called a wrap and we headed back to the dressing room.

After they changed, VJ took us to the stable behind the "palace." He harnessed a huge, sleek horse and brought it out to where we waited in a dusty paddock. Effortlessly, he mounted it bareback and reached down for Shami.

Noor pushed Shami behind her back. "He can't go up there. It's too dangerous."

"I want to go," said Aamaal.

"No," said Noor.

Shami tugged at Noor's shirt and said something in their language, giving her a pleading look.

Noor sighed. "Hold them tightly," she said sternly. "None of your fooling around."

VJ gave her a solemn nod, though his eyes sparkled.

Noor handed Shami up first, rattling off extensive instructions for both boys. Shami clutched the arm that VJ wrapped round his stomach.

Parvati handed Aamaal up, who settled in front of Shami and leaned forward to pet the horse.

VJ clicked his tongue and they were off at a leisurely walk, kicking up dust, which stopped me from following but didn't deter Noor or Parvati. VJ did three tours around the enclosure before lifting the children down.

"Next time I bring Eka," said Parvati.

Noor didn't comment as she was too busy dusting off Shami while simultaneously barking orders at Aamaal to stay away

from the horse. Aamaal ignored her and cooed at the horse, kissing its face. It nuzzled Aamaal's stomach, almost knocking her
over. VJ stayed close, ready to catch her, but had the good sense
not to provoke Noor further by touching Aamaal unnecessarily.

After a minor battle to separate Aamaal from her new pet, we
left the stable and headed to the parking lot. VJ texted his dad
that we were on our way, so Sanjay Patel was waiting for us at
the bus. He insisted we go back to the first building, where he
had lunch waiting for us. We were on the point of leaving when
the costume woman came running out of the palace, shouting.

"One of them took the necklace!" Her chest was heaving as
she reached us.

"What necklace?" asked VJ's father, calmly.

"The Jindan Kaur. She was wearing it." She glared at Parvati.

We all turned to Parvati.

"I am giving you. You are putting in box," said Parvati indignantly.

"That's true," I said. "I saw you put it in a box."

"It's not there now," insisted the woman.

"I'm sure it will turn up, Sheetal," said VJ.

"It will not turn up," she said heatedly. "I am not so careless
that I misplace expensive jewelry."

"Now, now, calm down," said Mr. Patel. "One necklace is not
serious. Surely we can replace it."

"It took weeks to have it made. It's a perfect copy of the
original."

My attention was diverted by Noor and Parvati. They'd
walked away from the group and were having their own discussion. Only because I was watching carefully did I notice
Parvati slip something into Noor's hand. I casually moved

closer and reached out to Noor. When I felt the necklace in my grasp I stepped away from them.

"I was going to give it back," I said, holding out the necklace. "I just wanted to try it on, since I didn't get a chance to dress up."

"You refused to dress up!" exploded the costume lady, snatching the necklace and giving me a foul look.

"No harm done," said VJ, taking my arm and steering me hurriedly in the direction of the bus. "Now, who's ready for lunch?"

We left the lady still sputtering as we piled in.

"I always love a happy ending, don't you?" said VJ's father, settling into the seat beside his son and giving him a warm look.

VJ turned away and stared out the window. Film star Sanjay Patel brushed a hand across his eyes as he failed yet again to win over the only fan he really cared about.

Grace

She doesn't do it for money she does it because she LIKES it!

I contemplated the message. This was my life, my new normal. Every morning, with the obsessiveness of an ingénue reading her reviews, I dumped my books in my locker, grabbed what I needed for the day, and trudged upstairs to the sixth floor girls' bathroom. In the fourth cubicle, the farthest from the door, I read the latest messages on a Hater Wall devoted entirely to me.

I knew it was stupid, if not masochistic. Who cared what a few bored girls wrote about me on a bathroom stall? In the past three weeks I'd been befriended by the hottest guy in school—the fact that he was gay only made it more perfect—and I was possibly making a new friend in Noor. The previous weekend, when I hadn't wanted to get undressed for our Bollywood debut, she'd somehow understood, and I know she appreciated me taking the heat for the stolen necklace.

She'd even suggested we get together this coming week.

But somehow these small wins couldn't outweigh the losses. I missed my brother and Tina. I missed having someone I could have a completely honest conversation with. Maybe I spent too much time alone in my room thinking about what I did. Things were still strained with my mom. It didn't help that I found myself constantly lying to her. I couldn't bear for her to know that I really had screwed up my life as badly as she'd predicted. I wanted her to think everyone at school had moved on, so maybe she would too. I claimed I had friends, never mentioned the bullying, and hid my wounds both inside and out.

I was basically shunned at school, but at least the snide remarks and crude messages on my phone and Facebook had dwindled to almost nothing. At times I could almost believe that my humiliation was forgotten, except for this, a wall full of comments. There were hundreds of them. Okay, if I'm being completely honest, as of that morning there were fifty-three. Yes, I counted. Who wouldn't?

They weren't all bad.

Seventeen of them were at worst neutral, girls asking stupid questions, like, *Does she really charge for it?*

Eight were positive. My favorite said, *Why don't you people get a life?* Though, arguably, that one could have been directed at me. It was exactly what VJ would have said if I'd told him about the wall. I preferred that he think—like my parents—that things had blown over. He expected me to be strong and fearless like him. If he'd known about the wall, he would have laughed it off and been disappointed in me that I couldn't do the same.

I read through the new comments, repeating the few positive ones in my head, trying to commit them to memory. It was a challenge I set myself every morning, and every morning, I failed. Hours and days later I could recall every cruel word while the kind ones always eluded me. Many of the comments were petty and mean-spirited. They said far more about the writer than they said about me, yet a part of me agreed with them.

They were substantively inaccurate: I wasn't giving BJs behind the equipment house at the pool, and I hadn't had sex with any of the many guys listed. I hadn't had sex with anyone, but I had been intimate. With a complete, still unknown stranger, I'd exposed my self and not just my body. I'd revealed my innermost thoughts, my fears and hopes. I'd treated my own soul like a commodity at a fire sale that I couldn't unload fast enough. As much as these girls hated me, they couldn't come close to how much I hated myself.

I jumped when I heard the bathroom door open and was glad I'd had the foresight to lock the stall. It was unusual for anyone to come in at that time of day. Being on the top floor, far from the lockers and cafeteria, this bathroom wasn't convenient.

"We were just talking. I asked him what he was doing this weekend."

The voice was familiar but I couldn't place it immediately.

"And how are my boyfriend's weekend plans any of your business?"

That voice I knew.

The only thing worse than sitting in a bathroom stall eavesdropping on someone else's conversation was realizing that the two someones were Madison and Kelsey. There was nothing I could say that would convince them I'd just happened to overhear by accident. And this almost definitely confirmed that they were contributors to my Hater Wall—not that I was ever in doubt.

"I was just making conversation," said Kelsey.

"Liar. I've seen the way you get all giggly around him."

"You're paranoid because of what Grace did. I'm not a slut like her."

Hang on. How did I get drawn into it?

"From where I was sitting you didn't look much better!"

Whoa! Madison was out for blood.

"Excuse me?" Kelsey sounded every bit as angry as Madison now. "You think I'd send naked photos of myself to a guy?"

"She didn't send them to a guy. She sent them to you!"

I held my breath. Was this the moment I'd finally find out what really happened?

"She didn't know that." Without even seeing her I could hear the smug pleasure in Kelsey's voice.

"Just stay away from my boyfriend," snapped Madison.

There was a shuffling and the sound of the door opening and closing. I gave myself a few seconds to calm my breathing before emerging from my hiding place. I walked past the stalls to the sinks and practically jumped out of my skin when I came upon Kelsey in front of the mirror, reapplying her mascara.

"You were listening?" she accused, rounding on me angrily.

I met her gaze. "You were the one who did it?"

I didn't have to say what "it" was. Her guilty look said it all.

"Not everything," she said, as if that should make all the difference. "I was the one you were texting with but it was

Madison's idea. She was the one who sent your photo to the entire school and pasted one to your locker."

"Why?"

She shrugged. "I guess she was jealous of you."

I didn't waste time challenging the ridiculousness of that assertion. "I'm not asking about her. Why did *you* do it?"

Her eyes cut to the door. I was blocking her way, but if she'd tried to get past me I would have let her. I had an overwhelming desire to burst into tears and I did not want to cry in front of her.

Kelsey beat me to it.

"I'm sorry," she sobbed. "I don't know why I go along with her. I just want her to like me."

I stepped forward and patted her on the back. Despite everything, I felt sorry for her. I knew exactly what she meant about trying to curry favor with Madison. I didn't think I'd ever stoop as far as Kelsey but I'd done my own share of sucking up. Madison may have been a mean girl, but she was the one who had to be placated if you wanted to fit into their group.

"Are you going to tell?" asked Kelsey.

I thought about it for a minute. "No, I just want everyone to forget about this."

"You're a lot nicer than Madison."

"That's setting the bar a little low, but thanks."

"You're kind of pretty too. At least you would be if you made more of an effort."

"We'd better get to class." I didn't wait to see if she was following as I walked out the door and headed downstairs.

It was an hour into second period when a messenger showed up at the classroom door with a note for me to report to the principal's office. I felt a rush of anxiety.

The first thing I heard when I stepped into the outer waiting room was Madison's voice. Twice in one day was twice more than I wanted. I couldn't imagine how this could end well for me.

"She's lying," she howled loudly.

The response was inaudible.

"Sit down there for a minute, Grace," said the receptionist.

Madison's crying got even louder as a door opened somewhere in the warren of offices. Mr. Smiley rounded a corner and beamed at me.

"Grace, how are you?"

"Fine," I said cautiously. Something told me that was about to change.

"Wonderful! Would you like to come with me?"

I got heavily to my feet and shuffled after him down the hall. I could see we were heading to the conference room, which was all too familiar. Madison's voice got louder with every step.

For some reason I didn't expect the room to be full. You'd think I would have learned from the last time. Both my parents, Mr. Donleavy, the school counselor, my homeroom teacher, another teacher who must have been Madison's homeroom teacher, Madison herself, and her parents all looked at me expectantly. If Mr. Smiley hadn't been directly behind me I would have turned right around and fled.

"Why don't you sit here with your parents, Grace?"

I slumped into the chair next to my mom and tried to make myself as small as possible.

"Madison, would you like to start?" asked Mr. Smiley.

"She's a liar," said Madison.

I was pretty sure she wasn't supposed to say that. I shot a look at Mr. Smiley, who was giving Madison a disappointed look.

"There's no proof she did it," said Madison's father.

Did what?

"Two other students brought this to my attention just today," said Mr. Smiley firmly. "And Madison has already admitted that she said mean things to Grace."

Madison glared at me.

"The sooner you apologize, the sooner we can move on," said Mr. Smiley to Madison.

"What will the consequences be if she admits it?" asked her father.

"We'll discuss that at a later time. First, Madison needs to apologize."

There was a long pause.

"I'm sorry," said Madison.

I was completely confused. What was she apologizing for, exactly? Kelsey had admitted to me that she was the one texting me. We only had her word so far that Madison had anything to do with any of it.

"That's okay," I said. I'd have apologized myself if it would have got us out of the room faster.

Mr. Smiley practically glowed, and there were a few sighs of relief around the table.

Mr. Donleavy didn't seem to be buying it though. "So, you're admitting you did all this, Madison?" he asked gently. "The texting, and sharing the photograph?" I was a little annoyed that he was being so nice to her, but it was a fair question.

"Sure," she said, which wasn't the same as saying yes, though only Mr. Donleavy and I seemed to notice.

"Well, that's it then," said Mr. Smiley. "Thank you all for

coming. Grace, you can go back to class. I hope we can all put this behind us now."

My parents and I stood up and filed out. They gave me hugs and congratulations, neither of which felt deserved. I still had a knot in my stomach. I knew for a fact that Madison was taking the fall for Kelsey on the texting. And none of this explained why Todd had been such a jerk the other day. For someone with no part in this at all, he'd certainly seemed eager to humiliate me.

I couldn't ask Kyle if Todd might have a reason to hurt me, since he still didn't know what I'd done, but there was nothing to lose by asking his former girlfriend, Anoosha Kapur. Kyle had told me that Todd had ruined their relationship. Maybe that was a clue.

I looked for Anoosha as soon as I reached the cafeteria at lunch. I was disappointed but not surprised to see her in a large group of popular girls. If I hadn't been so desperate, there's no way I would have gone up to them.

"Grace, I've been meaning to talk to you," Anoosha said as I approached. "How are you doing?" Her voice was full of concern. "Sit down."

"Could we talk in private?" I asked, avoiding the stares of the other girls.

"Sure." She stood up. "Watch my things," she said to her friends, and she followed me out of the cafeteria and down the stairs to the school's reception area. We sat down on one of the two couches.

"So, how are you really?" she asked.

"I've been better. I'm still trying to work out how all this happened. It's a little confusing. I was wondering if you know anything about Todd's involvement."

"Probably no more than you do. He came to school bragging you'd sent him a topless photo. No one believed him at first, till he forwarded it to a bunch of people."

"Wow! That's already more than I knew. So Todd thinks it was me who sent him the photo?"

"He did at first, but then we all heard about the sexting and realized someone had been leading you on. I'm sorry you got tricked like that."

"So Todd passed my photo on just to show off?"

"Partly, but he also hates your brother. You gave him a perfect opportunity for revenge. He had a crush on me last year and did everything he could to break Kyle and me up. One night at a party, I was drunk and I let him kiss me. I made a mistake, and Todd finally got what he wanted. Your brother dumped me. But even after we broke up I wouldn't go out with Todd. He's a bad guy, Grace."

There wasn't much left to say. Kelsey was the one doing the sexting, and Todd had sent my photo to the entire school to get back at my brother by humiliating me. Kelsey said it was Madison's idea, but she'd lied about Madison sending my photo to everyone, so maybe Madison wasn't involved at all. Mr. Smiley said two students had squealed on Madison. After Kelsey had admitted her involvement to me this morning she might have panicked that I'd change my mind about turning her in and decided to give Smiley someone else to blame. Todd was a slime for going along with her but, given what Anoosha said, it wasn't hard to believe he'd pin everything on Madison to save his own skin. With college applications looming, they both had a lot riding on maintaining clean records.

I followed Anoosha back to the cafeteria and took a seat at

my usual table. I was glad VJ wasn't there yet. I needed some time to think.

I felt Madison's presence before I saw her. She came up behind me and slammed one hand on the table, leaning in so our faces were inches apart.

"I know you're the one who told on me. Smiley wouldn't say who it was but I *know*!"

I was so shocked by the accusation that I didn't know what to say.

"First you try to steal the boy I like by sending him a boob shot, as if your flat chest would attract any guy, and then you accuse me of being behind it all. Do you really think a hag like you is a threat to someone like me? Why would I bother to take you down? You're already beneath me."

"Look, I know Kelsey was the one sexting me. Why don't we go tell Smiley together? You shouldn't be taking all the blame for this."

"Just because you're a rat doesn't mean I am."

"I didn't tell him you did it, Madison."

"Yeah, right, who else would do it?"

"Smiley said two students came forward, so it couldn't have been me. Maybe it was Kelsey and Todd."

"You really expect me to believe that? You tried to steal the boy you knew I liked, and now you try to drive a wedge between me and my best friend. You just don't give up, do you?"

"Ladies!" VJ arrived at the table, shouldered Madison out of the way and took the seat opposite me. "Are you joining us today, Maddy dear? Do say you are. I haven't seen a good catfight in weeks."

Madison barely noticed him she was so focused on me. "Do you know you got me suspended for three days? It's going on my permanent record."

She didn't deserve that. It was a serious consequence for something we both knew she didn't do.

"Well, maybe next time you'll think twice before being such a colossal bitch," said VJ.

Madison flinched. I felt a pang of sympathy as she turned and walked stiffly away. I was pretty sure she was trying not to cry, and I knew what that was like.

"She didn't do it," I said. "I think I should go to Smiley."

"Stay out of it," said VJ. "It's karma. She's done plenty to deserve retribution. You're too soft. You need to toughen up."

I nodded, but I wasn't sure I agreed. Maybe I needed to be tougher, but that didn't mean it was okay to jeopardize Madison's future for something she didn't do. I looked around for Kelsey and wasn't surprised to find her sitting with Todd, giggling. Had that been her endgame all along?

"Madison's taking the fall for Kelsey, and she thinks I'm the one who told Smiley it was her."

"Good. Maybe now she'll realize you're not someone she can push around."

He couldn't have been more wrong.

22

noor

Equal chances . . .

If she'd been old enough I would have sent Aamaal to school
alone the first day back from midterm break. I didn't want her
with me when I encountered my friends. I knew the stain of
who I was couldn't be washed away by medals, or even years
of friendship. I only hoped the parents of Aamaal's friends
would spare their young children the knowledge that a cher-
ished playmate was the daughter of a prostitute.

Only Gajra was waiting at the gate when we arrived. That
was unusual but not unheard of. Particularly after a break, the
other girls were often swept up in the excitement of sharing
details about their recent vacations. I cringed to remember the
fantastical stories I'd told them myself over the years. Would
they realize that every word was a lie?

Gajra opened the gate for me and hugged me as soon as I
stepped through. Then she bent down and hugged Aamaal as
well. Aamaal was startled but hugged her back. It was as if

Gajra were consoling us for a death in the family, which in a way I suppose she was. The family that I'd created, the one I desperately wanted to be true, was gone forever. Stripped of my past, I had no idea who I would be in this new future. I clung to the only thing I was sure of, Gajra's affection.

"Thank you," I said.

"For what, Noor?" She linked her arm in mine, as Aamaal raced off to find her friends. I watched her go and was relieved to see she was quickly absorbed into a game of chase.

"Shall we go see how everyone's holiday was?" asked Gajra.

It was the last thing I wanted to do, but there was no point delaying the inevitable. Arm in arm, we walked toward a cluster of my former friends. They pressed together at our approach like a flock of skittish pigeons.

"My father says it's improper for a girl like her to go to school with girls like us." Sapna kept her back to me but spoke loudly so I was certain to hear.

"My father says it doesn't matter where you come from, it only matters what you do with your life," said Gajra. "What is it your father objects to, Sapna—the fact that Noor bests you in almost every subject, year after year?"

"I'm the daughter of a doctor!" Sapna rounded angrily on Gajra, her hands balled into fists. "She's just a . . . a . . ." Poor Sapna was trapped by her own snobbiness. It would be unthinkable for a well-brought-up girl to even say the word "prostitute."

"She's just a what?" Gajra demanded fiercely. "A straight-A student? Our future valedictorian? Our future prime minister, perhaps? What is it you're trying to say?"

"Why do you defend her, Gajra? She's not one of us."

"You're right. She's smarter and works far harder than any of us. But who knows, if we're lucky maybe some of her perseverance will rub off. Didn't your father also come from modest beginnings, Sapna?"

Sapna turned crimson.

"What was your grandfather?" Gajra continued, "A taxi-wallah, isn't it?"

"That's a respectable job."

"Of course it is, and wasn't he lucky to be born a boy so every career option was open to him. Wouldn't it be wonderful if girls had the same opportunities?"

"Her mother could have been a maid, or a street-sweeper. There are other jobs for low-born women."

"Yet you only have to look outside the gates of our school to see whole families living on the street. Work is not easy to come by. Don't you listen to what our teachers tell us? Seventy percent of our population lives in slums, a quarter lives in absolute poverty. Would you really judge a mother harshly because she would do anything to provide for her children?"

"Perhaps you're the one who will be our future prime minister, Gaj," I teased, trying to lighten the mood. "You can certainly argue like a politician."

We all laughed—all but Sapna, who continued to glower at Gajra.

Gajra stared her down. "I want to live in an India that isn't held back by the prejudices of caste and color. Don't you, Sapna?"

Sapna looked from Gajra to the other girls. It was clear which one of them had won the day. She gave a grudging nod.

"All this talk of politics is making me bored," said Kiran. She sighed dramatically. "Come on, Noor, haven't you got a game for us?"

"I'm sure I can think of something." I looked around at the faces that had become so dear to me over the past eight years. For the first time they were looking back at me, the *real* me. They waited eagerly as I decided what we should play.

The rest of the day was like my first day of school. I entered every class, each new cluster of schoolmates, frightened of rejection. I needn't have worried. My friends cocooned me with their laughter, and most teachers went to great pains to congratulate me on my recent medals. There were a few who were awkward around me, but none mentioned the revelation of my origin. I collected Aamaal at the end of the day, confident we'd weathered the worst. She too had had an uneventful day and was full of stories of one of her friend's rabbits. It had had babies over the break, and Aamaal pestered me all the way home to let her have one.

When we entered our street I managed to distract her by giving her a few rupees to buy some greens for Lucky the goat. While she was suitably distracted I went inside to pick up Shami. The house was just waking up, but Deepa-Auntie already had Shami bathed and fed and was playing catch with him in the lounge. I was pleased to see Shami chasing a tightly balled sari. He was having one of his good days. The labored breathing that had hung on for weeks was finally responding to a new antibiotic.

I no longer took Shami to doctors. It was easier, not to mention cheaper, just to ask advice from the other aunties and buy what they recommended. I was pretty certain Shami had tuberculosis, and I knew he had the virus. I was determined he'd be one of the lucky ones who survived. He just needed to hang on a few more years. As soon as I got my school-leaving certificate, I'd get a job so I could afford the medicine and look after him properly. Three more years was all I needed. I knew lots of people with the virus who'd hung on longer than that, my ma included.

Shami squealed with delight when he caught sight of me. "Noor-di, Noor-di!" He hurled himself into my arms. I caught him mid-flight and swung him up onto my hip. I had a flash of anxiety that at four he was still tiny enough that I could easily support him with one arm.

I gave Deepa-Auntie a questioning look. "He's had a good day," she confirmed. "He took only a short nap today, so you might get him to bed early."

"Ma?" I asked.

"Still sleeping."

I set Shami down. Ma was getting harder and harder to rouse these days. Even Prita-Auntie had tried to talk to her about her drinking, and everyone knew Prita-Auntie was one of the biggest drunks on the lane.

"I'll be back in just a minute, Shami. You play with Deepa-Auntie."

"I want to come. I want to see Ma."

"She needs her tea first, Shami. You know she'll be happy to see you once she's had her tea." I hoped this was true, but Ma's moods had become as uncontrolled as her drinking. Even Aamaal, her clear favorite, could never be sure whether she was going to get a kiss or a smack. She'd taken to avoiding Ma altogether. She refused to even come inside to change her clothes after school until I told her it was safe. Often I had to bring her clothes down to her and she changed in the washing room, not greeting Ma at all.

I left Shami in the lounge and walked down the hall, careful to listen for Pran. I could hear some of the other aunties in the downstairs room that was just below ours. I poked my head in their door to greet them as I passed. A large rat scuttled toward me. It noticed me at the last minute, turned tail and disappeared down the corridor back to the kitchen. I paused at the bottom of the ladder. There wasn't the slightest noise from above. I should have asked if Prita-Auntie was still passed out as well. I quietly climbed the ladder and breathed a sigh of relief when I popped my head through the hatch. Prita-Auntie's bed was empty.

I scrambled up the rest of the way and walked over to Ma, who didn't stir, and watched her for a moment. Even in sleep the lines around her once-beautiful face drew her mouth into a perpetual frown. Several locks of lank, greasy hair had escaped from her braid and fell across her folded arm. Her body under the threadbare sari was little more than bones. It was hard to remember the way she used to be, so full of energy and determination. I used to pride myself on being like her.

Silently, I vowed that in three years I'd take her away from this life as well. I hoped it wouldn't be too late for her to regain some measure of who she used to be. At least she could live her final years in peace and comfort. We wouldn't need much, just a small room we could call our own, a kerosene cooker and, if we were lucky, running water and electricity. I'd seen rooms like that in Kamathipura, but my mother was not going to end her days among the men who had used her. I would take us as far from these fifteen lanes as it was possible to go. As Gajra had so recently pointed out, India had no shortage of slums. We'd make our home where no one knew us.

I reached under the bed for our stash of food and pulled out the tea, powdered milk and spices. I took her mug and our single pot from her bedside stand and returned to the ladder.

Ten minutes later I was back at her bedside holding a steaming brew of masala chai. Cinnamon scented the air, briefly overwhelming the usual, less pleasant odors.

"Ma." I gently shook her shoulder. It felt as if the bones rattled under my touch. She, on the other hand, didn't move at all.

"Ma," I said more loudly.

Her eyes peeped open. "Leave me alone," she groaned. "What time is it?"

"It's late, Ma, almost five. The men will be coming soon. Deepa-Auntie has already turned one away."

This was a lie but it had the desired effect. Ma hastily dragged herself into a sitting position, resting her back against the wall. "You haven't let her steal any of my regulars, have you?"

"Of course not, Ma, I would never do that." There was no point trying to defend Deepa-Auntie, who had never once accepted one of Ma's regulars, though many had approached her. Ma's mind traveled in deep grooves like a train, impossible to derail.

I knelt down and pulled out the box that stored our clothes and took out a salwar kameez for Aamaal. "Shami's doing well today, Ma. He's running around downstairs."

"I went to the temple last week. It's already working. Have you been this week, Noor?"

"Yes, Ma. Shall I go again?"

"Yes, go tonight. We must give thanks. Have you done your homework?"

"I'll do it now. I just need to feed the children first." I didn't tell her I was meeting up with Grace and Parvati, both of who were eager to hear about my first day back at school. Ma still didn't know about Grace, or why the school had decided not to expel me. She thought it was her own appeal that had convinced the principal to let me stay.

"Don't neglect your studies. You mustn't give them any excuse to try to get rid of you again."

I picked up the cup of tea she'd drained. "Would you like anything before I go, Ma? I could brush your hair or massage your feet."

"No, just send Aamaal up. I never see that child anymore."

I nodded, then leaned over and gave her a quick hug. She brushed me away.

I picked up Shami on my way out and found Aamaal, where I knew she'd be, still playing with Lucky. That goat was a better childminder than I'd ever be.

"Go inside and change, Aamaal. You can put your uniform away and give Ma a hug."

"Is Ma okay today?"

"Yes, I wouldn't have told you to go to her otherwise. Don't ask stupid questions."

She ran off and I immediately regretted my harsh words. It was my jealousy rearing up. The sight of Aamaal would cheer Ma in a way that I never could. I sometimes wondered if Ma actually knew Aamaal's father, maybe even loved him. I'd never known Ma to have a serious boyfriend the way many of the aunties did. She said a boyfriend was just one more man stealing your cash, which was true. Most aunties ended up supporting their boyfriends, even if the relationships didn't start out that way.

One thing was certain. Ma never loved my father, black dung beetle that he must have been. Whatever Gajra said about the new India, my too-dark skin, several shades darker than Ma's own, couldn't help but disappoint her. It was no wonder she preferred Aamaal.

When Aamaal returned, we headed for the café where Parvati and I had agreed to meet Grace. Parvati was supposed to be waiting for us in an alley just one lane over from our house. She wasn't at our meeting place, but I'd told her to go on ahead if Suresh was already on the hunt for her. I could only hope that was what she'd done.

The café we'd chosen was a long walk from Kamathipura. It was part of a large, modern chain, so a safe place for the foreigners to wait and the last place Suresh would think to look for Parvati. A single coffee there cost more than three times what a man would pay for our mothers. I wouldn't be wasting any of Ma's earnings on refreshments, so I bought Aamaal and Shami a couple of vada paav at a street stall on the way. The potato fritter in a bun wasn't a favorite of either of my siblings but at only ten rupees it was a regular standby.

I was disappointed, thirty minutes later, when we finally walked through the door, sweaty and tired, to find Grace sitting by herself. No Parvati.

"You came alone?" I said, glad she'd left VJ Patel behind.

She was at a table with four chairs. Aamaal immediately plopped herself down in one and looked around with interest. This wasn't the kind of place any of us was used to. I'd been carrying Shami on the long walk over, so I was happy to drop him in his own chair. Only when I'd sat as well did I notice other patrons eyeing us strangely. Most of them were in western dress. The few in salwar kameez wore the plain, tailored, high-fashion kind that I'd usually seen only on billboards, so unlike the boldly colored, ill-fitting, street-stall kind Aamaal and I wore.

"My mom doesn't know I came alone," said Grace. "I had to take a taxi because I told her VJ's driver was bringing us."

"He didn't want to come?"

"I didn't tell him." She smiled conspiratorially, but there was something forced about her smile.

I remembered VJ hadn't been paying attention when we'd made plans to meet. It had been at the end of the day, after we'd visited his father's studio. VJ had been lost in his own thoughts. It was obvious there was something wrong between he and his father. He seemed to resent it when his father showed off his studio, but VJ was the one who took us there, so he must have been proud of his father in some way. He'd seemed particularly angry when his father flirted with the young film star. I didn't understand why that upset him. His father showed far more restraint than I was used to seeing from men. Still, I knew what it felt like to be ashamed of a parent and proud of them at the same time.

"Where's Parvati?" asked Grace.

I hesitated. She didn't really know Parvati. I'd done most of the talking when we were all together. Parvati's English was good enough for scrounging a few rupees off foreigners on the street but not really up to serious conversation. Even if she'd had the words, Parvati would never have told them about Suresh.

"Perhaps she forgot."

Aamaal reached for the small menu that was wedged between the condiments in the center of the table. I snatched it out of her hands and replaced it where it had been. Grace took a sip of her drink. It looked like coffee but it was in a tall plastic glass with ice and a straw.

"Do you want one?" she asked. "My treat."

Aamaal and I said yes and no at exactly the same time. I repeated no and gave Aamaal a *watch out or I'll hit you* look.

"Shami wants that," said Shami. He pointed to a white frothy drink that was just passing our table in the hand of a chubby boy. But he spoke in Kannada. I was relieved that Grace wouldn't understand.

"You want a vanilla Frappuccino, Shami?" she asked, to my surprise.

Aamaal and I said yes and no at exactly the same time again. Grace laughed and stood up. I stood too.

"They just had dinner," I said. "They'll be sick if you give them anything else."

"I'll take that chance," said Grace, and she walked toward the counter.

I thought about chasing after her. Now that she was gone, the other customers were openly staring at us. I sat down and scolded both children until Grace returned. I was dismayed to see she was carrying two of the white mixtures and a third drink that looked like her own. She set that one in front of me and the white drinks in front of Shami and Aamaal.

I flushed with embarrassment. "I'm not thirsty."

Grace looked disappointed. "I've paid for it, so no point letting it go to waste."

I stared at the drink that cost many times the price of my mother, or as much as a month of medicine for Shami. Grace was right about one thing; I couldn't waste it. I took one sip. After the long, hot walk, the drink was like cool rain on a sweltering night. I took another.

23

Grace

I realized too late that I'd offended Noor by buying her the drink. I wasn't sure what I should have done. I couldn't very well have sat there drinking alone, especially with Shami and Aamaal looking on longingly. I tried to come up with something I could say to lighten the mood. I was sorry she hadn't brought Parvati and wondered if I'd done something to offend her as well. It was bad enough that everyone at school hated me; I wasn't sure I could bear it if Noor and Parvati didn't like me either. Maybe I should have brought VJ. Everyone liked him.

It was selfishness that had made me come alone. I needed a friend, a real friend I could talk to. I had to tell someone about the cutting. I wanted to stop but I wasn't sure I could do it on my own. The desire, ever since Madison had called me a hag, was almost overwhelming. I just couldn't get the word out of my head, and cutting had helped the last time. Maybe I wouldn't even have to tell Noor about the cutting. Maybe I could just tell her what Madison had said, and that would be enough to get it out of my system.

I'd tried to talk to VJ about it. He'd said that Madison was just lashing out and it was ridiculous to let it bother me. But VJ had never been anything but beautiful and popular. Madison may have been lashing out, but she'd voiced my deepest insecurities. Was I ugly? Was that why no boy had ever shown an interest in me? Her words had festered like an infected cut, far more painful than the ones I'd inflicted on myself. It had taken all my resolve not to add *ugly hag* to my previous inscriptions, but I wasn't out of the woods yet. Even as I sat looking at Noor across the table, the desire to cut was a time bomb ticking inside me.

"How is Parvati?" I asked.

"She is well, thank you."

Perhaps it was just her school-taught English, but the formality of Noor's reply seemed designed to keep me at a distance. She wasn't looking at me either, as she fidgeted with her straw. Parvati was definitely an uncomfortable topic of conversation. Maybe she'd told Noor she didn't like me. Noor had to meet me as part of her deal with Miss Chanda, but Parvati didn't. I suddenly felt embarrassed to have forced Noor into being my friend.

"How did your first day back at school go?" I asked, hoping she hadn't also been bullied. It couldn't have been easy walking into school with all her longtime friends knowing the truth about her for the very first time.

"It went well, thank you."

Another formal response. I looked around the café, trying to think of something else I could ask.

"Asmi is having rabbit with six babies. Asmi is wanting give me baby," said Aamaal.

"Really?" I could have hugged her I was so grateful someone wanted to talk to me. "That's really wonderful."

Aamaal gave her sister a triumphant look. "Noor say no."

I grimaced at Noor. "Sorry, I didn't know."

"We have no place to keep it." She hissed something at Aamaal in their language. Aamaal stuck out her lip. Her eyes filled with tears.

This just kept getting worse. How could I have been so stupid as to think Noor might like me when I couldn't even connect with kids from my own culture?

Shami said something to Noor in their language. Whatever it was, it didn't help. She responded, clearly annoyed at him as well.

"What did he say?" I asked, not really expecting she would tell me.

"He also wants a rabbit."

I wished I hadn't asked.

"I got called to the principal's office yesterday," I blurted, though the hope that I could confide everything was dying fast. "They think they figured out who pretended to be a boy and sent my naked picture all over the school, but they've got the wrong girl. Madison, the girl they've accused, didn't do it. It was her best friend texting me. And now the friend is making a play for Madison's boyfriend."

Noor cocked her head. I wasn't sure if she'd understood. Her English was really good but I'd been speaking quickly. I gave her a few minutes to respond. I don't even know why I continued when she didn't.

"I overheard the two girls talking when I was checking out my Hater Wall. It's this wall where everyone who hates me writes about how much they hate me. I think these girls are the ones who started it."

I paused. I couldn't believe I'd told her all that. What possible interest could she have in my pathetic little problems?

"I'm sorry," I said. "I don't have anyone to talk to." I blinked back tears and hung my head. It was mortifying.

Suddenly a tiny pair of feet were next to mine. I looked up and was eye level with Shami's unwavering gaze. He clambered into my lap and rested his head on my chest. I glanced at Noor. She smiled sympathetically, which only made me want to cry more. As usual, I'd messed everything up. I was supposed to be the one helping her, not the other way around. I put my arms around Shami.

"Can I ask you a question?" I asked.

Noor immediately looked wary. "What?"

"Did I do something to upset Parvati?"

"No." She shook her head. "Why do you ask?"

"I expected her to be with you. Why didn't she come?"

Noor took a napkin out of the holder in the center of the table and leaned over to wipe Shami's face. She took away the straw he was blowing through. Spitting on the napkin, she used it to wipe his sticky hands as well. She kept up a running commentary to him the entire time. Even without the translation I knew she was telling him off, but her voice was gentle, and he watched her as though she was the center of his universe. When she finished he slid off me, crawled onto her lap, put his thumb in his mouth and closed his eyes. I could still feel the warmth of him on my empty lap and couldn't help but feel envious. There wasn't a person in the world who would choose me first if they had other choices. I wasn't being self-pitying, it was simply the truth. Even my parents would have chosen my charming, successful brother if they'd had to choose just one of us. Heck, I'd have chosen him over me. I didn't blame them.

"It's not you," she said, returning to our conversation. "Parvati has a problem so she could not come today."

"Is it something I can help with?"

"It is a big problem. I am telling Parvati to speak to Chanda-Teacher but she will not. She also will not like it if I tell you."

I tried not to feel hurt. "Is it a secret?"

"Yes, it is *her* secret. If she wants you to know, she must tell you. I think perhaps you also keep secrets for your friends."

"I would, if I had any friends."

"I think you have a secret with Vijender Patel?"

"He's more of an acquaintance. He's nice, but we're not that close." I suddenly realized what she was getting at. Of course I was keeping a very big secret for VJ.

"Would you tell me what really happened when you returned to school?" I asked. "I've been worrying about you."

"Everyone was kind to me. My best friend Gajra told every-one we must treat each other the same. It does not matter who your parents are, or what caste you're from."

"Can I ask you something else?"

"You may ask. I may not answer."

I scanned the café and noticed several people watching us. It confirmed the suspicion that had been growing in me. "Why did you choose this café? It's a long way from where you live and it doesn't seem like . . . your kind of place."

Noor gave me an appraising look. She also glanced at the nearby tables. You could almost see the other patrons leaning in, trying to eavesdrop. We were the definition of colliding worlds: not east and west, but rich and poor. This café was a bastion of the rich. The people in here may have shared nationhood with Noor, but they were my people.

Noor stood up, shifting Shami onto her hip. "Do you want to see my home?"

"I thought you'd never ask." I jumped to my feet. "Time to go home, sweetie." I extended my hand to Aamaal, who took it as though holding my hand was the most natural thing in the world.

When we got out on the street my first impulse was to flag a taxi. I stopped myself just in time. Noor was showing me her world, so we'd do it her way.

Twenty minutes later I was seriously regretting my decision. Not taking a cab in brutal heat, when you have more than enough cash in your pocket, is just stupid. It had to be worse for Noor. She hadn't put Shami down once. Nor had she shown any of the annoyance I'd felt on the multiple occasions we'd had to walk in the street because everything from livestock to makeshift stalls had taken over the sidewalk. Several times I'd had to stop walking and jump out of the way to avoid becoming roadkill.

"Are we almost there?" I asked for the third time.

"We are close," said Noor, as she had the previous two times.

Finally we turned into a quieter lane, though that was mainly because it was so congested with people and animals that the cars could only inch along. I walked carefully, watching the ground, but had to look up occasionally to avoid collisions.

There was filth everywhere. Even the walls of the crumbling cement buildings were cloaked in a layer of grime. I knew, from my previous visit, that we'd entered one of the narrow lanes of Kamathipura, though being later in the evening it was busier and somehow different from before.

Though it was teeming with people, women were scarce. A few burqa-clad women fluttered quickly from stall to stall making their purchases before racing off. In contrast, the other women, in neon-bright saris, with fake jewels sparkling in their noses and ears, lounged in doorways or strolled slowly up and down the lane shouting out to passing men.

Many women greeted Noor, and she paused each time to exchange a few words. Her whole demeanor changed as she wove her way down the lane. Gone was the girl who'd perched uncomfortably on the edge of her seat in the coffee shop. Noor was at ease here. It was home.

At first I wasn't concerned when a boy, perhaps eleven or twelve, popped out from between two parked stalls and grabbed Noor's arm. She spoke to him as if she knew him, but her tone wasn't the same as the one she'd used with the women. She wasn't happy to see him. Had Shami not been asleep in her arms I felt certain she would have shoved the boy away.

"Is everything all right?" I asked.

The boy smirked at me. "My name Adit," he said in a heavy accent. "What is your name?"

I ignored him. "Is he bothering you, Noor?"

Noor looked pointedly at the boy's hand, still gripping the arm that was cradling Shami. He let go.

"Adit is a friend from when he was a child." It wasn't clear if she was telling me or reminding him.

"I am not child," said Adit.

"You think because you are a bully you are a man?" asked Noor in English, perhaps to put him at a disadvantage.

"I am telling Pran-ji where is Lali go."

"You tell Pran and you will be sorry, Adit." Noor spoke calmly and added a few words in Hindi; threats, I suspected.

Adit puffed out his chest but his eye twitched. I wasn't sure if it was nerves or a permanent condition. He spoke back to her in Hindi, throwing in a few English swearwords having to do with the female anatomy. She waited until he ran out of steam, replied curtly in Hindi and turned to me.

"My house is a little more down the street. We cannot go inside at this time but I will show you." She continued walking and I followed.

"Who's Lali?" I asked.

"Lali ran away from our house."

"Does Adit want to harm her?"

"He says he knows where she is. Probably he is lying."

Aamaal was still holding my hand, which by now was sweaty and not just with heat. I glanced down at her. She stared back with round eyes.

"What if he's telling the truth?"

"We must hope he is not," said Noor.

Noor stopped and pointed across the road. It wasn't clear which building she was pointing at. They were all narrow and tightly packed, sharing walls, like ramshackle row houses from a bygone era. Most were fronted by shops or workshops, though they were all so drab and cluttered it was difficult to figure out what many of them were selling.

"Which one's yours?"

"The entrance beside the car-fixing shop."

I looked skeptically across the road. There was a guy on the street with some kind of loud power tool that he was using on metal. None of the various pieces of metal strewed in haphazard piles nearby looked as though they'd come out of a car, but it was the only thing in sight that might have fit her description. It did have a darkened, open doorway to the left of it. It also had bars extending out from the second-floor windows like cages. There was a woman sitting in one of them looking out over the street.

"It's like she's in a cage." I hadn't meant to say it out loud and immediately wished I could take it back. What if Noor mistook my meaning?

"Yes."

"Why doesn't she come out?"

"Some women are not allowed outside."

"They aren't allowed outside . . . ever?"

"Lali was not allowed out."

"How old was Lali?"

"Older than me, younger than you."

I gasped.

"Do you have a phone, Noor?"

"I have Parvati's phone but I am not using it. I am keeping it safe for her."

"But you could use it, if you had an emergency, if you needed me?"

Noor looked at me strangely. "Needed you?"

I didn't know how to explain my fear. Perhaps it was the young boy's aggressiveness, or the horror of a world where young girls were locked away, only to be taken out to be played with like toys from a cupboard. Noor had explained that her mother had chosen not to force her into prostitution, but for how long? She'd also said that her mother believed there was nothing wrong with sex work, that it was even expected for the women in their community.

"Do you know Parvati's number? If you give it to me, I'll put it in my phone and then ring you. Then you can save my number."

"It is very kind of you but I am not needing help, Grace."

"Then do it for me, so I don't worry."

She reluctantly gave me Parvati's number. I rang it immediately.

"When you turn on her phone, you'll see my number as a missed call." I hoped I wasn't insulting her by explaining that.

She leaned over and hugged me with her one free arm. I was so startled by the gesture I welled up. It was ridiculous to be so emotional. I really didn't know what had come over me lately. Since my public shaming, I seemed to choke up at the slightest provocation. It was no wonder Noor doubted I could help her. I was barely coping with my own life, and my problems were nothing compared to hers. But in that moment I vowed to myself that if she ever was in trouble, I wouldn't fail her.

24

Grace

Over the next couple of days I almost put Madison's comments out of my head. While Noor and I hadn't talked about Madison, other than my brief rundown of Madison taking the fall for Kelsey, seeing Noor's life had put my own in perspective. I thought less about my own troubles and more about Noor. I found my mind wandering to daring if unrealistic scenarios in which I rescued her entire family from poverty. I still checked out my Hater Wall every morning but there had been no new comments since Madison had been suspended, and I no longer felt the need to reread the old ones.

I felt only a little nervous arriving at school on Friday morning. Madison would be back from suspension. I hoped, like me, she was ready to move on, but I feared she might still be looking for payback. The frustrating thing was that I did feel guilty. While I wasn't responsible for getting her in trouble, I'd let her take the fall for something I knew she hadn't done.

Thirty minutes into the day I received a note to report to the principal's office. I wasn't at all surprised to see Madison when I was ushered into the conference room. Mr. Smiley and the counselor were the only other people there. I was directed to the seat across from Madison's.

"Thank you for coming, Grace. We wanted to give you and Madison a chance to clear the air before she resumes classes."

Madison and I avoided eye contact.

"Who'd like to go first?" asked Mr. Smiley.

"Perhaps now that Madison's had a few days to reflect on her actions, she has something she'd like to say to Grace," prompted the counselor.

Madison's silence filled the room.

"Grace," said the counselor, undaunted, "perhaps you'd like to tell Madison how her actions affected you."

My own silence joined Madison's.

"We have to talk this out, girls," said Mr. Smiley. "We're not leaving here until we do."

"Is someone going to send out for pizza?" I asked.

It was a failed attempt to lighten the mood. Madison's lips didn't even twitch.

"Well, at least we're talking," said Mr. Smiley optimistically. "So, why don't you go first, Grace. How did Madison's actions make you feel?"

My hands were resting in my lap. I pressed gently on my thigh, where my feelings were inscribed for my eyes only. It ached a little.

"I'm over it. I'd just like to put it behind me."

Mr. Smiley looked disappointed. "Madison, do you have anything to add?"

Madison met my eyes for the first time. My mouth went dry. Her gaze shifted to Mr. Smiley. "I've learned my lesson, sir."

"And what lesson was that?"

"That I shouldn't betray my friends."

There was a long pause. Mr. Smiley was obviously trying to decide whether I was the betrayed friend that Madison was talking about.

"That's good to hear," he finally said. "Isn't it, Grace?"

"Terrific."

"Well, girls, you can go back to class."

Madison and I filed out. I was glad we were heading to different classes. My heart was still pounding from the malevolent look she'd given me back there. I planned to peel off the second we passed out of the office doors, but she grabbed my arm.

"Do you know that in addition to destroying my college chances you got me grounded for six weeks? You show off your skanky body to the entire school and I get punished. You know what you are? You're a dis*grace*."

She stressed the last syllable in case I couldn't work out that she was doing a play on my name.

"I don't know what to say. I already apologized for flirting with fake-Todd. I offered to go to Smiley with you to tell him Kelsey was the one texting me. It's not my fault you chose to take the blame." But I'd let her. Was it my fault?

"Unlike you, I don't betray my friends."

"What do you want from me, Madison?"

"I want everyone to know the truth about you."

"What truth? That I sent a topless photo to some random person? That I'm the least popular girl in school? Unless they've been in a coma for the past three weeks, I can assure you they do know."

"You're right about that. Your *dis-grace* is legend."

I wrenched my arm out of her grasp and walked away. I thought she'd hurl some parting shot but she didn't. She saved that for later.

The rest of the school day passed without incident. That was the way I thought of it, as if incident were the norm and lack of it was noteworthy.

I got home to find Mom at the door, as she always was these days. If hawkeyed concern was supposed to make me feel loved, it wasn't working. All I felt was suffocated.

"Did you see Madison today?" she asked. That was her greeting. No hello.

"Yeah, Mr. Smiley called us both in."

"Really? He should have told me he was going to do that. I would have come."

"It went well, Mom. Everything's okay between us now."

"What did she say?"

"She apologized."

"As if that's enough for what she did!"

"It is enough, Mom. It's over."

"What about the other kids?"

"What other kids?"

"What are kids saying about what you did? Are they treating you differently?" She'd asked me this question every day for two weeks. By now she had to know what I was going to say. Just like I knew what she was going say.

"No one's said anything. They've forgotten about it."

"Forgotten?! I assure you they haven't forgotten." And there it was. Whether other kids were still being mean or were really moving on, the one person who would never forget was my mom. To give her credit, she was sounding less accusatory and more resigned, so perhaps we were making progress.

"I'm going to take Bosco for a walk," I said. The reason for the change in subject was not lost on her.

"I'll come with you."

"I need some time alone, Mom."

"We can talk about your birthday. What would you like this year?"

"Can you buy me a new life?"

"Grace!" Mom looked devastated. I shouldn't have said it.

"Sorry, I'm just joking." I gave her a hug. "I'll be back in fifteen minutes. Please stop worrying." If she ever found out about the bullying, much less the cutting, she'd never let me out of the house.

She hovered in the doorway while I fetched Bosco and followed us out to the elevator lobby. I could tell she was debating whether to insist on coming. It wouldn't have been the first time. The relief when the elevator doors closed, leaving her behind, was almost as intense as the feelings I got from cutting.

By the time I got back, Dad was home and we sat down to dinner. Mom happily relayed my lie that things had gone well with Madison. Dad, with his own brand of vigilance, asked for details, which unfortunately required further lies. He was skeptical when I said that Madison wasn't angry, so I told him that Madison and Kelsey had invited me to eat lunch with them again.

Finally they moved on to what I wanted for my birthday. Truthfully, there was nothing I wanted, but Dad loved spoiling us with presents so I came up with a few suggestions. Then

Mom started badgering me about having a party. It was her version of spoiling. I regretted lying about Madison and Kelsey when Mom practically insisted we invite them over to help me celebrate.

"It's important to show you have no hard feelings," said Mom.

"But I've already made plans with Noor and VJ," I improvised.

"Well, they can come too. You can have as many people as you want."

"Let me talk to them and get back to you."

I escaped to my room shortly after. My excuse—homework—was legitimate for once. I had a ton. It was close to eleven by the time I broke the back of it and could turn to my nightly ritual of checking Facebook for new hate messages. I hadn't had any for a week, so I wasn't even nervous when I saw an invitation to join a Facebook group, until I saw the name. I shouldn't have clicked on it.

I'm not sure what I expected. I do know that when the page opened with my topless image, in full living color, my world turned black. I slid off my chair and sank to the floor, putting my head between my bent knees. I took deep raggedy breaths but couldn't stop my heart from pounding or my head from spinning. It was everything Mom had predicted. My half-naked image was now on the Internet. Available for everyone to see. Forever.

Finally I pulled myself up and sat down again at my computer. The possibility that my parents might see this page made me feel physically ill. I grabbed the trash can from beside my desk and held it on my lap, in case I threw up, while I scrolled through the forum. I had to know how bad it was.

It was bad.

Every comment was more heinous and humiliating than the one before, as if they were competing to see who could be the crudest. It was hardly surprising, given the name of the group.

DissGrace.

Madison may not have engineered my original downfall but she was definitely behind this. With a three-day suspension she'd had time on her hands, and judging from the comments, the page had been up since the very first day. I will say one thing for Madison: she knew how to rally support. She wasn't the only one who thought I was an ugly hag.

It was a long while before I turned off my computer, and a long while after that before I walked over to my bag and fished out the knife. It was lucky I'd kept it. It had been over a week since I'd inscribed Todd's appraisal. I'd been thinking about returning it to the kitchen. Even without Noor's support, I'd been feeling stronger. I'd thought I was done. I'd hoped I was.

This was my longest inscription yet, seven letters, two words. I was careful to line up the *U* with the *S* and the *L* so I had to wrap the rest of it around the back of my thigh. It was awkward. I thought about the femoral artery. It was so accessible, and I had the right equipment.

I knew now that people at school were never going to forget I'd stripped off for a total stranger. My image on the Internet would be an eternal reminder. The bullying wasn't going to stop. The only way to end it was if I ended it. I could make it look like an accident, though my parents wouldn't be consoled by the idea that I'd accidentally bled out while etching *UGLY HAG* into my thigh.

I had to take a break after a couple of letters to go fetch tissue so I didn't bleed on my bedspread. Wasn't I lucky to be so wealthy and well cared for that I had my own en suite bathroom? It was yet another privilege I had over Noor. I'd been insane to think I could ever tell her about this. The absurdity of voluntarily carving up my own flesh was staggering, and yet I couldn't stop. I played with my life, while she struggled for hers. She must never know.

Bosco watched from the foot of my bed, my only witness.

"What do you think, buddy? Am I crazy? Wouldn't I be doing everyone a favor by ending this tonight?"

His soft brown eyes held silent reproach.

"You'd still have Mom. And Kyle will be home at Christmas. You know, when he returns you're going to want to be with him anyway. This was never more than a temporary arrangement."

My phone pinged from inside my bag. It was probably my brother again. His timing was uncanny. I had to force myself to walk over and take out my phone. I didn't put down the knife, certain this was going to be something else I'd rather not read.

I was wrong.

The text was brief and to the point.

go to zoo sunday? noor

I sat down at my desk chair and stared at the letters I'd just finished chiseling into my flesh. They shone crimson in the light of the overhead lamp. I swiped my tissue over the *A*. I'd cut a little too deep; it was still dripping. I looked back at the message and read it again.

what time? I asked.

10 am at the flamingos

"Flamingos, Bosco, what do you think of that? I can't check

out before I've seen the flamingos." I put the knife back in my bag and returned to the bed, plopping down, phone still in hand.

ok

Bosco heaved his lazy self to his feet, padded closer and dropped his head into my lap. I lay down and curled around him, my face buried in his soft woolly fur. The steady rise and fall of his chest lulled me to sleep.

25

Noor

Without a matriarch . . .

It was my idea to visit the zoo. Grace seemed lonely and in need of a friend, but it was Parvati I was most concerned about. More and more she was succumbing to Suresh's domination. She rarely bothered to fight him anymore, as if she too believed he owned her. I'd seen so many spirits crushed among the girls and women in my community. I couldn't bear to see it happen to Parvati.

Parvati had always loved the zoo. We'd discovered it together years ago, a refuge from our lives. I wasn't sure how she'd feel about sharing it with Grace but she didn't hesitate.

"Are you sure she'll like it?" asked Parvati.

"No," I said honestly. "I think she will like doing something with us though. She was sorry you didn't come last week."

A shadow crossed Parvati's face and I cursed myself for reminding her.

"Was the café very grand?" asked Parvati.

"It was a waste of money. The zoo is much nicer," I reassured her.

Unlike the café, the zoo was cheap, even if we paid to get in. Of course, Parvati and I never did pay. Years ago we'd found a back entrance where we could sneak in for free. In the cooler months, I would take Shami and Aamaal whenever I had the bus fare. Recently, though, Shami's illnesses had sapped my cash reserve. The large grounds were like walking through an ancient forest. The trees were twisted giants, covered in vines and moss. I imagined that many of them, like the zoo, were over one hundred years old. It was one of the few places we could go where people weren't fighting over every inch of pavement.

Most of the cages were empty, and more animals were gone each time we visited. Only the signs were left to suggest what might once have been there: lions and rhinoceros, leopards and tigers. It must have been something to see all those animals in real life, but on the bright side, the zoo had fewer visitors now, and the animals that were left had become old friends.

"I want to see the bear," said Aamaal, staring, bored, at the flamingos. "And the deer and the spotted dog."

"He's not a dog, Aamaal." I was hoping she'd forgotten about the hyena. It was the one animal I did not like to visit.

"Do you think she'll bring Vijender Patel?" Parvati asked anxiously. I wasn't sure if she wanted to see him or was scared he would come—Parvati never flirted with boys anymore. She didn't even speak to them, if she could avoid them. I used to wish she was more cautious. Now that she was, all I felt was longing for the girl she used to be.

"I don't know. She didn't bring him to the café."

"And the monkeys, and the rhino—"

"The rhino's gone, Aamaal. I explained that."

"Did she say why he wasn't there?"

"Did you remember the lettuce for the hippo, Noor-didi?"

"Yes, Aamaal, but I've told you we really shouldn't feed him.
If we got caught—"

"Do you think he's ever been to the zoo before? With his
money, I bet he can see hippos and tigers in the jungle."

"There they are!" I said loudly. Vijender had come. I shot a
look at Parvati. Her once-open face was unreadable.

Aamaal wrenched her hand from mine and ran toward
Grace and VJ. I was on the point of calling her back when
Shami wriggled from my arms and followed her. VJ had
already dropped to his knees by the time they reached him. It
was typical of his arrogance that he assumed they were running to him.

VJ swept both my siblings into a big hug. My stomach
clenched to see Aamaal in his arms. I had to remind myself that
not every male was a threat. I hadn't shared my suspicions
about VJ's preferences with Parvati. Perhaps I should have. It
might have put her at ease.

As we came up to them I was shocked to hear Shami burbling
about a cricket match he'd watched on TV. I felt a stab of jealousy
that he'd chosen to tell VJ about his new interest rather than me,
but I couldn't help smiling when VJ dissected every play Shami
described, and Shami glowed with excitement. Perhaps the film
star could do some things for Shami that I could not. I just hoped
VJ understood that if he ever did anything to hurt my brother
I'd make him sorry he ever met me.

"So, what are we going to look at first?" asked Grace.

"The spotted dog," shouted Aamaal in Hindi. Though I'd

coached her to speak English when we were with the foreigners, I was happy in this instance that she'd forgotten.

"Let's start with the hippo," I said, also in Hindi. "He's much closer and we have food for him." I didn't add that I'd deliberately chosen our meeting place to be as far from the hyena as possible.

"Shami want to see spotty dog," agreed Shami. Fortunately he spoke Kannada. Shami still got his languages mixed up. He was fluent in three and had begun to learn English as well.

"What's that, little man?" asked VJ. I knew he'd cause trouble.

"Shami want to see spotty dog," Shami repeated, this time mostly in Hindi.

"The spotty dog it is, then," said VJ, as if he were in charge.

"Why do they have a dog in a zoo?" asked Grace.

"It is not being dog," said Parvati.

"It's a hyena," I said. "But really we should leave it till later. It's on the other side of the zoo."

"I want spotty dog," insisted Aamaal. She tugged on VJ's arm.

VJ scooped up Shami and placed him on his shoulders. I was on the point of objecting in the same moment that Shami squealed in delight. VJ put a hand on one of Shami's dangling legs and took Aamaal's hand with the other.

"Are we ready to go?" he asked cheerfully.

I crossed my arms. What an irritating boy he was.

"Which way do you want to go, Noor?" asked Grace.

VJ, Aamaal and Shami pinned me with identical imploring looks.

"All right," I said grouchily, "we will see the hyena first."

"Yes!" VJ crowed, swinging Aamaal's arm up in a victory punch.

VJ set off with my siblings at a slow trot, deliberately bouncing Shami up and down. Shami giggled and shrieked with far more enthusiasm than I'd ever seen in him before. It made me sad and happy at the same time.

Grace, Parvati and I followed. Parvati looked glum. I wasn't sure if she was wishing she'd brought Eka. We'd agreed, since we were spending the bus fare to come this far, that she would look for a place to sleep in this part of town tonight, far from Suresh.

"Shami seems to have taken to VJ," said Grace, calling my attention to where VJ had stopped to let us catch up and was passing the time swinging each of my siblings around like propellers on a helicopter.

"He is too rough with them."

"They seem to like it."

"Yes, they liking," agreed Parvati.

"I could give you a go," VJ teased.

Parvati flinched.

I started walking again, giving my brother's flying feet a wide berth.

Fifteen minutes later we reached the hyena. I swallowed my disappointment to find him still there. Many animals at our zoo died from poor care and malnutrition; I imagined it was a welcome release. Every time we came I hoped the suffering of this miserable creature had ended. He paced his tiny iron cage with a glassy-eyed despair that I'd seen too often in my own community. His tongue lolled out of his open mouth, skin stretched taut over jutting bones. I looked at my sister, who had come to stand beside me. Her anguished face was only part of what I hated about visiting the hyena.

Her hand found its way into my own. "Tell him the story, Noor."

The story was the other part.

Shami, who had been in VJ's arms, asked to be put down and

ran to take my other hand. It was our tradition to tell the story together. I was embarrassed to tell it in front of the foreigners but I couldn't disappoint Shami and Aamaal.

"You come from a proud line of hyenas," I began in Hindi, looking directly at the hyena. "Your mother and your aunties all loved you. Your sisters hunted while you stayed at home and played and slept and learned what it was to be a little boy hyena, beloved, in the paws of your community."

"Because girl hyenas are stronger and fiercer," said Aamaal, who knew the story well.

"Yes," I agreed.

"But hyena families stick together forever," said Aamaal. "That's why he's so sad. He misses his family."

"When will his mummy come, Noor?" asked Shami.

"Not yet, Shami," scolded Aamaal authoritatively. "We haven't told him the bad part yet."

"What are they saying?" asked Grace quietly. VJ played translator.

"One day some bad men came and stole you from your mother," I continued.

"Because mummy and sisters were out hunting," added Aamaal.

"But your mummy and sisters never stopped looking for you."

"Your sisters would never forget about you," said Aamaal pointedly to Shami.

"And one day they'll find you," I said to the hyena.

"Because family sticks together, right, Noor-di?" asked Shami.

"And a family isn't a family without a mummy," added Aamaal.

"That's right, one day we'll come and this hyena will be gone, but we won't feel sad because we'll know his mummy and sisters have come for him."

"Don't worry, darling, your mummy and sisters are on their way," said Aamaal to the hyena. "I wish I could give him a hug," she said to me.

"Well, who's for ice cream?" asked VJ. "My treat!"

"You don't have to treat us," I said.

"I am wanting ice cream," said Parvati, summoning a smile. For once I felt a rush of warmth for the film star.

"I'm treating everyone, even Gracie here. She could use a little meat on her bones."

Grace flushed and quickly turned away. Even VJ noticed.

"Everything all right, Grace?" VJ gave her a curious look. "You're not upset that I called you bony, are you?"

"You need to learn when to keep quiet," I scolded. "There is a small restaurant down this path." I took Grace's arm.

Grace and I dropped back, letting VJ go ahead with my siblings. "You are feeling embarrassed," I said.

"No, it was no big deal. Where did the story come from?"

"The first time we came here Aamaal was so sad because of the hyena that I made up a story about his family rescuing him. Later I asked my teacher about hyenas. Their families really do stay together and look after each other, just like people. I think that is why he has become crazy. He is lonely."

"You're a good sister."

"I am certain you are as well."

"Maybe I used to be."

We enjoyed another hour at the zoo before I had to take Shami and Aamaal home. I let VJ give us a ride. It was much quicker, and I worried Shami's flushed face might indicate more than excitement. The car dropped us at the end of our street.

"Can you meet next week?" asked Grace. "On Friday night, maybe?"

"I think so."

"I was thinking maybe we could have a meal somewhere."

I hesitated, but I could see it was important to her, so we agreed on a falafel place. It was on the edge of my neighborhood and not too expensive. If I set aside a little money all week, I might be able to afford something.

Deepa-Auntie met us the minute we walked through the door of our house. "Thank goodness you're back, Noor. Your ma isn't well. I think she should see a doctor."

"I'll talk to her," I said.

"Shami want to see Ma," said Shami.

"Not right now, Shami-baby," said Deepa-Auntie. "Let Noor go first."

I hurried to the ladder, scrambled up and peeked over the top. Ma was flat on her back with her eyes closed. The heat, even with the fan going, was stifling. I climbed the rest of the way and went over to the bed, perching uneasily at its foot. She didn't stir. I reached for her wrist. She had a pulse but her flesh was burning up. I noticed she had a sore on her lip again, heavy with pus.

I crawled under the bed and pulled out the fixings for tea and a tiny folded paper of pills that she didn't know about. I would dissolve some into her drink. To please her I also took the small jar of home remedy that she swore by. Shami called it her magic powder. If only it was magic, I thought traitorously. I wondered how many more illnesses like this her body could endure before death took her. Each time, she returned from them a little weaker.

I left her sleeping and made my way down the ladder, heading to the kitchen. Adit was standing in the hallway.

"She's sick again," he said.

"It's nothing. A cup of tea will revive her."

"Nishikar-Sir was asking about you."

The owner of the brothel. My heart stopped but I held myself tightly, determined not to show my fear.

"Why would he be asking about me?"

"Did you really think he wouldn't notice you forever? Your ma earns so little now. You must have seen this coming."

"You seem to take pleasure in this, Adit."

"It's just the way things are. Your mother was stupid to send you to school. You're just a girl."

"You're a boy, yet your mother didn't bother to send you to school."

"It wouldn't matter. An education is more useful for a boy, but both our fates were written before we were born. If I'm lucky, Pran will let me stay on here as his assistant."

"You call that luck, to live off the women who are trapped here?"

"What do you expect me to do, Noor? I also must provide for my family."

"I don't know who you are anymore, Adit. The boy I knew was a fighter. He would not have given in to a fate he didn't choose. There is a whole world of possibilities beyond our fifteen lanes. Don't you want more for yourself?"

I didn't give him a chance to respond. I could see my words had hit home as his cheeks colored. I pushed past him and went down the hall to make my mother's tea.

26

Noor

The big boss . . .

Ma must have known that Nishikar-Sir had asked about me, though she gave no sign of concern. She was a respected woman in our home and in the community. As powerful as he was, I was not such a valuable item that Nishikar-Sir would risk the anger of the entire Devadasi community, not to mention the non-Devadasi sex workers, by selling me without Ma's permission.

Still, I couldn't ignore his interest entirely. I'd seen it often enough. If Nishikar-Sir had decided he wanted me, the pressure on Ma would begin. But Ma had worked hard to give me a good education, and her pride wouldn't allow her to accept that her daughter needed to take over the work because she could no longer bring in enough customers to provide for her children. So over the next few days, I kept my worries to myself, making light of it whenever Deepa-Auntie tried to broach the subject. I don't think she would have let it go so easily if we hadn't both been distracted by the return of Lali-didi.

She was brought back in the night. There were as many accounts of how it happened as there were people to tell the tale. What was certain was Adit's part in it. He really had known where she was, and for the promise of a job he gave her up.

Lali-didi went back to the lockup. We were all forbidden to speak to her, but there wasn't a woman or girl in the house who obeyed. No matter how many times Pran or Binti-Ma'am chased us away, we kept a round-the-clock vigil outside the box that was her prison. We spoke to her constantly, told her what was happening in the outside world and made plans for her release. Some of us promised her wild things that we could never bestow.

Lali-didi herself spoke little. She didn't cry either, even when Pran went inside the box with her. Her silence echoed off the walls of our home in a way that her tears never had. It spooked Pran. Over the week of her confinement he went to her with decreasing frequency and none of his usual malicious glee. He tortured her with the dogged determination of a man completing a distasteful task. We all suspected Nishikar-Sir had ordered it.

On the day she was released, Pran came into the outer room, walked straight past Shami and me sitting on the floor, went to the door of the box and unlocked it. He didn't speak to us. I'm not even sure he saw us. He turned and walked straight back out. Shami and I jumped up. Other than Pran, we were the first to see Lali-didi since her return to our house.

"You're free, Lali-didi," I called out. "Pran isn't here. You can come out now."

After a few minutes of silence, I climbed up on the stool and poked my head through the doorway. Lali-didi was a shadow in the farthest corner. "Come out," I said gently. She didn't budge.

I hated the box. My fear of it had only grown over the years. But I had no choice. I climbed in. Shami's face appeared in the open doorway.

"Shami want Lal-di," he said.

I reached over and hauled him in as well.

"It's over, Lali-didi. You have to come out now. You're safe." Of all the many lies I'd told in my life, that was perhaps the biggest.

"It is over, isn't it, Noor?" she said.

"I swear I'll get you out of here, Lali-didi." Silently, I added her to my list of people who would someday share my small room in a distant slum.

"We're almost the same age but I'm not like you," she said. "I can't even write my own name. I've never been to school. My brother sold me to the brothel in Calcutta. My family was glad to be rid of me. You have a future. This is all I'm good for."

"You're wrong. It's not too late for you to go to school. When I get out, I'll make a life for all of us." The tears streamed down my face. I had to make her believe me.

Shami patted my leg. "Don't cry, Noor-di. Come out, Lal-di. You're making Noor-di sad."

The shadow moved. I reached out my hand and Lali-didi took it. We maneuvered awkwardly past Shami and out of the box. He crawled to the door and I lifted him down.

Lali-didi was thinner than I remembered her. Her crocodile arm had completely healed, but I wondered if the wounds inside her ever could. She looked around bleakly, squinting at the light. I left Shami to guard her while I went to the bottom of our ladder to shout for Deepa-Auntie.

She came running, as I knew she would, and followed me back down the hall to the lock-up. I was surprised to see Ma and several other aunties right behind her.

"It's a crying shame," Prita-Auntie muttered, waiting her turn to embrace Lali-didi. "The girl's not strong enough for the life. Any fool can see that."

For the rest of the evening, the aunties clucked around her as if she were a precious object, easily broken. Lali-didi drank the tea they served and sat quietly while they washed and brushed her hair, but her despair was written on her body. Nothing anyone did could dislodge it. Pran made a futile effort to send her customers that night. But he couldn't stand up to the entire house when the entire house united against him. Lali-didi got a single night of peace.

The day after Lali-didi emerged from the box, Nishikar-Sir returned to our home. It was Friday night, the evening my siblings and I were supposed to meet Grace for dinner. We were late leaving the house. I'd spent more time than usual sitting with Lali-didi after school. Like never before, I was aware of the narrow gap in our ages and the vast gulf in our life experiences. I was fearful of what she might do to herself.

I stayed with her until her first customer arrived, even though it meant my siblings and I would have to run to make it to the restaurant in time to meet Grace. She'd texted me twice since the zoo to confirm the meeting. I didn't know why it was quite so important to her.

When I got downstairs, Shami reported that Aamaal had a

sick stomach and was in the washroom. Together we went to stand outside the locked door. I could smell the problem from the hallway.

"Are you okay in there, Aamaal?"

"No."

"Try to hurry, we're running late."

I held myself back from scolding her, though I was genuinely getting worried about the time. Shami sank down to the floor to wait but I paced in frustration.

I was just on the point of texting Grace to let her know we'd be late when I heard loud voices coming around the corner. It didn't even occur to me to think of Nishikar-Sir. I'd been so absorbed by Lali-didi's tragedy, I'd forgotten my own danger. But when I heard a harsh male voice call my name, I felt a stab of fear. There was one way out of the building and that was in the direction of the man calling my name. The only hiding places I could get to quickly were the toilet, which Aamaal was currently occupying, and the washing room beside it. The washing room was a tiny closet, not more than four feet square, completely devoid of anything but a tap and a drain. Anyone looking for me would find me the second they opened the door, which left only the room Aamaal was currently befouling.

"Shami, you need to tell the men that I've gone out to fetch you dinner."

"Shami having dinner with Grace."

"I know, baby, but Noor needs to hide from the bad men. Can you help Noor hide?"

Shami's brow creased. "Noor-di hide," he said solemnly.

As quietly as possible I tapped on the latrine door.

"Let me in, Aamaal. It's an emergency."

"I'm not finished" came her surly reply.

"Please, Aamaal. I need to come in, quickly!"

She unlocked the door just as I heard the voices rounding the corner. I slipped in and locked it behind me. I wasn't sure if I'd been spotted. The smell in the room made me gag but it also filled me with hope. If I could find someplace to hide I was certain the men wouldn't give the room any more than a very brief once-over.

"Pran and Nishikar-Sir are coming, Aamaal," I whispered, looking down to where she was crouching above the hole. "They can't know I'm here."

She nodded in understanding. It broke my heart at how easily she accepted a dangerous situation.

"If they open the door, I will stand behind it," I whispered. "You must make sure they don't open it too far. Can you do that?"

She nodded again.

"Hello, Shami." Voices were just on the other side of the door. I recognized Pran's. "Where's Noor, Shami?"

"Noor-di buy kebabs," said Shami.

I had to smile. I almost never bought kebabs. We couldn't afford them, but they were Shami's favorite. If I got through this, he was definitely getting kebabs tonight.

"Would she leave them alone?" asked another male voice. It had to be Nishikar-Sir.

"She wouldn't leave them on the street but she'd leave them in here if she was just going out to get food," said Pran.

"I told you I wanted to see her. Why would you let her go out?"

"I'm very sorry, Nishikar-Sir, I didn't know you were coming tonight, you didn't—"

Pran's obsequious pleading was cut short by a loud thwack.

"Do you think I have time for your excuses, you useless mule? Go find the girl and bring her to me."

"She might be in there, Nishikar-Sir."

"Why didn't you say that in the first place? Are you trying to hide her from me?"

There were two more loud cracks, accompanied by Pran's whimpers. I had to admit I felt a grim satisfaction in hearing him get beaten.

I jumped at a sharp rap on the door and I pressed against the wall.

"I'm in here!" shouted Aamaal.

"Is that you, Aamaal?" It was Pran again, though his voice sounded different than I'd ever heard it, weak and frightened. "Where is your sister?"

"She went to buy food," said Aamaal.

"Why did she leave you two here?"

"I have bad diarrhea. Do you want to see?"

If I hadn't been so terrified, I would have laughed.

"These children are more effort than they're worth," snarled Nishikar-Sir. "I hope you charge Ashmita double to let them stay here."

I bristled with indignation. We were already charged for every bucket of water, the rental of Ma's bed, a share of the electricity and we bought all our own food. What more could we be charged for?

"Of course, Nishikar-Sir, we'll certainly do that."

"I've been offered a good price for the girl, Pran. I'll be back for her before morning. When she returns, lock her up."

My blood pulsed in my ears. It was true, then. That was his plan. I was trembling so much I had to sit down on the filthy, urine-stained floor.

"I understand, sir. It's just that I think Ashmita was hoping to delay a little longer. The girl's a top student, medal-winning."

"Education is wasted on girls. It only gives them expectations they have no right to. Ashmita's delayed long enough. How old is the girl, thirteen, fourteen? Does Ashmita plan to wait until the blossom has wilted? She's worth less every day."

"But the Devadasis, sir, they support each other. If you anger one—"

"Let them experience my anger! The Devadasis are born to be whores. They should know their place. If Ashmita cooperates, the girl can continue to work here. If she doesn't . . . well, I have brothels all over the country. I'll send her away and Ashmita will never see her again. See how she likes that!"

"Ashmita's been a good earner for—"

Again Pran was cut off. The door reverberated as something slammed into it. There was a muffled grunt.

"Ashmita will be dead within two years. Her earnings are already a fraction of what the young girls bring in. The lounge is full tonight because you got the young one back. We need more like her. We're doing the lot of them a favor by training the girl. Everyone expects something for nothing. Who does she think will feed those brats once she's gone?"

Loud footsteps receded down the hallway. I rose heavily to

my feet and put a cold hand on the door. I was on the point of opening it when Shami spoke.

"Why are you sitting there, Pran-ji. Do you feel sick?"

Clever boy. I didn't know Pran was still outside.

"Shut up!"

There was scuffling, at first quiet and then louder.

"Let go, Pran-ji."

"You're coming with me. It's long past time I introduced you to a little place where your sister spent many nights at your age."

No! I threw open the door and took in the scene in an instant: Shami was twisting and cowering away, trying desperately to escape as Pran dragged him down the hall. I saw the familiar light of excitement in Pran's eyes as the tears rolled down Shami's face. My little brother, who'd endured countless injections, a life of wracking coughs and constant illness, who never complained, never cried. I ran after them and leaped on Pran's back, pummeling him.

"Let go of him!" I screamed.

Pran dropped Shami as he turned his attention to me, raising his hands to ward off my blows while trying to grab my swinging arms at the same time. I felt rather than saw Aamaal join the fray. Pran howled in pain. I knew Aamaal had bitten him. I'd suffered her bites myself on many occasions. He lashed out, and I heard the sickening crack of his fist hitting flesh. It wasn't my own, so it had to be one of my siblings'. I turned to look and saw Aamaal flying through the air. She cracked against the wall and dropped to the floor. She lay still, whimpering. I left Pran to rush to her but he grabbed me from behind and threw me to the ground. As he bent over me Shami leaped on his back, a whirlwind of teeth and nails.

"Go get Ma, Shami," I gurgled as Pran easily shook him off and dragged me to my feet, one hand clutching my hair, the other encircling my throat.

Shami was off, scampering down the hall. Pran didn't even notice.

"You've been trouble since you were a child." Pran pulled me after him in the opposite direction. "I hope Nishikar-Sir does send you away. I'll be glad to be rid of you."

There was only one place we could be going in that direction. The box.

"No, Pran-ji," I pleaded. "You don't have to lock me in there. I won't try to escape. Just let me look after my sister." I craned my head over his shoulder, trying to see Aamaal. She hadn't moved from where she'd fallen. Her arm was twisted underneath her body in a way that looked physically impossible. "Please, Pran-ji, I beg you."

He laughed. "You're going to be doing a lot of begging over the next weeks, little Noor."

"STOP!" My mother had come. She rushed forward with an energy I hadn't seen in weeks and gave Pran a hard shove that made him release me, though he took a chunk of my hair with him. I winced, then ran to Aamaal, still flat on the floor.

"What do you think you're . . . ?" Ma broke off midsentence when she caught sight of Aamaal. In seconds she was at my side. "What has he done to her?" she demanded.

"She attacked me," said Pran, coming to stand over us. "You're lucky I didn't do worse."

Ma wasn't listening. She gently raised Aamaal so she could

free her trapped arm but it dangled uselessly from her shoulder. Aamaal moaned.

"It hurts, Ma," she said.

Ma laid her down again, positioning the floppy arm at her side. "Stay still, child," she said. "Noor, go get a dupatta. We need to bind it."

I jumped up, grateful to have my old ma back and taking charge. Even Pran stepped aside to let me pass as I ran to the ladder. I clambered up, only slowing when my head was above the level of our floor. Deepa-Auntie and Lali-didi were entertaining customers. I was as quiet as possible as I rushed past their closed curtains. Ma's own bed looked recently vacated. I knelt down and pulled out our box of clothes, taking Ma's cleanest and least worn dupatta. For a moment I wondered if she'd object, but this was Aamaal. I was sure she would have made the same choice.

I raced back to my sister. Shami and Ma were on the floor comforting her. Pran stood nearby. I helped Ma use the dupatta to bind Aamaal's arm tightly against her chest.

"We must take her to the hospital. Noor, go out to the main road and bring back a taxi."

"Noor's not going anywhere." Pran suddenly came to life, crossing his arms and spreading his legs in a stance clearly intended to prevent our passage.

"What are you talking about, flea-on-a-rat's-backside? Noor needs to help me take her sister to hospital. Can't you see you've broken Aamaal's arm?"

"You can go but Noor stays here."

"Why should I leave her? What's it to you?"

"Nishikar-Sir wants to meet her."

"For what purpose?" Ma knew the answer. There could be only one.

"He wants to sell me," I said, before Pran could come up with a lie.

"Not without my permission," said Ma coldly.

"There'll be trouble if she's not here when he returns, Ashmita. I won't let him take her tonight but we must let him see her, so he doesn't think you're openly defying him. Then tomorrow we can all discuss what is to be done." Pran's voice was uncharacteristically reasonable. I felt a prickle of fear.

Ma gave him a hard stare. She too was suspicious. Aamaal moaned again. Ma got unsteadily to her feet, Aamaal in her arms. For the first time I realized what this fight had cost her. Though the drugs I'd been slipping her had helped, she was still weak.

"Please let me go with them, Pran-ji," I pleaded. "I promise I'll come back."

"I'm sorry, Noor," he said, sounding genuinely regretful. "I can't do that. You must meet with Nishikar-Sir tonight. But I promise I won't let him touch you until your ma returns."

Ma looked from Pran to me, her face creased with indecision.

"I'll be back soon, Noor. If I go quickly I might return before Nishikar-Sir gets here. Look after your brother."

I held my breath, rigidly holding myself, so the tears would not fall.

"I'll be back soon," she repeated. "She had better be here when I return, Pran, or you will experience the true meaning of trouble."

Ma swept past him and disappeared around the corner and

out of sight. The harsh glare of the fluorescent light gave Pran's pointed features a maniacal glow as he advanced toward me. Shami hid behind my leg. I put a reassuring hand on his shoulder.

"If you go quietly, Noor, I won't beat you."

"You don't need to lock me in, Pran. I'll wait for Nishikar-Sir and my mother."

He laughed. It was the most chilling sound I'd heard all night.

"You'll be gone long before your mother returns, Noor. I'll make sure of that."

"You wouldn't dare. Ma will be furious."

"Perhaps, but she'll get over it. We both know which daughter she loves, Noor. She's always treated you as little more than a servant. I'm surprised you aren't looking forward to getting away from her. You'll have your own life, your own money."

"Before or after I've paid back my purchase price?" I scoffed.

"Don't worry, you'll work in another of Nishikar-Sir's brothels, possibly in Calcutta or Bangalore. Wouldn't you like to see a bit more of this great country of ours? There will be no purchase price because he already owns you. A share of your earnings will go into your own pocket from the first day. Who knows, perhaps someday you'll earn enough that you can send for the little brat." He nodded at Shami.

I hoisted Shami onto my hip and tried to walk past him. "I've heard enough, Pran. I'll wait outside for my mother."

"You will do what I tell you, Noor, or I'll wring your brother's neck, like you should have done the day he was born, sickly runt that he is."

I hesitated. Pran made a grab for Shami and we scuffled, Shami kicking out with his little legs, but even united we were no match for Pran. He had Shami out of my arms in seconds. We squared off, him holding my squirming, clawing brother, and me, my arms empty. I thought my heart would stop; the pain of seeing Shami in Pran's clutches was that great. My pride, watching Shami's determined struggle not to give in, was matched only by my agony. It was a struggle I'd witnessed every day of his life.

"All right," I said. "Let him go. I'll go with you."

Grace

I wanted to recreate my fifteenth birthday. That's my excuse. It was the best birthday I'd ever had. Up till then most of my birthdays had been little-kid birthdays: specifically, unpopular little-kid birthdays, by which I mean I celebrated with my family.

By my fifteenth birthday I still didn't have enough friends to have a party but I did have one exceptionally wonderful friend who was determined to make my birthday special. Tina said it was time we had a sophisticated grown-up evening, no parents allowed. She chose a real five-star restaurant, with napkins and fine china. She even had to make a reservation. We both got dressed up and put on makeup. We had a good giggle when we got to the place and the hostess realized it was just us.

Tina ordered truffles crostini and roast duck; I ordered scallops almandine and grilled salmon. We were both dismayed to discover truffles were just expensive mushrooms. They tasted hideous so we shared my scallops. The only rule was that everything we ordered had to be something we'd never tried before—new experiences to celebrate the new me. Tina said turning fifteen was like teetering on the precipice of adulthood. Sixteen was an adult. Fifteen was a practice run. The excitement of dating and college and careers seemed just around the corner. We couldn't wait.

I didn't tell Noor that Friday was my sixteenth birthday. I didn't want to pressure her or make it into a big deal. But it was a big deal, bigger than she could possibly have imagined. The past few weeks had been a nightmare. I couldn't believe that all my hopes and expectations of who I'd be on my sixteenth birthday could have imploded so dramatically in such a short space of time. I thought maybe with Noor I could recreate some of the magic of my friendship with Tina.

As usual it took many lies to convince my parents to let me spend the evening with Noor. It wasn't just that she was a sex worker's daughter, though that did worry them. More than that, they no longer trusted me to make good decisions without adult supervision. I told them Parvati and VJ would be there as well. I thought they might be more encouraging if it seemed that I was developing a group of friends. It didn't help. They didn't know any of my new friends, so their overprotective paranoia was in overdrive.

Mom insisted on talking me through my plans multiple times. If I hadn't known better, I'd have suspected it was the lawyer in her trying to trip me up in a lie.

"And you're going with VJ's driver?"

"Yes, that's why I'm walking to his house."

"Why can't our driver take you?"

"It's like last year, Mom. *VJ*'s taking *me* out, like Tina did."
I knew that would get to her. Mom was almost as devastated
by my loss of a best friend as I was.

"Maybe I should call VJ's mother," said Mom.

"Please don't embarrass me, Mom. I need to go out with
friends like a normal teenager."

Mom sighed. The Achilles' heel for both my parents was
always the same. They wanted my life to be perfect. To
control them, the only real challenge was to figure out how
to convince them that giving me what I wanted would
ensure that.

I spent considerable time deciding what to wear. I didn't
want to dress super-fancy like last year but I did put on one of
my prettiest Indian print dresses and a bit of makeup. I wasn't
trying to show off. I just wanted to look my best. I hoped Noor
would notice and tell me I looked nice. If it felt right, I'd admit
it was my birthday. Maybe after the falafel place we could get
cake somewhere.

When I was ready I did a quick turn in front of the mirror.

"What do you think, Bosco?" Bosco, asleep on my bed as
usual, raised his head and looked at me. "I'm sixteen. Can you
believe it? I want you to know things are going to be okay from
now on. I really like Noor and I've got VJ. So you can stop worrying about me."

I wasn't at all sure if this was the truth, but I wanted it to be.
I went over and gave his ears a reassuring rub, kissed him and
headed to the kitchen to say good-bye to my parents.

Dad was sitting at the table. "Your mom tells me you're
going out with VJ and some girls from the NGO tonight," said
Dad, trying to sound as though he wasn't crushed.

I walked over, hugged him and kissed the top of his head. He gave me a one-armed squeeze and I stayed a while with his arm around me.

"We can go out tomorrow night, Dad. It'll give you more time to plan something really super-special."

"Your mom and I could take you all out tonight for something super-special."

"We've already made plans, Dad. I'll do something with you guys tomorrow."

"It won't be your birthday tomorrow."

Mom made big eyes at him across the table.

"I'm sixteen now, Dad. Sometimes I want to be with my friends."

"You'll always be my baby girl."

"John!" said Mom in a reproving voice, though she was no better.

"You're such a dork, Dad."

I gave him a final hug before I pulled away and headed for the door. Both my parents jumped up to follow.

"If you run into any trouble, or if anyone says or does something that makes you feel uncomfortable, just call us," said Mom, hugging me at the door. I'd already told her VJ was gay. It was probably the only reason she was letting me go.

"We're just going to get pizza, Mom. Nothing is going to go wrong."

Dad opened the door and gave me another hug. "Happy birthday, my girl."

"Thanks, Dad. Love you."

I walked to the elevator. I didn't need to look back to know they were still at the door watching me.

I walked down the block before hailing a taxi. I'd already lied to my parents that VJ lived just around the corner. It would be just like them to watch out the front window.

The drive to Kamathipura took an hour, which was longer than usual. Friday night traffic in Mumbai was always terrible. I had trouble spotting the falafel place Noor had described. It was smaller than I'd expected but also a bit nicer. Most of the food outlets in Kamathipura were little more than counters with no place to sit. This one looked like a proper restaurant though it was open to the air, with just a few large overhead fans for cooling.

I was a few minutes late and disappointed that Noor wasn't already there. There wasn't a single woman in the place. I sat down at a table as close as I could get to the door, though there were only eight tightly packed tables and most were occupied. I'd been sitting about fifteen minutes when I noticed the server behind the counter staring at me. It was one of those places where you have to go up to the counter to order. He must have been wondering what I was waiting for. I got out my phone.

already at restaurant. U far? I texted.

I waited for an answer. A group of men came in and took the last empty table. I could feel the counter guy's eyes on me, though I was careful not to look his way. Men from other tables were gawping at me as well. I suddenly felt exposed in my flimsy Indian frock. I should have just worn jeans. My face burned with embarrassment. I looked at my phone again. Noor was almost thirty minutes late. I'd never felt so pathetic.

restaurant crowded. u here soon? I typed.

I waited.

And waited.

And waited.

Another fifteen minutes passed.

Nothing.

So far this was the worst birthday ever. Maybe I should have gone to her house but I didn't have the courage to walk through Kamathipura alone at night. Surely if she'd had to cancel she'd have let me know. I couldn't continue to sit there if I didn't get food. The counter clerk was clearly talking about me with one of his servers, gesturing angrily. I flushed with embarrassment. They were going to throw me out any minute. I got up and went to the counter to order a falafel and water, though I really only wanted the water. The heat, combined with my anxiety, was making me queasy.

I couldn't bear the thought of going home and giving up on this night, though it was obvious Noor wasn't coming. I'd had such stupidly high hopes, not only for my birthday but for our friendship. I took my food back to the table and proceeded to consume it as slowly as possible. It was close to eight, two hours after we were meant to meet, when I sent one final text.

can only wait a few more minutes. hope u ok

The last statement was both true and not. I was genuinely worried about Noor. She lived a precarious life. Maybe something bad had happened to her. At the same time, it seemed too coincidental that she'd have a serious problem the very same night we'd agreed to meet. A far more likely explanation was that she'd decided she didn't want to have dinner with me. On reflection, she hadn't seemed that keen. I was the loser trying to force my friendship on her. Why should she want to be my friend? No one else did.

So, on my sixteenth birthday, I sat alone in a run-down restaurant, surrounded by men openly ogling me, wishing I could disappear.

Noor didn't like me.

I felt foolish that I'd expected anything more and betrayed because I really did like her and Shami and Aamaal. What was so wrong with me? My eyes stung with unshed tears. I only wanted to be her friend. Was that too much to ask? I felt like screaming or hurling my half-eaten falafel across the room.

I didn't.

I had a better way to release tension.

The washroom sign was to the right. I picked up my bag and headed over. I was grateful to find the door unlocked, but disappointed, when I stepped inside, to discover it filthy and foul-smelling. I took the knife from my bag. Fortunately, I was wearing a dress—easier access. I hiked it up, gingerly leaned against the wall and bent my leg, bringing my canvas within reach. The first letter was an obvious choice.

T

It couldn't be anything else. My poem was almost complete.

I thought long and hard about the next letter. I wanted to write *traitor*, an indictment of Noor. But this was my epitaph, not hers. It needed to describe me, and when I realized that, I came to another realization. The word was obvious, as obvious as what I needed to do next. I'd known all along it would come to this. Even the location felt somehow right. My parents wouldn't find me. Strangers would clear me away like so much debris.

I etched an *E*.

My father's face, his disappointment as I'd left the house this evening swam into view.

The *R* took more time. My hand was shaking.

I looked around the small room. Maybe I should leave a note.

I started on the *M* but my hands were shaking so badly now I had to stop. I felt light-headed.

My phone buzzed. I looked at my bag. Who could be calling at a time like this?

"You're too late," I said grimly.

I finished the *M*.

My phone rang again. What if it was my mother checking up on me?

I glared at the bag. The ringing was interminable. Every time it ran through the limit of rings, it would start afresh moments later. In my frustration I'd made the downstroke on the *M* too deep. Blood dripped down my leg.

Whoever it was, they weren't giving up on me. It had to be my parents. It would be typical of my mom to somehow intuit something was wrong. Or maybe it was my dad making a last-ditch effort to convince me to spend my birthday with them. It could even be Kyle or Tina, wishing me a happy birthday. I put the knife under the tap and rinsed it off. The phone continued to ring as I dried the knife, reached for my bag and dropped it in. My phone, nestled inside, glowed and bleated like a living thing. I took it out and checked the caller ID.

It was Noor.

I put the phone to my ear and answered.

"Hello."

28

Noor

A small triumph . . .

The only light switch for the box was on the outside. It would have cost Pran nothing to turn it on. He didn't. In the silent darkness, with no room to move, the smell of sweat mingled with sex and blood was magnified. I thought I might suffocate. It would be some kind of victory if he found me dead. Too bad I wouldn't be around to enjoy it.

There was no need to explore the limits of my prison; I'd seen it often enough. I could do nothing but wait. My own thoughts were an unwelcome companion. I worried about Aamaal. Would they be able to fix her arm? Could Ma afford it? I worried about Shami. Before Pran took me away I'd told him to go to Deepa-Auntie. I could only hope that he had.

I worried about myself. My life was over. I would rather be dead than submit to the men who used Ma. I didn't give in to tears. I was beyond them.

"Noor-di?" It was Shami.

"What are you doing here, baby? I told you to go to Deepa-Auntie."

"Should I bring her here, Noor-di?"

"No, Shami, that would only get her in trouble. Just tell her where I am. Tell her Pran has broken his promise to Ma."

"Okay," said Shami. I heard the faintest footsteps as he left.

Only a few minutes had passed when I heard noises again.

"Noor, what has he done to you? What are you doing in there?" Joy coursed through me at the sound of Deepa-Auntie's voice.

"He's going to sell me. Nishikar-Sir has ordered it."

"No! That can't be. Your ma would never allow it." It was Lali-didi this time. It was good to hear her voice, but they had to leave before Pran caught them. How had they got rid of their customers so quickly? Surely that would arouse suspicion.

"Pran hurt Aamaal. Ma took her to hospital. He plans to hand me over to Nishikar-Sir before she returns."

"I won't allow it!" said Deepa-Auntie.

"No, you mustn't confront him! He'll hurt you."

There was silence, followed by whispering between Deepa-Auntie and Lali-didi.

"Noor, do you still have Parvati's phone?" asked Deepa-Auntie.

"It's in my pocket."

"You must call the foreigner. We have a plan."

Over the next ten minutes, we talked through their idea. It was outrageous, and I wasn't sure Grace or Vijender Patel would agree. There was only a small chance it would even work, but it was my only chance.

It was already almost eight o'clock. We had agreed to meet

for dinner at six. Grace would be back home by now. Would she even be allowed to come out again?

She didn't pick up the first time I called. I tried again. It rang and rang then went to voice mail. She had to answer. I couldn't give up. Maybe she didn't keep her phone with her all the time like I did. She lived in a proper house where her valuables weren't in constant threat of being stolen.

The seventh time I called, Grace answered.

"Hello." Her voice was wary.

"Grace, you have to help me." The words spilled out. "I'm locked in a box. You need to come here and bring Vijender Patel."

"Noor, what did you say?" The phone crackled. I could hardly hear her.

"A box. He'll need to pretend he wants a prostitute and then come and break the door. He should ask for a young girl, that's important. Do you remember I told you about Lali-didi? He must get to her."

"Noor, I don't understand—"

"He's going to sell me tonight, Grace." I was in tears now.

"Who's going to sell you?" The line crackled, beeped and went dead.

I hit redial several times and repeatedly got the recorded message telling me the caller was out of range. I cried as quietly as I could.

"Are they coming?" asked Deepa-Auntie. I could hear the doubt in her voice.

"I don't think so. I couldn't make her understand."

"I'll find your ma, Noor. I'll check every hospital."

"No, you can't. Pran will punish you if you take the night off."

"When your ma finds out, Pran will have bigger problems than me. I'll go down the street talking to men. He won't realize what I'm up to until I'm long gone."

"It's too dangerous, Deepa-Auntie. Please, don't."

Her bark of laughter was harsh and unlike her. "I've lived with danger since the day the men came to my village, Noor. The only thing that kept me going was you and your brother and sister. You give us all something to hope for. If you can escape, maybe someday we all can."

"It's true, Noor," agreed Lali-didi. "Some day you'll be an important person, more powerful than Pran or Binti-Ma'am, or even Nishikar-Sir. On that day we will laugh in their faces and walk out the front door."

The weight of their expectations could have felt like a burden, but it had the opposite effect. Their dreams only strengthened my own.

"Be careful, Deepa-Auntie."

"Don't worry, Noor-baby, I'll be back before you know it."

I leaned my head against the wooden wall and prepared to wait. The time passed slowly. Shami kept vigil outside. For a while we played a guessing game. As the hour grew late, his responses became more infrequent and his words jumbled. Finally, I ordered him to go to sleep. His silence, after wishing me good night, was almost immediate. At first it was comfort enough that I could picture his small body curled up beside the stool under my prison door.

I checked the time on the phone many times and chided myself for wasting the battery. I wished I could have slept as well. Some ninety minutes after Deepa-Auntie's departure the phone rang. My fingers trembled as I answered it.

"Noor?" It was Grace. "I'm outside your building." Her voice was as clear as if she were just outside the box. "VJ has headed inside."

"He's inside?" All at once I realized the rashness of my plan. VJ might be a rich film star, but he was a boy, sheltered and inexperienced. He didn't even like girls. If I could figure that out, surely a man with Pran's experience would realize.

"Shami!" I called through the wall.

"Yes?" I was surprised by how quickly he woke up.

"You must go tell Lali-didi that the plan is happening. VJ Patel will be asking for her."

"I'll tell her, Noor-di," he said eagerly. The patter of his feet retreated.

I looked at my phone. It was nearly ten o'clock.

I checked it a dozen times over the next thirty minutes. Finally, I heard the approach of footsteps and whispers.

"Are you in there, Noor?"

It was Vijender. I broke into a cold sweat. I was relieved and terrified at the same time.

"Hurry," I said. "Pran could show up at any moment."

"I bought us some time. Pran recognized me but I used it to our advantage. I promised him five times Lali's price to clear your room and I said if anyone disturbed me before I was finished, then the deal was off." There was a loud scraping along the doorframe.

"Are you okay in there, Noor?" It was Lali-didi. My heart pounded as I considered the danger I'd placed her in.

"You must come with us, Lali-didi," I told her, though the racket from VJ hammering a wedge between the door and frame may have drowned out my words.

"I need to go back to the lounge, Noor. You know how suspicious Pran is. He'll be worried about his money. Sooner or later he'll come looking to make sure VJ hasn't snuck away without paying. VJ has given me money for him. Perhaps it will be enough to distract him awhile longer. Should I take Shami with me?" she asked.

"No!" I couldn't bear to not see Shami before I left. "I want to take him with me."

"We can't take him tonight, Noor. It's too dangerous," said VJ.

"I promise I'll keep him safe," said Lali-didi.

"Shami want to go with Noor-di." I didn't know if he was pleading with me or them. My heart ached. What had I been thinking? I couldn't leave Shami.

"Good luck, Noor. We're going now . . ."

"No!"

"Bye-bye, Noor-di." I knew him so well. He was holding in his tears, as he had so many times before. I reached out to him in the darkness.

"Make us proud," said Lali-didi. They were her final words to me.

I shoved my fist in my mouth to stifle the sound of the sobs that wracked my body.

Minutes later, with a shattering of wood, the door fell open and VJ's head appeared in the opening. He registered surprise when he saw the state of me but quickly recovered. There was no time to delay.

VJ extended his hand to help me down. "Hurry. We haven't much time."

"Shami?" Grief overshadowed my fear.

"We'll come back for him, but we must go now."

He didn't need to tell me that, but where could we go? There was only one exit, and it meant getting past the lounge without being seen. We'd never make it.

"Follow me," said VJ. He ran in the only possible direction. I followed but was still shocked when he got to the ladder that led to our room. Suddenly we heard distant shouts coming from the direction of the lounge.

"Quick, Noor!" said VJ, taking the rungs of the ladder two at a time.

We were going to get caught. There was no way out from the second floor. Still I followed him, scaling the ladder faster than I'd ever done. I stopped in my tracks when I got to the top. Adit was waiting there.

"Come on, Noor." Adit gave me an impatient look. "I did what you asked," he said, turning to VJ, who was running across the room to the window.

"Good man." VJ dug in his pocket and pulled out a wad of cash, tossing it onto the nearest bed. Adit trotted over, snatched it up and pocketed it.

VJ was leaning out the window, where the metal cage prevented escape. I could hear the sound of running feet from the floor below. I raced over to join VJ. It took me a moment to realize there was something different about the window. The screws had been removed from one side and the metal bars pushed out from the wall, creating an opening just large enough to squeeze through.

I shot a look at Adit, who smiled proudly.

"Pran will beat you for this if he doesn't kill you," I said.

"Maybe I won't give him the chance. You were right when you said there's a whole world beyond these fifteen lanes. Why should you be the only one to escape?"

"Enough talking," snapped VJ. "You need to go first, Noor."

"We're going to jump?" I said, aghast.

"Not exactly." VJ picked up a bundle from the floor. Only then did I realize it was a rope made out of knotted dupattas. Some were so tattered it would be a miracle if they didn't tear and break.

"You go first," he said. "I'm heavier. This might not hold my weight."

I took it from him, steeling myself not to look down as I swung my legs out the window and squeezed through the bars. It took every ounce of my courage to push off and drop. For just a second I panicked and hung helplessly, my feet dangling in midair. I didn't know what to do, but suddenly I heard Pran's voice. He was in our room. It spurred me to action. Planting my feet against the wall, I leaned out and scuttled down.

I looked up to see VJ and Pran grappling at the window. For a moment Pran's face disappeared, and in that same instant VJ was over the side and coming down twice as fast as I had.

There was no time to worry about what had happened to Adit as VJ grabbed my arm and pulled me across the road. Grace was there, waiting by the open door of a taxi. We jumped in, amid the bellowing of many voices. I was shaking with terror.

The car moved off immediately but it was Kamathipura, and speed was impossible. We locked our doors, but Pran emerged from our house and chased after us. Within minutes he'd reached the car and was banging on the window. I was grateful to be sitting in between VJ and Grace, and I was more grateful still that Pran was alone. No one was coming to his aid, though I had no doubt Binti-Ma'am had to be out on the street by now, though too fat and lazy to give chase. She was probably planning the beating she'd give me when I was dragged back to her.

Pran's screaming and banging accompanied us to the end of our lane. At any moment, I was certain he'd smash through the glass. I think the taxi driver had the same concern. He kept leaning on his horn and shouting at Pran to stop. Had VJ not ordered him to keep moving, the driver would have got out of the car to fight Pran off. Finally, when we turned onto the main road, Pran had to give up after he was almost swiped by a speeding car.

I didn't turn to look at him as we roared off. I felt no satisfaction. My small triumph over Pran seemed like nothing compared to my fear for those I'd left behind.

Grace

"Are you okay, Noor?" I asked. My heart was still racing.

She nodded but seemed strangely subdued.

"You're still frightened."

"I left them all. I left Shami."

"You'll see them again soon." I tried to sound confident.

The roads got wider as we left the heart of Kamathipura, and I began to think through what to do next. I'd have to take her home, unless she went with VJ. He could smuggle her into his house more easily but I doubted she'd be very happy about it. I glanced at her. She was staring silently out the window. We were passing a collection of tarp-covered lean-tos under a bridge. Noor's tension was palpable.

"Stop," she said.

"Stop what?" I asked.

"Stop! Stop the car!" Clearly agitated, she barked something in Hindi directly to the driver.

He pulled off the road and she fumbled with the door handle.

"What's wrong?" asked VJ.

"We must get Parvati."

"Where's Parvati?" I asked.

"There." She pointed back to the settlement we just passed.

"It's late, almost eleven o'clock. Is this a good time to be dropping in on her?" I didn't add the fact that I was already unsure what the future held for Noor. The last thing we needed was Parvati as well. Miss Chanda had told us there were rescue homes for girls in danger of being trafficked but I wasn't sure that applied to Parvati.

"You are right, it is too early," said Noor.

"For what?" asked VJ.

"To help Parvati escape from Suresh. He will be awake. We must wait."

"Who is Suresh?" I asked. "And why would Parvati need to sneak away from him?"

"He takes money from men to let them do things to Parvati. He is very dangerous. He has a knife."

I jumped when someone tapped on the window but it was just an old man. I rolled down the window and gave him a ten-rupee note. It was dark under the bridge and it gave me the creeps. If there were potential murderers around, I wasn't sure it was safe to hang out there. I was also starting to worry about what I'd say to my parents. It would be midnight soon. I needed to get home.

"Well, I guess we wait," said VJ.

"Are you sure Parvati will leave with us?" I asked.

"She must."

"Okay," I said, wondering what fresh lie I could tell my parents to explain missing curfew by several hours.

I dialed Mom's cell. She picked up on the third ring.

"Grace, Dad and I were just talking about you."

Why didn't that surprise me?

"Are you having a good time?"

"Fabulous!" I forced as much enthusiasm into my voice as I could muster. "In fact, VJ's asked me to spend the night. We're watching some of his dad's old movies. They've got a full-size screening room. It's so cool, Mom. You have to see it sometime. Can I stay, Mom, please?"

Noor raised an eyebrow.

There was a long pause and some whispering with my father. She could have saved herself the effort. I knew what they were saying. They wanted me home safely tucked into bed but were thrilled that I sounded so happy.

"Can you put VJ's mom on the phone, sweetie?"

"Sure, Mom, no problem."

"She wants to talk to your mom, VJ," I said loudly, while giving Noor a pleading look.

She nodded and took the phone.

"Hello, it is very nice to speak with you," said Noor in a mature voice that was not her own. I gaped at her.

I didn't hear my mom's response, though I probably could have guessed it.

"Of course," responded Noor. "She is a good girl. I am so happy to have such a friend for VJ." Then she listened for a while. I could practically feel my mother's enthusiasm coming through the phone line.

"No, no," Noor continued. "We are happy to have her to

stay with us. It is a great honor. Yes. Thank you. Good-bye."

She handed the phone back to me without a word and looked out the window.

"I'm really sorry I made you lie for me."

She turned to me with a small smile. "I understand. Sometimes I also do not tell my mother everything."

I sighed in relief.

We waited three hours while the streets cleared and the neighborhood fell silent. The taxi driver reclined his seat and slept. VJ had promised him far more money than he'd make in several nights of driving, so he was good-natured about the change in plans. VJ did his best to distract us with stories of life in the film industry, often tinged with an underlying sadness, a lot of broken dreams and betrayals. Up till then I'd thought he dabbled in the industry to please his father, but his ability to go to the heart of a story made me rethink that. Perhaps he just needed to be behind the camera instead of in front of it.

Finally Noor deemed it late enough to go looking for Parvati.

"Everyone will be sleeping now," said Noor. "Many boys are using heroin and they are drinking. Once they sleep, they do not easily wake."

We got out of the car and approached the squatter settlement. Lights from the bridge overhead provided enough illumination to see that many people didn't even have the luxury of a lean-to covered with plastic tarp. Whole families slept right on the pavement, their few worldly goods bundled around them.

We picked our way carefully between bodies and the tent-like structures. Even this late, the heat was oppressive. The windowless polyethylene homes must have been stifling. Noor stopped and put a finger to her lips. A few steps on she raised her hand. VJ and I stopped while she went a little farther on her own, rounding a lean-to, so we could see only the top of her. She crouched and disappeared.

She was gone for what felt like a long time, though it was probably not more than ten minutes. Finally she reappeared and came round the front of the lean-to. I felt weak with relief to see Parvati behind her. I could see why Noor was concerned for her. Her hair was a straggly mess and her clothes dirty and disheveled. It was the look in her eyes that was most disturbing though. She looked hunted, like an animal that's been chased to the point where it has lost all hope of survival.

She nodded to us but didn't speak. I think she had no words for the torture she'd endured. She fell in step behind us as we walked to the edge of the camp. We were almost on the point of leaving when she stopped, though I didn't notice at first. Noor touched me on the shoulder and I turned to find Parvati standing stock-still, as if she didn't dare take the last step to freedom. Noor walked back to her and took her hand, murmuring in a soothing tone. Parvati shook her head. She leaned close and whispered something to Noor, turned around and wove her way back the way she'd come.

Noor came to stand beside us. "She is coming. She forgot something. I told her to leave it but she said it is important."

VJ and I exchanged looks. Every second we delayed increased the chances someone would wake up and confront us. In fact, I was certain I'd seen movement in the shadowy interior of a nearby lean-to. Any minute now I expected someone to raise the alarm.

We waited almost twenty minutes. Twice I suggested going

back to look for Parvati but Noor was resolute that we must wait. I was just on the point of going after her myself when we saw movement from the direction of Suresh's lean-to. Sure enough, Parvati came into view. She was running as quickly as possible in the crowded space, leaping over debris and dodging shelters. It was more than her energy level that was different.

"Is that blood?" I whispered to VJ.

"I don't think it's tomato sauce."

As she came closer the smell of it wafted off her. She paused again at the edge of the encampment, where she'd stopped before. Her final look around was one of triumph and satisfaction. Blood was spattered on her kurta and smeared on her face. There were specks of it on her trousers and sandals. In one hand a knife glinted in the lamplight. Blood dripped from its tip.

"I want we are leaving now," she said.

"Well, all right, then," said VJ, approaching her carefully. He held out his hand. "Shall I just hold on to that for you?"

She looked at it as if seeing it for the first time. "I think I must be throwing."

"That sounds like a wonderful plan." VJ still held out his hand. She placed the knife in it, careful to hand him the hilt.

Noor took Parvati's arm and gently led her to the car. VJ and I followed at a distance.

"What are we going to do?" I asked in a low voice.

"You heard the lady. We throw it away."

"It's evidence."

"Of what? I didn't see anyone commit a crime. Did you?"

"You know what she must have done."

"The only thing I know is that she was gang-raped and tortured and the guy we've left behind was responsible for that."

We reached the car. Noor and Parvati were already inside.

"It's not right, VJ. Vigilante justice is not the solution."

"Maybe not, but I'm not going to turn her in. Are you?"

We made the trip home in a fraction of the time it had taken us to reach Kamathipura. The streets were virtually empty. We decided we'd all go to VJ's house. He lived in a mansion on the seafront, and the guard was in the employ of his family and wouldn't jeopardize his job by telling stories of a bloodstained girl arriving in the early hours of the morning.

VJ brought clean clothes for Parvati to change into. I suspected he got them from a maid. They looked too modest to be his mother's. Noor and I both went into the bathroom to help Parvati clean up.

We were all exhausted from the evening's events. VJ had offered us separate bedrooms but the three of us flopped down together on a king-size bed. As tired as I was, I lay awake for a long time wondering what the morning would bring.

30

Noor

Unexpected poetry . . .

I wasn't sure what woke me. When I sat up, Parvati was coming out of the bathroom. Her hair was brushed and neatly braided. She wore the clothes Vijender had given her the previous night. She nodded toward the hallway. I got up and followed her.

"You're leaving?" I asked.

"You know I must."

"What will you do?"

"I'll find a job, work as a maid or clean the streets. I'll do anything." She considered her words. "Anything but *that*."

"Vijender's family is rich. They could help you."

"What have I told you, Noor? Foreigners and films stars—you can't trust them."

"But they rescued us."

"And I'm grateful, but I've looked after myself for as long as I can remember. I'm not going to put my life in the hands of strangers now, when I have everything to lose."

"Suresh is dead, then? You're sure of it?"

"There's no doubt." She gave a cheerless smile.

"You'll need money. I don't have much but I—"

"I don't need money." She pulled a wad of bloodstained cash out of her pocket. "This will get me to the other side of the country. I've heard Calcutta is a good place to disappear."

"Was that his?"

"It was mine. I earned it."

"You must take your phone." I tried to hand it to her, but she wouldn't take that either.

"You keep it, Noor. Someday, when they've stopped looking for me, I want to be able to contact you."

I pulled her into a fierce hug. "If you ever need anything . . ." My voice broke as I stifled a sob.

She pulled out of my arms and we faced each other. A lifetime of memories passed between us. She was dry-eyed, but her face twisted with the misery of our parting.

I wanted to see her out. She wouldn't let me. We walked together to the end of the landing. I watched her disappear down a grand spiral staircase that looked built for a cinema heroine.

When I returned to our room Grace was sitting up in bed.

"Where's Parvati?"

"She left."

"Why?"

"You know what she did to Suresh."

"VJ's family is powerful. They could help her."

"The risk is too great. She did a crime. Money cannot change that. And she is a low-caste girl. Money cannot change that either. There will be many who think that what Suresh did to her was not so bad. They will want to punish Parvati. I know it is hard for you to understand, but for us things are not always easy."

Grace looked down at her lap. I hoped I had not hurt her feelings.

"I have something to show you," she said, a strange hesitancy in her voice.

She crossed her leg and hiked her dress up over her thigh. At first I saw only a mess of cuts and wondered what kind of accident could have left such wounds. I sat down next to her for a closer look. Only then did I realize the cuts formed words. It seemed impossible. I waited for an explanation.

"It's an acrostic," she said.

"What?"

"A kind of poem. We did them in middle school. You see, in one direction it forms the word *slut* and in the other, the first letter . . ."

Her words trailed off. She must have seen the look on my face. She had carved words into her own flesh. I thought of the many scars I'd seen on the girls and women in my community—I'd never seen anything like this.

"I am not understanding," I said. "What is *hag*?"

"It's like a witch."

"And *term*?"

"I was going to write *terminal*, like *dead*. I changed my mind."

"Why did you do this, Grace?"

"I was ashamed. I felt so alone."

"But this . . ."

"It was stupid. It only made things worse. Now I have this to be ashamed of as well."

"Do your parents know?"

"How can I disappoint them again?"

I wasn't sure how to put my thoughts into words. I felt as if I were watching her standing on a bridge, looking over the side. She was safe for the moment but that could change in an instant; the desire to jump could become too strong.

"You must tell your parents," I said.

"I know." She sighed heavily.

We heard quick footsteps in the hallway and VJ rushed in through the open doorway.

"Where's Parvati?" he demanded urgently. "The police are here!"

31

Grace

I told VJ about Parvati's disappearance on our way downstairs. He led the way into a large living room with seating for at least thirty people. I wondered if the cops felt as intimidated as I did. There were three of them seated on one side of the room. Across an expanse of Persian silk carpet sat VJ's dad and a stunning woman who must have been his mom. VJ's parents stood up when we entered and greeted us warmly. VJ sat next to them and Noor and I took seats nearby.

"As I was saying," VJ's mother said firmly, "you cannot question these children until their parents arrive."

My heart jumped out of my chest. Had she called my parents already? I wasn't sure I was ready to talk to them.

"At this time we only need to speak to the girl Parvati," said the oldest policeman. "Are you Parvati?" he asked Noor.

"No, she's not," said VJ. "We don't know where Parvati is."

"When did you last see her?"

VJ hesitated.

"She left many hours ago," said Noor.

"Do you know Suresh Asari?" The officer's tone became considerably less polite when he addressed Noor.

"Yes, he is the boy who raped my fourteen-year-old friend and made her do sex work."

The officer was momentarily thrown off balance by Noor's directness. "Do you have proof of this?" he demanded flatly.

"Why? Will you charge him?" Her face gave nothing away.

"You were seen at the encampment under the Grant Road Bridge tonight."

Noor eyed him calmly.

"Suresh Asari was found murdered shortly after you left."

"This has gone far enough," said VJ's dad. "If you have further questions, you may speak to my lawyer."

"That's fine, Mr. Patel, but you have no rights over this girl. We're taking her with us."

"This child is a victim," snapped VJ's dad. "You aren't taking her anywhere without me."

"The only victim here is a murdered boy under a bridge."

"She's just told you that the child you're looking for was raped and trafficked!" VJ's mom exploded.

"We have only her word, and what does she know of these things?"

"I grew up in a house where minor girls do sex work," snapped Noor.

"And where would that be?" The officer leaned toward Noor, while one of his younger colleagues flipped open a notebook and prepared to write.

Noor was slow to answer. She looked from the officers to me and back again.

"What will you do if I tell you?"

"We will raid the establishment." He seemed to think this answer would please her. It didn't. Her face was wreathed in anxiety.

"What will you do with the women who are working there?"

"If they're not minors and haven't been involved in trafficking, they'll be released."

"They will not be charged for doing sex work?" she asked suspiciously.

"No."

"I want to get Shami and Aamaal out," she said to me. "Pran will be very angry at my escape. He may hurt them. And I need to save Lali-didi. What do you think I should do?"

Though I didn't entirely understand Noor's distrust of police, I understood her struggle. Her mother and her community might disown her for instigating a police raid.

"This may be your best chance to get justice."

Noor stood up and addressed the officers. "I will tell you where I live. But I must go too."

VJ and his parents stood as well. "I'll go with you," said VJ.

"No, you won't," said his parents in unison.

"I'll go," said VJ's father. "Noor, you will ride with me."

The senior officer started to object but VJ's father raised his hand. "It's not negotiable."

"I'd like to come," I said.

"Your parents will be here any minute," said VJ's mom. "You must be here when they arrive." My heart plummeted.

I walked Noor to the front door and gave her a hug. "Good luck," I said.

"You too." She gave me a meaningful look.

I went back and sat down. VJ's mom left the room, saying she was going to organize breakfast.

"When my parents come, would you mind leaving us alone?" I asked VJ.

"Of course," he said. I was grateful he didn't ask for an explanation.

Minutes later we heard voices coming down the hall. A servant showed my parents in. They rushed to me, enveloping me in a family hug.

"I'll go see how my mom's doing with that breakfast," said VJ.

We sat together on the couch, Mom and Dad on either side of me.

"Gracie, why did you lie to us?" demanded my mom before I had a chance to speak. "You should have told us what was going on last night. You could have been killed."

This was so far from what I was worrying about that I was momentarily thrown.

"Mom," I said, taking a deep breath, "there are a lot of things that I should have told you."

I crossed my ankle over my thigh and hitched up my dress.

Mom gasped. Dad was perfectly silent. I couldn't bear to look at either of them, so I looked at what I'd done.

I wondered if the scars would be there for the rest of my life, like my topless image on the Internet. Was it yet another thing I'd have to explain to my own teenage daughter someday?

Finally I peeped at my mother. Her face was rigid with shock. She was barely holding it together. I put my arms around her and was relieved that she hugged me back.

"I'm so sorry, Gracie. How did I let all this slip past me?"

"Give me a little credit, Mom. I'm a teenager. Slipping things past you is what I live for."

"Grace, that's not funny!" Her voice sounded more like her, though, so it couldn't have been unfunny.

I marshaled the courage to pull out of my mom's arms and looked at my dad sitting silently on the other side of me.

I wish I hadn't.

Tears were streaming down his face.

"My baby girl," he said miserably.

"Aw, Dad, you're such a dork." We hugged, and stayed like that for a long time.

32

Noor

Freedom . . .

The minute we entered the outskirts of Kamathipura I began to question whether I was doing the right thing. All my life experience told me police were the bad guys. I'd seen them take bribes from the overlords who controlled us, while arresting and abusing the people I cared about. How would this time be any different?

As Sanjay Patel's silver Porsche cruised down our narrow lane, I felt every person on the street watching me. Our small lane was already clogged with police cars. It seemed the entire force was converging on my home, though the ones who'd arrived before us had only the lane number. They milled about impatiently peering in every open doorway.

I jumped out the second our car stopped, not even thanking Vijender's father. My only thought was to disappear into the crowd in the vain hope that no one would know I was the traitor. Despite what the cops said, I knew the aunties, and even my own mother, would be arrested along with Pran and Binti-Ma'am, even if it was only temporary. Brothels were illegal. The cops weren't going to take the time to figure out who were the victims and who were the criminals.

Unfortunately, my role in the raid was not yet over. A cop caught me before I got very far and hauled me back to the officer in charge.

"Is this your house?" he demanded.

I was so terrified I could only nod.

He put a loudspeaker to his mouth. "Let's go!" he shouted to the legions of cops flanking him.

It seemed impossible that so many people could fit inside our house but they stormed the door with purpose, rushing in like a rising tide. I tried to follow but was held back, so I watched in horror as, one after another, everyone I loved was dragged out in handcuffs. The women who shared my room were among the last. The awkward access, up and down our narrow ladder, must have slowed the cops, but it didn't deter them.

Prita-Auntie was first. She frothed at the mouth she was so enraged. It took three men to get her in a van. She kicked one of them in his private parts. I cringed to imagine how he might retaliate when they got her to the station.

Ma was next. She was too weak to fight.

"It's my ma," I screamed, struggling with the cop who was holding me. He seemed to understand and let me go. I rushed to her, putting my arms around her waist. It wasn't my intention to impede her captors but only beg her forgiveness, but they pulled me off her and threw me to the ground.

"Ma," I cried, prostrate on the pavement, as she was hustled past. "I'm sorry, Ma!"

"Find Aamaal and Shami!" she shouted. She struggled. One of the cops lost his grip. She looked back at me. "Keep them safe."

I scrambled to my feet and raced after her. "I'm sorry," I cried. I needed her to understand. "I'm sorry."

Both cops had hold of her again. They half-pushed, half-lifted her into the back of the van to join Prita-Auntie. Prita-Auntie was crying now. She looked scared. Ma stumbled and fell to her knees, off balance with her hands cuffed behind her. For a moment she just sat on the floor, defeated, as if she hadn't the energy to lift herself onto the bench. I tried to climb in to help her but one of the cops shoved me aside.

"It's my ma!" I screamed, but he held me fast.

"Leave me," Ma shouted. "I'm all right. Go!"

"Noor!" It was Deepa-Auntie, suddenly beside me, also in cuffs. I hugged her, though she couldn't hug me back.

"It's my fault," I said.

"You did well, Noor. Your ma's right, go find your Shami and Aamaal now."

The cops hustled her away.

Ma still hadn't uttered a single word of forgiveness, but I left. My siblings were more important. They were why I'd brought the police. I ran back to the entrance to our house. No more adults were coming out. I hadn't seen Binti-Ma'am or Pran.

Some children were already in vans, separated from their mothers and aunties. I raced back and forth on shaky legs from one vehicle to another. I couldn't see Shami or Aamaal anywhere. I returned to our house, where two cops guarded the entrance.

"I need to go inside," I said. "My brother and sister haven't come out yet."

"The house is clear," said one of the cops. "There are only policemen in there now. Check the vans."

"I've checked them all. Please, let me past."

"No one's allowed back in."

I looked wildly around for someone to help me. Finally, I spotted the cop who'd interviewed me at VJ's house. I ran to him and explained the situation. I was hysterical. I'm not sure I made much sense, but he followed me back to the entrance and ordered the guards to let me through.

The house felt strangely unfamiliar, though I'd left less than twenty-four hours before. The noises and smells that had filled my childhood were gone. It seemed impossible that my history could be expunged so quickly and completely. I crept down the hallway and peeked around the corner to make sure the coast was clear before rushing for the ladder. I was up it as fast as I'd ever climbed and found my siblings exactly where I knew they'd be, huddled under the bed, their arms wrapped around each other though poor Aamaal had one arm in a cast.

"Come out now." I knelt on the floor, leaned down and reached for the entwined mass of them. Aamaal shuffled them both out of reach.

"Ma said to stay here," she said.

"She didn't mean forever, Aamaal. Just until I came for you."

"That's not what she said."

"I peed," said Shami in a tiny voice.

"It's okay, Shami-baby, we'll get you cleaned up. But you must come out now."

"Not till Ma comes," said Aamaal.

"She's not coming back, Aamaal," I said, with a mixture of guilt and exasperation.

"Where's Ma?" asked Shami, his voice trembling. He'd been holding back tears a long time.

I did the only thing I could. I slid under the bed and lay next to them, pulling them into my arms. Shami was sandwiched between us. I rubbed Aamaal's back. Her body shook as she finally let herself cry. Shami put his thumb in his mouth and burrowed into me. I felt his chest rise and fall against my own. I wished we could have stayed like that forever, but I could hear the officers banging around downstairs, their shouts filling the air. This wasn't our home anymore. We had to leave.

"Come on," I said. Wiggling backwards, I dragged them with me, stood up and helped them both to their feet. "It's time to go."

We walked cautiously to the ladder, listening for sounds before we wordlessly descended. I took a final look around, knowing I would never see this place again. I waited for the relief to wash over me but all I felt was sad. Whatever else it was, it was my childhood home. I could hear voices from the direction of the lounge—stern, joyless voices. I took each of my siblings by the hand and we walked in the opposite direction, past the washroom, the kitchen, to the small room at the end of the hall.

I had to see it one last time, commit it to memory as one might revisit the scene of a murder. It was the site of so much sadness. Shami and Aamaal didn't question where we were going. Their steps didn't falter as we entered the outer room. My brave little siblings stood with me in front of the box.

The noise was nearly imperceptible, yet unmistakable. All

three of us held our breath as we strained to listen. It came again. The wooden crate, little more than a coffin, was not empty.

It didn't make sense. The door was closed but it wasn't locked. Why would anyone choose to be inside? The light was off. Even with the morning sun filtering into the outer room, it would be pitch-black in there. Could a rat have got in? It wasn't impossible. They got in everywhere else.

I let go of my siblings' hands, hopped up on the stool and opened the door. I jumped back quickly. If it was a rat, it would scurry away. I didn't want to be in its path.

We waited.

Nothing.

The noise had stopped. Yet I knew there was something in there. The hair rose on the back of my neck. The presence inside the box waited just as we did. My siblings' hands found their way back into my own.

"Hello," I said.

Silence.

"Is someone there?"

Suddenly I remembered that I hadn't seen Pran or Binti-Ma'am outside. Was it possible they were hiding in the box? It made sense. The police wouldn't think to look there. It was the perfect hiding place. Only someone very familiar with our home would think of it. I was ablaze with outrage that Pran or Binti-Ma'am would be saved from arrest by the very thing they'd used to destroy the souls of others. I let go of my siblings, got back up on the stool, switched on the light and climbed inside.

I wasn't prepared for the sight that greeted me.

Lali-didi sat on the filthy mattress, leaning back against the blood-spattered wall.

"What are you doing in here?" I asked. There was something beyond the fact of finding her in such a strange place that made me uneasy.

"Just resting."

"In here?" I couldn't keep the astonishment out of my voice. She smiled weakly.

"I've brought the police, Lali-didi. Everyone has been arrested, but you don't need to worry. You're a minor. You'll get sent to a rescue home."

"Good for you. I knew you would save us."

"So you'll come out now," I said.

"Not yet."

"But you're free, Lali-didi. You don't ever have to be in a place like this again. You're free."

"Not yet."

I didn't know what to say. Lali-didi had often been a mystery to me but I was more perplexed than usual. My disquiet grew.

"You're going to have a wonderful life. Everything's going to be okay now."

"Do you know how many times I've been raped, Noor?"

I didn't answer. I couldn't.

"Ha! Neither do I. I can't count beyond one hundred. It was many hundreds though, I can tell you that."

"It's over, Lali-didi."

"I can still feel their touch on my skin. I can still smell them, even after I bathe, like their stink seeps out of my own pores."

"You can go to school. You can be happy." Tears were sliding down my face. Lali-didi's eyes were dry.

"I am happy, Noor. I've waited for this day a long time. You marched in just as I knew you would and closed the doors on this house of torture. I planned for this from the moment you escaped last night. You came more quickly than I expected. Thank you for that." Blood dripped out of her nose. She wiped it away but it only seemed to make it bleed faster. "You should go now."

"Lali-didi, what's going on? What have you done?"

She held up a can of rat poison that had slipped down on the far side of her.

"No," I gasped. "Not now, Lali-didi. You're going to get your freedom."

"Yes I am, Noor. Yes I am."

I crawled over and pulled at her arm. "We have to get you out of here. We'll go to the hospital. There's still time."

She wouldn't budge.

"Good-bye, Noor." She crumpled before my eyes. For the first time I noticed blood leaking from her ear.

"Lali-didi," I sobbed. "Please don't do this." I pulled at her arms, even as I felt her limbs go limp.

I don't know when my siblings joined me in the box or how long we sat there. We didn't hear the heavy footsteps enter the outer room or the voices urging us to come out. I don't remember leaving Lali-didi, or climbing in a van. I don't remember the police station or the day and night we spent in detention while our futures were being decided.

Everyone I loved was in prison, everyone but Lali-didi. Only she was free.

33

Noor

What I will remember . . .

I'm woken by the mattress creaking above me. I slide out of bed, careful not to disturb Aamaal, and stand up. I have to climb up the first rung of the ladder to get my head high enough to see Shami on the top bunk. His eyes are wide open.

"Are you okay, baby?"

"My stomach hurts."

"Do you need to go to the bathroom?"

"I'm not sure."

"Well, let's give it a try."

I pull down his cover and step off the ladder to give my seven-year-old brother space to climb down. I put my hands out to catch him in case he stumbles. He's wobbly but manages to get down without mishap. His body is still adjusting to a new higher-dose medication. We've been through it all before, the diarrhea, nausea and fatigue.

I follow him into the bathroom and sit cross-legged on the

floor while he sits on the toilet. There's no shyness between us. I've ministered to his ills since he was a baby. I'll continue for as long as he'll let me.

"Do you think Ma is watching us?" asks Shami.

"Well, hopefully not right now." I smile.

"Maybe she's already been born again. She could be a baby bunny."

I chuckle. Shami can think of no better incarnation. He dotes on Aamaal's rabbits.

"Noor-di?"

"Yes?"

"I haven't done much good in my life. If I died right now, I wouldn't come back as a bunny, would I?"

"You're not going anywhere for a long time," I say firmly.

"I'd probably come back as a pigeon. No one likes pigeons. There's too many and they all look the same. I bet a lot of naughty boys come back as pigeons. Noor, if I was a pigeon would you still recognize me?"

"Of course."

There's a quiet knock on the door. I stand up and open it.

"Everything all right in here?" Karuna-Auntie pops her head round the door.

"His stomach is giving him trouble again."

She walks in, leaving the door open, and strokes Shami's hair. I only hope Varun-Uncle and Nanni are not behind her. It's the hazard of living with a houseful of doctors; poor Shami has no privacy. If I'd had any idea what we were getting into I might have thought twice about moving in with them. I wouldn't have refused—they're our salvation—but I might have thought twice.

Aamaal and I spent six weeks in protective custody after Ma's arrest. For all that time, we weren't allowed to see Shami, or anyone else. Shami was put in a home for HIV-infected kids. Luckily, since it was private and not state-run, it had liberal visiting privileges. Grace and VJ visited every day.

We all missed Ma's funeral, though it was nothing to speak of. She was given a pauper's cremation when her body was found in an alley barely a month after she got out of jail. She'd spent two nights locked up. The only people who did less time were Pran and Binti-Ma'am, who had mysteriously disappeared not an hour before the raid. Prita-Auntie was sentenced to three years for helping train underage girls. Deepa-Auntie spent several days in jail while it was decided whether she was in the country illegally. When she was finally released, Nishikar-Sir was waiting to install her in another brothel. It might have seemed like good fortune that Ma didn't meet that fate, but she had nowhere to go. With our home closed and her own health failing she lived on the street.

Some days I think Ma died of a broken heart. With her livelihood and children gone she had no way to survive and nothing left to fight for. Other days I remember the woman who endured endless nights of pain and humiliation to look after me and send me to a fee-paying school. Ma rarely praised me and never once said she loved me. She always insisted my destiny was both bleak and inevitable. Yet she kept my medals hidden in the hem of her skirt and fought anyone who tried to limit my dreams. Perhaps she died because her heart had filled to capacity. She knew the battle was over and she had won.

Karuna-Auntie came back into our lives by accident. She was doing volunteer checkups at the HIV home and discovered

Shami. She recognized him, though he didn't remember her. I'd dragged him to so many doctors, and it had been over a year since he'd seen her. Only when she reminded him of their shared passion for *manga an' napple* did he figure it out. It didn't take long for her to get the details on all of us.

She appeared at our rescue home one afternoon, standing in the doorway of the musty room that doubled as a bedroom and lounge for thirty girls. I knew her immediately, though I didn't acknowledge her. I waited to see why she had come. The disappointment would have been too much if it had been a random coincidence.

The ache of missing Shami had become unbearable. I was close to the desperation of those girls I'd read about years earlier who'd broken their legs trying to escape their rescue home. Had it not been for Aamaal, I would have tried it. I remembered Karuna-Auntie's compassion and prayed she was there to help us.

Her eyes lit up the second they fell on me and she walked straight over.

"Hello, Noor." She plopped down onto my mattress on the floor. "Do you remember me?"

Aamaal, who was never more than a few feet from me the entire time we lived in protective custody, looked up from the schoolwork I'd assigned her.

"Yes," I said.

My eagerness must have registered on my face. She looked pleased. In addition to being separated from my beloved brother, we hadn't been allowed out of the home to go to school. Prison could not have been more punitive.

"You never came back to see me. I always hoped you would."

"You would have taken my brother away." I didn't state the obvious—that I'd since brought that misfortune upon myself.

"I saw Shami yesterday."

I sat up straighter.

"How is he?" demanded Aamaal, closing her book. "How did you get to see him? Can you take us?"

I didn't speak. Aamaal had asked every question in my own heart.

"I thought perhaps we could discuss a more permanent solution."

My breath caught in my throat.

"I live with my brother's family and my mother. My mother and brother are both doctors. My brother has a wife and two children. Thankfully she's not a doctor. That would be a bit tiresome, wouldn't it?"

She paused, but when we didn't respond she continued. "We're a crowded household but we're happy. I think you would like my nieces, Noor. The eldest is studying her standard twelve. The younger is in standard eight. You're in standard ten now, aren't you?"

I blushed when I remembered the lie I'd told her.

"Standard nine," I mumbled.

"So what do you say?" Her penetrating eyes were full of kindness, just as before.

I was confused. What was she asking?

"Would you and Aamaal like to come live with us?"

Her offer was beyond my wildest hopes. "What about Shami?"

"Oh, he's already agreed," she said breezily.

Aamaal jumped up. "Yes, YES, YES!"

"Wait a minute, Aamaal," I cautioned. "How long would we live with you?"

"I've never married, Noor. The idea of deferring to a man never sat well with me. Having my own children, on the other hand, is something I've always wanted. I like you, Noor. I have a feeling you and I are not so different. And, of course, I've been smitten with Shami from the moment I met him. Now that I've met Aamaal, I can see you're an irresistible lot, you Benkatti children. I'd like to become your guardian. What do you say?"

It was a week beyond that before the legal work was completed and we came home to this apartment. I laughed when Usha-Auntie, Karuna-Auntie's sister-in-law, showed us to the bedroom we now share and apologized that all three of us would have to share a room, and Aamaal and I would both sleep in the lower bunk. It took her weeks to accept that, to us, everything about the way they lived was luxurious.

Finished on the toilet, Shami goes to the sink to wash his hands. I stand up to supervise. He isn't thorough if I don't keep an eye on him. Karuna-Auntie follows us back to the bedroom and climbs up the ladder to tuck Shami in and kiss him good-night. I switch on my night-light and pick up my Biology textbook. In two weeks I'll write the medical school entrance exam. With three doctors constantly testing me, I'm confident I'm ready, but I enjoy studying, which is lucky as it'll be another seven years before I'm fully qualified.

Karuna-Auntie leans down and plants a kiss on my forehead. "Sleep is just as important as study, Noor," she whispers. "Don't stay up too late."

"I won't."

She walks out, leaving our door slightly ajar. I stare at the page in front of me but my mind wanders.

Grace will return to Mumbai soon for her summer holidays. I'm looking forward to being together again. She graduated last year and went home for university. VJ and I have planned a welcome dinner for her.

VJ graduated two years ago and has been a rising star in Indian cinema. Last year he was in a British coproduced movie that was an international hit. When he was nominated for an Oscar everyone said his fame would eclipse his father's. He went to America for the ceremony. The paparazzi found it quaint that he brought a high-school friend as his date.

All of India watched with pride as Bollywood's heartthrob won the prize. Since VJ had remained a fixture in our own lives, our whole family was gathered around the television when he took the stage to accept.

He began his speech by thanking his father and mother. Then he thanked us, his adopted siblings. He said his brother Shami had taught him everything he knew about courage; I was surprised to discover we had that in common. I smiled when he said his sister Aamaal had taught him to live life to the fullest. It may have been true, but I'd never known the film star to have any problem living big.

I was nervous when he mentioned me. He said I'd taught him that if the future was not written as you wanted it to be, then you must write your own story. I thought about that for a long time. My life hadn't been the straight canal to the sea that Ma had predicted, but neither had it been Deepa-Auntie's mountain river full of unpredictable twists and turns. Many hands had guided my journey, not the least

FIFTEEN LANES ~ 293

of them Ma's. I'd had some luck, but more than that, time and again, I'd had help. I couldn't have written my story without that.

Last of all, VJ thanked his high-school sweetheart, the love of his life, Luca D'Silva. The camera panned to the beautiful boy in the audience who blew him a kiss.

It caused a media storm that went on for months. Some said VJ's public disclosure would end his career. VJ said it launched it. He's moved behind the camera now, to tell the stories that matter to him. His father is financing his first film, a documentary on sex trafficking. He and Luca live together. They talk of getting married if it ever becomes legal.

Grace has grown stronger with each passing year. Counseling and finally confronting Kelsey and Todd, the masterminds of her downfall, helped her to move forward, but that was only a small part of her recovery. Grace and I spent her last two years in Mumbai volunteering at the NGO in Kamathipura, Sisters Helping Sisters. With Chandra-Teacher's help we've started literacy classes for sex workers. Deepa-Auntie was our first student. When Chandra-Teacher offered Deepa-Auntie a job as an outreach worker and helped her break free from Nishikar-Sir, Grace and I learned as much about the importance of confronting bullies as Deepa-Auntie did. Grace plans to become a human rights lawyer. I pity anyone who persecutes the powerless on her watch.

This summer she's bringing a boy with her who wants to intern at our NGO. Grace doesn't call him her boyfriend but I think he's important to her. Grace didn't date throughout high school. While the wounds on her leg have healed, not all damage is visible. I teased her that this boy must be serious if she was bringing him to meet us, but she just laughed and said, "He's a bit of a dork."

"Noor-di." Shami interrupts my thoughts. I get out of bed and step up on the ladder.

"Are you all right, baby? Is the light bothering you?"

"My stomach still hurts."

I climb up the ladder and settle myself next to him, leaning on the headboard. "Roll on your side. I'll stroke your back."

It's the rare night that I can't put him to sleep with a back rub.

"Noor-di?"

"Go to sleep now."

"Just one question."

"Okay, but only one."

"If I die and get born into another family in Kamathipura, will you still recognize me?"

"You're not going to die."

"But will you recognize me?"

I don't tell him the truth—that when we lived in Kamathipura, and in the years since, I've seen all of us reborn a thousand times. I see myself in the hopeful school-going girls with their scuffed shoes and faded uniforms, and Aamaal in the wide-eyed stares of young girls who know too much about abuse and too little about love. I see Shami in the wizened faces of children haunted by disease. I used to dream that one day I would have a home where I could shelter all the people that I loved, but every day, the list of people I want to save grows longer. There are already too many to be contained by four walls and a roof, so I've changed my dream. I've opened a room in my heart that I reserve for the women and children of Kamathipura. Its size and scope have no limits.

"Of course I will recognize you," I say. "Now go to sleep."

"Just one more question, Noor-di, and then I promise I'll sleep. If I'm born into another family, will you still love me?"

I pull him into my lap. He's so tiny and light he still fits easily. "If you come back as a bunny, or a pigeon or a child of Kamathipura, born to another family, I will find you, Shami. And I will always love you."

Author's Note

I first started volunteering with sex workers' daughters in Kamathipura, the largest red-light district in Asia, in March of 2013. Though I've had training in working with victims of sexual violence, I wasn't so naive as to think I was going to transform the lives of the girls I worked with. Still, I wasn't entirely prepared for the level of violence and degradation they're routinely exposed to. More disheartening still is the extent to which a large portion of society has turned its back on them. Time and again I've heard stories of girls being shunned, even asked to leave school, when it was found out their mothers were sex workers—no matter that the vast majority of their mothers had been trafficked into the life and were victims themselves.

Early in my work with the girls, I had the opportunity to edit a countrywide report on sex trafficking produced by Dasra, a leading Indian strategic philanthropy organization based in Mumbai. Suddenly my personal experiences and observations had a broader context. Though government figures are lower, according to Dasra's research, there are an estimated 15 million people in India who have been trafficked into sex work. More than a third are children, some as young as nine years old, sold into sexual slavery to satisfy an increasing demand for younger girls. Daughters of sex workers are at particular risk.

In a decade where India has seen unprecedented growth and a decrease in the percentage of the population living below the poverty line, sex workers have experienced falling wages, an increase in the number of child prostitutes and a significant decline in life expectancy. NGO workers in Kamathipura estimate that 60 percent of sex workers are HIV-positive. Many children are born infected. Tuberculosis and other diseases related to poverty and overcrowding are also rampant.

Some day I will leave India, as I have left so many other countries, but I'll take with me the memory of girls, full of hope and determination, who against all odds dream of a future beyond the fifteen lanes of their red-light community. I'll remember their mothers, who chided me for my abysmal Hindi, and the chai-wallah who, despite the congestion of goats, cows, people and all manner of vehicles, always managed to save me a parking space outside the night shelter where I worked. But for now I look forward to the hugs and shrieks of "Susan-didi!" that will greet me tomorrow night when I return to my girls in Kamathipura. I still have no illusions that I've transformed their lives, but I have no doubt they've changed mine.

SJ Laidlaw
Mumbai, February 2015

Acknowledgments

It took close to two years to write this book, because it was challenging to find the light in a story too dark to tell.

I'm very grateful to the Canada Council for the Arts, not only for financial support but for the tacit endorsement that this story was worth the struggle.

I feel extremely fortunate to have worked on yet another book with my wonderful editor at Tundra Books, Sue Tate. As always, Sue provided the perfect combination of intelligence and empathy, cheerleading and honesty.

Also at Tundra, I appreciated the wisdom of my former publisher, Alison Morgan, and I'd like to mention a young intern, Sarah Essak, who was an early champion of Noor's story, even in its darkest incarnation.

This was my first time benefitting from the keen eyes of Catherine Marjoribanks, who copyedited this book, and Tundra's managing editor Elizabeth Kribs. I'd like to thank them both.

While this book is a work of fiction, it's based on lives that are all too real. Those stories were collected from many sources, but two women in particular illuminated my work with their insights. I'm grateful to Manju Vyas, who has dedicated her life to the women and girls of Kamathipura, and Namita Khatu, whose energy and smile never faltered despite the daunting task of helping the most downtrodden in a city where more than a quarter-million people live on less than thirty cents a day.

I'd also like to thank Sudarshan Loyalka, who sixteen years ago started the small NGO in Kamathipura that became my second home in Mumbai, Apne Aap Women's Collective (www.aawc.in). His vision and commitment continue to inspire all those around him.

Unwittingly, two good friends, Neera Nundy and Deval Sanghavi, cofounders of Dasra, provided assistance when they invited me to attend a countrywide conference of anti-trafficking NGOs and asked me to edit their report on sex trafficking in India. Also at Dasra, I'd like to thank Pakzan Dastoor, who oversaw the report and lent me books. I swear I'm still planning to return them.

Finally, as always, I thank my husband, Richard Bale, who reads every draft of my work from the most abysmal beginnings. He is perhaps the only person whose relief when a book is finally finished equals my own.